Abigail's Secret

D1056802

by

MARILYN TURK

To Nicole,
May God richly bless you!
Marilyn Turk

Candlelight
Romance
LOVE INSPIRED BY
HIS WARM GLOW

ABIGAIL'S SECRET BY MARILYN TURK
Candlelight Fiction is an imprint of LPCBooks
a division of Iron Stream Media
100 Missionary Ridge, Birmingham, AL 35242

ISBN: 978-1-64526-262-6
Copyright © 2020 by Marilyn Turk
Cover design by Hannah Linder
Interior design by Karthick Srinivasan

Available in print from your local bookstore, online, or from the publisher at:
ShopLPC.com

For more information on this book and the author visit: http//:www.marilynturk.com

Brought to you by the creative team at LPCBooks:
Bradley Isbell, Shonda Savage, Leslie L. McKee, Jessica Nelson

Library of Congress Cataloging-in-Publication Data
Turk, Marilyn.
Abigail's Secret / Marilyn Turk 1st ed.

Printed in the United States of America

Praise for *Abigail's Secret*

Who doesn't enjoy the beauty of a lighthouse and the lure of the rocky coast of a Maine island? While reading *Abigail's Secret*, I was moved into thinking the lighthouse and its island are metaphors for brokenness and loss, that bring back wholeness and love, while revealing 'Abigail's Secret'. To quote, "She (meaning Abby, Ms. Turk's heroine) was connected to the island as if it, too, were a relative." Readers of contemporary romances will want to add this novel to their list of favorites.

~Rita Gerlach
Author of the *Daughters of the Potomac* series

A lighthouse. A new friend. A family secret. *Abigail's Secret* delivers a sweet story of family relationships and new beginnings, with a bit of mystery thrown in. Turk skillfully weaves past and present into a story sure to touch your heart.

~Anne Mateer
Author of *Wings of a Dream*

Fans of Marilyn Turk will enjoy this cross-generational tale that bridges together two strong women through many years of love and loss. Readers will root for them both as they learn to shine their light."

~Julie Cantrell
NYT and USA TODAY bestselling author of *Perennials*

Marilyn masterfully weaves mystery into a sweet romance, tender family love, carefully researched World War II history, and a lighthouse!

~Susan G Mathis
Award-winning author of *Devyn's Dilemma*

Abigail's Secret is a sweet, clean romance with mystery woven throughout. I loved the intrigue of the romantic development between Abby and Carson along with the background setting of a lighthouse with historical significance. The surprise ending was an actual surprise that I doubt anyone could anticipate. Love blooms and grows in *Abigail's Secret* and I'm so glad to recommend it.

~Kathy Collard Miller
Speaker and author of over 55 books including *God's Intriguing Questions:*
40 Old Testament Devotions Revealing God's Nature

The past confronts the present in this lovely harbor-front tale of second chances and new beginnings.

~Ruth Logan Herne
USA Today Bestselling author

In *Abigail's Secret*, author Marilyn Turk has spun yet another delightful tale of mystery, intrigue and romance. I greatly enjoyed stepping into the seacoast town of Hope Harbor and following the lives of the characters there. Whenever I had to put the book down, I couldn't wait to pick it up again. A thoroughly satisfying read!

~Ann Tatlock
Novelist, children's book author and blogger

ACKNOWLEDGMENTS

Although a work of fiction, much research went into this book to capture the realistic setting and the accuracy of the historical background.

Hope Harbor, Maine, is not a real place but my visits to the quaint town of Bar Harbor, with its seasonal shops and small-town bed and breakfasts, fueled my imagination. The Hope Island Lighthouse is not a real lighthouse either, but my husband and I toured many lighthouses in Maine, and the setting for the one in this book reminded me of the Bear Island Lighthouse. Thank you, Chuck, for taking me on those wonderful trips.

I'd like to thank the people I know who've worked to renovate abandoned lighthouses and keepers' quarters, such as the ones at Little River Light in Cutler, Maine, where my husband and I had the privilege of being volunteer caretakers for two summers. Timothy Harrison, Kathleen Finnegan, Terry and Cynthia Rowden put hours of labor into beautifully restoring Little River.

Carson Stevens and his dream of owning a lighthouse was inspired by real lighthouse owner Nick Korstad. Nick's own dream has come true through his purchase of several lighthouses, including two he has restored as bed and breakfasts, Borden Flats, Massachusetts, and Big Bay Point, Michigan. Nick was kind enough to share some of his experience in renovating lighthouses so that I knew what challenges were involved.

I was blessed to have my son Bret Lyttle as an advisor. His expertise in construction management helped me to understand the construction of old buildings, and what kind of things could go wrong in the renovation process.

Finally, I thank God for giving me the idea for the story and the connections to make it real. He is the source of all creativity, and I'm thankful he shared a little bit of it with me.

DEDICATION

"The Lord is my light and my salvation—whom shall I fear? The Lord is the stronghold of my life—of whom shall I be afraid?" Psalm 27:1

Chapter One

Hope Harbor, Maine
Present

The last place Abby wanted to be was a cemetery.

She practically dragged five-year-old Emma up the hill where the ceremony was taking place. Late. Again. One more check on the failure chart. Avoiding the eyes of the others present as they watched her force her way to the front, she slid into the only empty chair, pulling Emma onto her lap. Emma set her ever-present Wonder Woman Build-a-Bear on her own lap.

Abby scanned the crowd, only recognizing a couple of folks from town. Who were all these people? Did they know her grandparents? She hadn't expected so many to come to the grave-marker ceremony commemorating their service as lighthouse keepers. After all, her grandmother had died twenty-five years ago when Abby was ten years old. And her grandfather had died before that, long before Abby was born.

A state senator and several other men waited behind the temporary podium, and alongside them stood the Coast Guard representatives in their navy-blue uniforms. When the man with a chest full of medals approached the podium, Emma tapped on Abby's arm.

"Who's that, Mommy?"

Abby leaned over to whisper in Emma's ear. "I don't know his name, but we need to be quiet now."

"Is he a soldier like Daddy was? He's wearing clothes kind of the same."

Abby's heart squeezed. Even though Kevin died when Emma was

only three, his now five-year-old daughter still remembered him, helped by the photos displayed in their apartment. Every time Emma saw a uniform, regardless of the branch of service, she thought of her father.

Had it only been two years since Abby had been in another cemetery as Kevin's military service was honored?

The officer welcomed those in attendance, naming a few dignitaries, then family members. Abby took a quick glance around. Were there any other family members besides herself and Emma? As far as Abby knew, she, her mother, and her daughter were the only surviving family members of lighthouse keepers Abigail and Charles Martin.

And if Mom hadn't begged her to go, Abby wouldn't have been here either. But with Mom's poor health, the chilly April air wouldn't have been good for her.

"Please, Abby. If Granny Abigail were here, she'd appreciate your presence at the ceremony," Mom had pleaded. "I wish I were up to going myself."

If Granny Abigail were here, there wouldn't be a ceremony, Abby had wanted to say, but she agreed to attend to please her mom. And maybe Granny, too, if she watched from heaven.

As the next dignitary approached the podium, Abby's mind wandered. Granny Abigail had been one of her favorite people in the whole world. Abby loved to hear her stories of being a lighthouse keeper, both before and after her husband drowned. Granny had such a zest for life, even with all the hardships she faced and raising a daughter alone at the same time. How had she managed? Where did she find the strength?

Abby was a widow now, too, raising a child on her own, but besides their shared name, that's where the similarities ended. Granny had lived in more difficult times, but Abby's life was easier. At least compared to Granny's it was. But she'd left her life in California after Kevin died because it felt too hard to handle alone. She'd run back home hoping to find herself again and help take care of Mom at the same time. Helping others made her feel needed, even though Kevin had always made fun of her for doing it. And except for that one time ... She sighed. Why did she feel so drained? If only she'd inherited Granny's strength. Where had Granny found the strength to carry on?

The overcast sky did little to lift her mood as she glanced around at the weathered headstones. She shuddered as a brisk spring breeze ruffled the air, and she drew Emma even closer, hoping their combined body heat would keep them both warm.

"Years of dedication …" Words drifted through Abby's thoughts, turning her attention back to the speaker. What would Granny think about being honored for her service? A smile crept across Abby's face as she imagined her grandmother's response.

Plum foolishness! Why should someone get a medal for doing their job? That's what Granny Abigail would say. She had loved being a lighthouse keeper despite the demanding position. But proud? She spoke of her late husband with pride as if his position at the lighthouse had been more important than hers, even though she assumed the same duties after he died. But *her* stories were as awesome as any Abby had ever heard.

The elderly gentleman beside Abby passed her a program of the service. When she turned to thank him, he pointed to a man standing near the end of the row. Abby made eye contact with the stranger who nodded back, a slight smile appearing between his trim mustache and close-cut dark beard. Heat flushed her face with the realization that he had watched her long enough to notice she was without a program. How embarrassing. Here she was, the only living relative present aside from Emma, and she didn't even know the agenda.

She gave a slight nod and attempted a smile in return before lowering her gaze to the program. Even though she'd only had a brief glance at the man, she'd seen enough to notice how good-looking he was. Black hair curled over the collar of his brown leather bomber jacket, framing a face that harbored light-colored eyes. She cut a sidelong glance and noticed he wore dark blue jeans over hiking boots. Was there a chance he was a distant relative of hers she didn't know about? He certainly hadn't known her grandparents since he looked to be about the same age as herself.

"Mommy, can I read it?"

Abby shushed Emma and held the program open in front of her daughter. She studied the program and tried to focus on the order of events. One of the dignitaries approached the two tombstones beside the podium and laid a wreath on each one. Next, a man named Timothy Harrison was introduced as the editor of *Lighthouse Digest* magazine. He took the podium and explained the significance of the lighthouse plaque, saying that all members of the military had such markers noting their service, but only recently had lighthouse keepers been awarded the same honor.

The magazine editor then unveiled the brass marker that was attached to a rod in the ground beside the tombstones, and a Coast Guardsman inserted an American flag into the marker. As the officer saluted the flag, the flag—assisted by the gentle breeze—waved its own salute in return. Abby bit back tears as she remembered Kevin's ceremony. At least she didn't have to see a flag-draped casket again.

Her attention returned to the speaker as he remarked that although many lighthouse keepers were assisted by their wives, few widows ever received the title of head keeper once their spouse died. He emphasized Granny taking up where her husband left off—no small task for a young mother. Abby's heart swelled with pride hearing her grandparents' accolades. They were special people—heroes and lifesavers. Why didn't those noble genes pass down to her? She swallowed the lump in her throat.

As the ceremony drew to a close, the audience was asked to stand as the color guard marched away. Abby placed Emma beside her, and they stood at attention until the service ended. Afterward, out of politeness, Abby was compelled to introduce herself to the people in charge.

She stepped toward the editor and extended her hand. "I'm Abigail Baker, the granddaughter of Charles and Abigail Martin. Thank you so much for honoring them in such a wonderful way."

Mr. Harrison's eyes brightened as he gripped her hand. "I'm so happy to meet you. I knew your grandmother. She was a remarkable woman."

Abby nodded. "Yes, she was. I wish I had known her longer, but she died when I was a child."

"I'm Emma!" Never shy, Emma extended her little hand up toward Mr. Harrison, who leaned over and grasped Emma's hand with both of his.

"It's very nice to meet you, Emma," he said. "So you're the great-granddaughter."

Emma looked up at Abby with a questioning gaze.

"Yes, Emma is my daughter."

The man glanced at Abby, frowning. "Is your mother ..."

"Mom would have liked to be here, too, but she struggles with COPD and just couldn't handle the walk out here."

"I'm sorry to hear that. Please give her my regards. I met her many years ago when your grandmother was still with us."

"I will. Thank you again." Abby turned to leave and noticed the man who had handed her the program standing a few feet away. Was he waiting to speak to Mr. Harrison too? As she started walking to the car, he caught up to her.

"Excuse me. I don't mean to intrude, but I wanted to meet you."

Startled, Abby nearly tripped over her feet. "Me?"

"Yes, I heard you say you're the granddaughter of the Martins."

"That's right. I'm Abby Baker."

"I'm Carson Stevens. I recently bought the lighthouse where your grandparents served."

Abby's mouth fell open. "You bought the lighthouse?"

"Well, technically, I bought Hope Island, which includes the lighthouse and all fifteen acres."

"Oh." Abby tried to envision the island from the last time she'd seen it many years ago. "Why? Are you going to live there?"

"Eventually. I'm restoring the keeper's house and plan to turn it into a bed-and-breakfast."

Her grandmother's house a B&B? "Is it big enough?"

"Sure. It'll have four guest rooms when it's finished."

"Mommy, I've got to go potty."

Abby glanced down at Emma, recognizing the telltale dance that signaled time was running out before an emergency occurred. Her face heated as she glanced back at Carson. "Sorry, but we need to hurry."

Abby scooped Emma up in her arms and began trotting down the hill. Carson ran alongside. "I was wondering if you'd like to go out to see the lighthouse some time."

"I don't know when I can, but … call me." Abby huffed as she ran, then crossed the street to the corner café in search of a restroom.

***

Well, so much for making a great first impression.

Watching Abby's long brown hair flying as she dashed away from him, Carson shook his head. Was it his imagination or was she really fast? Sure, the cute little girl's urgent need was more important than having a conversation with him, but it still felt like Abby couldn't get away from him quickly enough.

He could chalk it up to lack of practice. After all, being stuck in a cubicle with a computer all day and visiting lighthouses when he had any time off hadn't given him much of a social life. Not that he'd wanted one since Jennifer broke their engagement. In the year since, he must have become socially inept. But he had hoped to meet the descendants of the Martins and was so excited to find out Abby was their granddaughter. Maybe he'd come on too strong. He only wanted to know more about the former keepers at the lighthouse he bought. It didn't hurt that she was so attractive. He'd just have to relearn how to talk to women.

Carson headed to his truck parked around the corner. She'd told him to call her, but she didn't give him a number. How was he supposed to find her? He pulled out his phone and did a quick search for Abby Baker. Nothing showed up. He didn't even know if she lived around here. After climbing into his truck, he sat a moment before starting the ignition. *Think, Carson. There must be a way to find her.* He thumped the steering wheel. Had he blown his chance?

The image of Abby carrying her little girl down the hill wouldn't leave him. What was the girl carrying? A teddy bear with clothes on? Not only was he clueless about women, he was even less familiar with children. Although the girl did remind him of his little sister Dana when they were kids. Carson smiled at the memory, then shook his head. Hard to believe Dana was a mother with kids of her own now. Two boys and another child on the way. He should try to see them more often, but there was always something else he needed to do, and they lived in Colorado, a long way from Maine.

Carson checked his watch and flinched at the time. He was supposed to meet a contractor in a few minutes and discuss the Hope Island renovation. Work on the dock should be completed by now. How anyone ever landed on that island alive was beyond him. In fact, the island had a reputation for being "unlandable." Carson never ceased to be amazed at how people in the past dealt with problems without the help of modern conveniences. The floating dock he was having installed would be more durable and functional than the previous piers that had been torn apart by waves. Once the dock was ready, supplies could be sent over for the construction.

Carson pulled up to the local coffee shop, Mo's Beans. The aroma of fresh-brewed coffee greeted him as he entered the establishment. He glanced around the room and saw a man sitting on one of the couches who waved at him, then stood. Carson walked over and shook the man's extended hand.

"You must be Nick. I'm Carson."

"Nice to meet ya. Go ahead and get yourself some coffee, and we'll go over this." He pointed to a chart spread out on the table before him.

At the counter, Carson studied the creative coffee names listed on the blackboard behind the counter. "Don't you have any just plain coffee?"

"Sure. That'll be Mo's Joe." The full-bearded guy with the man bun pointed to the name on the board. "What size? A Little Joe, a Big Joe, or the Most Joe?"

Carson pointed to a cup, hoping he wouldn't have to remember which Joe it was. The guy nodded, grabbed a cup, and poured coffee into it. Carson reached in his pocket. "How much?"

The guy shook his head and waved him off. "You're new in town, so the first Mo is on us. But if you want some Mo Joe, you have to pay."

Carson took the cup wondering what planet he was on before returning to take a seat beside Nick.

Nick put his hands on his knees and faced Carson. "Okay, this is the situation. You know the place is in pretty bad shape, so we have to practically tear the whole house apart. The one thing you have going for you is the foundation. It appears to be solid. We laid some traps out there to catch the varmints so we can seal up the holes where they got in."

"Varmints?" Carson wasn't sure how to define the word.

"Yeah, you know—mice, squirrels. They've had the place to themselves for a while, and we have to get them out. Those things can chew up a house. And the yard is filled with voles, you know those little critters that eat all the plant roots and tunnel all over the yard."

Carson nodded, imagining the house overrun with rodents. Not a very welcome attraction for a bed and breakfast.

"Once we get them out, we'll have to replace the roof. Don't do any good to work on the inside if the roof leaks, and I'm sure it does."

"How long will it take to put on the new roof?"

"We should get it done by next week if the weather holds out." Nick swigged his Joe. Or was it his Mo? "Then we'll have to tear out the interior before we can start putting in new walls, flooring, plumbing, and electrical."

Dollar signs danced through Carson's head. Noticing a legal pad with numbers on it, he pointed. "Is that the cost for the whole renovation?"

Nick lifted the pad and held it for Carson to see. He choked and almost spit out his last sip of coffee. "Wow. That's higher than I estimated. Any way to get the costs lower?"

"Oh yeah." Nick laid the pad down on the table and faced Carson. "The more you do yourself, the less men I have to pay on the job. You ever do this kind of work before?"

"No, sir. But I'm about to learn how." He'd do whatever he could to reach his goal and good Lord willing, he'd prove all the doubters wrong.

Chapter Two

Abby dropped by her mother's house after the memorial service. Hercules, Mom's tortoiseshell watchcat, greeted them as she and Emma walked into the kitchen. Mom sat at the table with an open Bible. Abby plunked down her keys and purse while Emma ran over and hugged her grandmother.

"Hug Wonder Woman too!" The child extended her bear.

Mom complied with a big smile. "So how was it? See anyone we know?"

Abby shook her head. "You might have known more than I, but I did speak to someone who knew you. Timothy Harrison."

"Oh yes. He's the one who sent me the letter about the service. His magazine did a story on Momma a while back." She looked around the kitchen. "I have a copy here somewhere, if I can remember where I put it."

Abby glanced at the counter. "Got any coffee?" She walked to the coffeemaker, lifted the partially empty pot, and sniffed it before putting it back down. "You really ought to get one of those coffeemakers that just makes one cup at a time. You don't drink enough to keep a whole pot fresh."

Mom waved her hand. "Don't need something new to make coffee in. That one is just fine. Make yourself a fresh pot if you want."

Abby shook her head. "I don't want that much. I'll just drink some water instead." She took a glass out of the cabinet, filled it from the tap, then came back to the table and sat down across from Mom.

"Did you eat today? I have some deli meat if you want a sandwich," Mom said.

Frowning at the suggestion, Abby said, "No, thank you. I'll grab something later."

"Well, you ought to eat something. You're getting too thin."

Abby grimaced. Not this same conversation again. "I eat plenty, Mom. I just run it off."

"Emma, do you want a cookie? There's a fresh batch of chocolate chips in the cookie jar."

"Mommy, can I have some?"

"You can have just one." Abby walked to the counter and lifted the lid on the cookie jar, releasing the scent of sugar and chocolate chips. As she held the jar down so Emma could choose one, Abby reminded herself to pick up some lunch for the two of them on the way back to their house. Truth was, if it weren't for Emma, she'd forget to eat at all. Funny that there had been a time when she would have eaten a handful of the cookies by herself before she started eating healthy. But she carried the jar to Mom who selected one, then Abby returned the container to the counter before coming back to the table.

Emma climbed into one of the spindle-backed chairs at the round kitchen table and pretended to feed her bear the cookie.

"So Mr. Harrison was the only person you talked to?" Mom said between nibbles on her cookie.

Abby nodded then froze. "Actually, I did meet someone else. Did you know someone bought the lighthouse? Well, actually, all of Hope Island? He said his name is Carson Stevens."

"Is that right? Seems like I saw something about that in the paper a while back. Wonder what he plans to do with it."

Mom's memory wasn't as sharp as it used to be, but Abby couldn't believe Mom hadn't told her the lighthouse had been sold.

"He said he wants to turn the keeper's house into a bed-and-breakfast."

Mom laughed. "That old place? I can't believe anyone would want to stay there."

"I'm sure he'll have to do some major work on it to make it ready."

"I haven't seen it for over fifteen years. Your father and I used to take the boat out and drive by the island sometimes. The lighthouse looked so sad sitting up there all alone and empty." Mom's wistful expression tugged deep on Abby's heart. Life had changed so much since then. Did her Mom feel as desolate as the lighthouse she described?

"He asked me if I wanted to see it."

"Who?" Mom's attention had drifted, probably back to the island.

"Carson Stevens, the guy who bought the property."

"That was a kind gesture. You should go. Is he a nice man?"

"I didn't have much of a chance to talk to him, but he seemed nice enough." Abby gasped. "Oh! I told him to call me, but I forgot to give him my phone number."

Mom coughed a few times before getting her voice back. "Hmm. Well, let's ask around at church tomorrow. Maybe somebody knows how to reach him."

No doubt someone in town would know. One of the good things about living in a small town was that everyone knew everybody. Which was also one of the bad things about living in a small town, one of the reasons she'd moved to California when she graduated from college. Funny how her perspective had changed, because now the idea that everyone knew everybody made Hope Harbor seem like a safe place.

"I will." She pushed her chair back. "We need to go. I have errands to run and laundry to do. Can I pick anything up for you at the store?"

Mom pointed to a list on the refrigerator. "Yes, if you don't mind, I do need a few things."

Abby grabbed the list and extended her hand toward her daughter. "Come on, Emma."

"Give me a hug before you go." Mom reached her arms out to Emma, who gladly filled them.

Before walking out, Abby turned back. "I'll bring your groceries tomorrow when I pick you up for church, unless you need them before then."

Mom nodded. "Tomorrow will be soon enough. I'll try to be ready. It would be easier if you still lived here."

Easier for whom? Abby wasn't going down that road again. She'd lived with Mom the first three months after she moved back but had desperately craved the freedom of her own space. Mom wasn't so bad off that someone needed to stay with her full time. Even though Mom wanted her company, Abby hoped a daily visit would suffice. She'd come back to Maine to help her mother out, and Abby did all she could. But she had to make it on her own again, easy or not.

She leaned over and kissed her mother on the cheek. "I'll be here at nine o'clock. Love you."

As Abby drove to the store, she spotted Mo's Beans ahead. A good strong cup of coffee would be great right now.

"Mommy, I'm hungry," Emma whined.

Abby sighed. Mo's didn't offer anything for children, so Abby opted not to stop. She probably didn't need coffee this time of the day anyway, so she should just go home and make a salad for her and Emma.

The next morning Abby arrived at her mother's a few minutes early, expecting a delay. Mom moved so slowly now, becoming winded easily, which made getting dressed for church a major ordeal. Of course, Mom wouldn't go to church without dressing to the nines. She was highly offended by the casual attire of most of the congregation, especially the teenagers who wore jeans. Fortunately, Abby had a couple of easy-fitting dresses she could slip on and wear with sweaters or scarves, guaranteed to pass Mom's inspection.

Emma enjoyed going to church too and liked dressing up as much as her grandmother. The child was very particular about her clothes, especially for a five-year-old. In fact, unlike Abby, she would wear a dress every day if it were up to her. Today, she wore a pink-and-green-striped dress with a pink ruffle along the bottom and a matching pink bow in her dark ringlets.

"Mommy, Wonder Woman Bear needs some dress-up clothes for church."

"But then she wouldn't look like Wonder Woman," Abby said. More clothes and the bear would have a bigger wardrobe than Abby's.

"That would be her secret. You know, like Superman who hides his S under his other clothes."

Abby smiled. How did she have such a clever child?

Emma insisted on sitting in church between Abby and her mother instead of going to the children's worship. She contented herself with drawing while the minister spoke, and when the congregation sang, Emma added her own tiny voice to the throng, despite not knowing the words. She invented some in the process, amusing both Abby and Mom, who glanced over her head to smile, not bothering to correct the little worshipper.

As they stood to leave, Emma pointed to the back of the room. "There's that man from yesterday."

Abby's gaze followed the direction of Emma's finger, and she saw Carson Stevens walking toward the exit. He looked even better today than yesterday. Maybe now she could give him her number. But how was she supposed to do that? Chase after him and blurt it out? Besides, she had to help Mom out of church and to the car. Had he even noticed her there?

When they got outside, Abby scanned the parking lot but didn't see him. Maybe she should just forget it. She didn't have time to go to the island with him anyway, between her work at the preschool and Mom's appointments.

"Let's go to the Pound," Mom said, referring to the local lobster restaurant, after they were all in the car. "I'd love to have a lobster roll right now."

"Sounds good. Rick's?"

"It's the best, but we might have to wait a while, with the church crowd and all."

"I don't mind the wait if you don't. At least they have a playground for Emma to run around in and some picnic tables outside where we can sit."

"Then let's go to Rick's," Mom said, and Abby aimed the car in that direction.

***

Carson drove around the parking lot of Rick's Lobster Pound, searching for an empty space. The place was packed. Maybe today wasn't a good day to try this restaurant. He was about to leave when he spotted Abby sitting next to an older woman at a picnic table outside. Maybe that was her mother. Had she lived at the lighthouse too?

Now he could get Abby's number. Would that be rude? *Man up, Carson. Just do it.* What's the worst thing that could happen? He wasn't asking her for a date.

A car in the row beside him backed out, leaving a space open, obviously a sign he was supposed to stay. *Thanks, God.* He parked the car and walked the half mile to where Abby was sitting. She and the other lady had their backs to him as they looked toward a playground beside the restaurant. A quick glance in that direction and he spotted Abby's little girl. He cleared his throat.

"So we meet again." Did that sound as lame to them as it did to him?

Abby spun around, and her cheeks pinked when recognition registered in her eyes. "Oh, hello." She tapped the older woman, who was already checking him out and squinting her eyes like she was trying to figure out who he was. "Mom, this is the man I told you about. Carson, right?"

"Yes, Carson Stevens." At least she remembered his first name. He extended his hand.

The older woman still looked confused. "Remember, Mom? He's the person who bought Hope Island."

Abby's mother's eyes widened, and she nodded. "Yes, I did hear about that. So you're the one who's going to fix up the old place?"

"Yes, ma'am. I plan to turn it into a bed-and-breakfast."

The woman shook her head and smiled. "Imagine that. I'd sure like to see how you're gonna do that."

"With a lot of work. I met with a contractor the other day who told me about everything that needs to be done. But once it's finished, it'll be beautiful. You'll have to come see it."

"Lots of memories in that place." Her gaze drifted as if she were reliving some of them.

"So you lived there when your parents were the lighthouse keepers?

I'd love to hear about it some time." Carson attempted to regain the woman's attention.

"Come over to my house any time you want." The lady coughed and pointed away from the restaurant. "I live on Cedar Street, just down the road."

"Thank you. I may take you up on that."

"Mom, I'm sure Mr. Stevens will have his hands full with the work at the island."

Was she trying to keep him away? "That's true, but I will be staying in town while we're doing the work."

The hostess called a number and Abby said, "That's us. I better get Emma."

"Popular place. The food must be pretty good," Carson said, as Abby scurried away.

"They make the best lobster rolls. And their blueberry pie is out of this world." Abby's mother nodded her affirmation. "Hey, why don't you sit with us? Or were you meeting someone else?"

Carson shook his head. "No, I'm alone." Boy, was he ever. "I'd love to join you." Hopefully, Abby wouldn't mind. "Excuse me, what did you say your name was?"

"Oh, please forgive my manners. I'm Grace Pearson."

"Nice to meet you, Mrs. Pearson."

"You can just call me Grace."

Carson smiled. "My parents always told me to address my elders by Mrs. or Mr. I'm not sure I could call you by your first name."

"Suit yourself. Everybody around here calls me Grace though."

Abby came back with Emma and said, "Let's go inside and claim our table." She eyed Carson curiously as he helped her mother to her feet.

"Carson's eating with us." A look of surprise crossed Abby's face, and then she shrugged and reached for her mother's arm.

"You go on with Emma. Carson will help me up the stairs." She smiled up at him. At least he'd impressed Abby's mother.

After they were seated at the table and placed their orders, Emma piped up. "I saw you at church today."

"You did? Where were you?"

"I was in church, too, silly." She focused her attention on coloring the page their waitress had given her, along with some crayons.

"Well, Emma, I'm so sorry I didn't see you or I would've said hello."

"You were way in back and left before we did."

What a cute little girl. Pretty observant too. Had Abby seen him there too?

Grace's eyebrows lifted. "Have you come to our church before?"

"No, first time. Just thought I'd check out the churches in town."

"That won't take long. We only have four." Grace pointed her finger at him. "Next time you come to our church, you can sit with us."

"Thank you, I will." He glanced at Abby, who gaped at her mother's invitation. It seemed a good time to change the subject. "Mrs. Pearson, uh, Grace, when was the last time you visited Hope Island?"

A faraway look caught her eyes. "Back when my husband was alive, we did a lot of boating, so we passed the island several times. But we never stopped. You know, it's pretty hard to land a boat there. Besides, we didn't want to trespass on someone else's land."

"It's been government property for years, that is, until they decided to sell it this year. The Coast Guard has been managing the light since your mother left, but they haven't taken care of the buildings or the property."

"That's a shame. It used to be a beautiful place. My mother took great pride in the way she cared for it. In fact, back when the lighthouse service ran things, she said they'd come by and inspect it to make sure it was clean, even the house, and she always passed with flying colors."

"So you haven't stepped foot on the property for a long time."

"Probably fifteen, twenty years. As a matter of fact, I think the last time I was on it, Abby went with us." She faced Abby. "How old were you, Abby?"

"I was in high school."

"Then you both need to see it again."

Grace shook her head. "I don't see how I can climb in and out of a boat, much less climb up the hill to the lighthouse. But Abby could go."

"I want to go!" Emma paused in her coloring to look up.

"Maybe you can come too—after we get the place ready for special guests." He looked at Abby. "What do you think, Abby? We have a new dock now, so landing's not a problem anymore. Would you like to see the lighthouse and keeper's house before it's restored, like maybe next week?"

Abby glanced at her mom, then Emma on the other side of her. "I work at Emma's preschool during the day, so I don't know when I can."

"What about Saturday? Would you be free next Saturday?" He wasn't giving up that easily. Something in his gut told him she needed to go with him.

Grace touched Abby on the arm. "Abby, Emma could spend the day with me." Looking past Abby to Emma, she said, "Emma, why don't you and I make cookies or bake a cake next week?"

Emma's eyes widened. "Can we make a chocolate cake?"

"Of course we can."

Carson almost felt sorry for Abby now that Grace had taken away her excuse. He put on his best sad-puppy look, hoping she'd give in.

"All right, then yes. Yes, I'll go. I would like to see the place again."

Carson slapped the table. "Great! Then it's settled. Oh, you better give me your number so I can call you later in the week to tell you what time I'm picking you up." He whipped out his cell phone, fingers poised.

Chapter Three

When Abby took her mom home after lunch, she changed into her running shorts, a T-shirt, and sneakers. She needed to work off her meal, not to mention get some time alone.

"We're going to play Candy Land," Emma said from the living room as she tugged her favorite game out from under her grandmother's coffee table.

"Are you sure you're not too tired to watch Emma, Mom?"

Mom stood at the kitchen counter making a fresh pot of coffee. Waving her off, she said, "We'll be fine. Emma and I are going to have fun, aren't we, Emma?"

"Yes, ma'am." Emma brought the game to the kitchen table, took the lid off, and began setting up the board. "I'll be the ice cream cone! Grandma, what piece do you want to be?"

"Hmm. I'll be the marshmallow." Mom poured her coffee, then came to the table and sat. "You go on now, Abby. Enjoy your run."

"All right. I shouldn't be gone more than an hour and a half."

"No hurry. We'll be right here." Mom's coughs followed her words, reminding Abby of her health issues. Was it selfish of Abby to leave Emma there, to have some time by herself? But Mom didn't want to be treated like an invalid. And she enjoyed spending time with her only grandchild.

Abby leaned over and kissed Emma. "You be good for Grandma, okay?" Emma nodded, preoccupied with making the game pieces dance with each other.

"Thanks, Mom." She kissed her mother and left the house, sprinting along the street toward town, setting off the local bark patrol among the neighborhood dogs. Hopefully they were all restrained and wouldn't run after her. As she turned a corner, the sea came into view, and along with it, a sense of the freedom Abby relished. It was as if she were running away from her life, but not really. She'd always enjoyed running, and it was something she and Kevin had shared. She crossed the street before she reached the row of shops that lined Main Street with their crisp awnings. The shops were closed today but would be open tomorrow on Monday. That would change when the tourists arrived, and Sundays would become a day for businesses to take advantage of the extra foot traffic. Passing by the four-faced Howard clock with its wrought iron pedestal standing guard by the town square, she headed away toward the trail that skirted the coastline.

Running up and down the small hills formed by the rocky shore had become her favorite activity since returning home, and it invigorated her with new energy. A cool spring wind tingled her skin as she inhaled the scent of salt air. Here her thoughts could be drowned out by the gentle waves splashing along the shoreline. Abby embraced the solitude after passing a few people strolling the path. Unlike her community in California, Hope Harbor's residents weren't runners. In fact, life here was much slower in general. But Abby didn't mind being different, the only runner in town.

She ran several miles before hitting the steepest part of the trail. Sucking in the aroma of fir trees, she followed the trail that entered the woods before emerging again at the top. Her leg muscles contracted as she clambered up the challenging incline. At the peak, she relaxed and took in the sweeping view of the ocean before her. A huge boulder offered a place to sit and allowed her the opportunity to blend in with the peaceful, almost spiritual, environment. Up here where it was quiet, she thought she could feel God near. If she were good at praying, this would be a good place to do it. Surely He knew how much she appreciated the scenery.

Before her, the panorama stretched for miles. A few sailboats dotted the water beyond the harbor where lobster boats were moored until they went back to work the next day. Beyond the boats, small islands were scattered as if God had thrown a handful of rocks into a puddle.

One of those islands was Hope Island, but she wasn't sure which one it was from her perch above the water. They all looked like a clump of fir trees sitting on a pile of rocks, but Hope Island was supposed to be the farthest one from the shore.

She couldn't see the lighthouse or keeper's house from that perspective either, because the buildings were on the opposite side, facing out to sea with trees blocking the view of the structures from the mainland. From here, the islands didn't seem so far away, even though some were several miles out. From her understanding, Hope Island was about seven miles away. Boats provided quick access to and from the islands, most which only had occupants during the summer months when the vacation cabins were open. When the sea was calm, kayakers paddled to the various islands. But when the water was turbulent, not even a motorboat would attempt a trip. What would it have been like to live on the island without easy transportation? Her own grandfather had drowned when his small boat capsized in rough water.

Except for the unpredictable sea, the idea of being isolated from civilization wasn't completely unattractive. As an only child, Abby was used to being alone. That was one reason she had handled Kevin's deployments better than some military wives. But at least she had easy access to other people if she needed it. Unlike Granny Abigail, who managed a lighthouse and cared for a small child by herself. Abby couldn't conceive of handling those responsibilities on a remote island by herself. Especially after losing her husband who had previously been responsible for handling the lighthouse duties. How did she do it? How did she carry on without him? If only Abby could talk to her and find out.

Abby hadn't even thought about visiting the island since she returned, forgetting the place as if it only existed in the past. But Carson Stevens had bought it. And he offered to take her to see it again. A bubble of lost excitement welled up in her chest, urging her to accept Carson's offer. She really did want to go, to experience being on the island like her grandparents and her mother had been. Would she be surprised or shocked? No doubt, the years would have taken their toll on the buildings. But there was more than seeing the buildings that drew her.

She was connected to the island as if it, too, were a relative. Although she'd never lived there herself, her ancestors had, and maybe she'd feel that connection when she set foot on the island again. Would she feel Granny's presence or sense her strength?

But why had Carson invited her to go? She was a complete stranger and certainly couldn't contribute to his work. Unlike Mom, she'd never lived there, so she didn't even have any information to share about the lighthouse, unless she could recall one of Granny's stories. Of course, Mom was more than willing to share her stories with him.

A twinge of nerves stirred her heart. Did Carson consider her acceptance of his invitation as a date? She hoped not. Dating was not in her plans. Although he had a pleasant smile, he wasn't cocky or overly friendly, thank God. In fact, he seemed a little bashful. Not like Kevin, who had more than enough self-confidence and swagger. But there had only been one Kevin, and he was gone. Everything might not have been perfect between them, but he had been her husband and Emma's father. A tear trickled down her face as the pain of loss and loneliness once again squeezed her heart.

A rogue wave hit the shore, splashing high enough to sprinkle Abby with sea mist. She jumped back from her seat on the rock, her attention redirected to the present. Abby settled her hands on her hips and glanced skyward. "Okay, God. I get it. It's time to quit having these pity-parties."

She brushed off the dirt from her hands and glanced at her exercise watch. It was time to head back. Maybe it was time to quit running away and start running toward something. What, she had no clue. But maybe a trip to the island would help her out.

***

Carson drove toward the boat dock, glancing at Abby sitting in the passenger seat. Her hands were tucked between her legs as she stared ahead.

"Thank God, it's a nice day." Was that the best he could do for conversation?

She nodded. "It's beautiful."

Beautiful was definitely a better word for the sunny, clear day. Speaking of beautiful, his passenger could rival the weather. *Stay focused, Carson. Let's not get distracted from the reason you're here.*

"Hope I remember how to drive a boat." Okay, that got her attention as she whipped her head around, mouth agape.

"You don't know how to handle a boat? Then how have you been getting to the island?" Her eyes couldn't get much wider.

Carson laughed, faking bravado. "Some of the local guys have been carting me back and forth in their lobster boats. But I decided I needed to buy my own boat. So I did."

"You bought a lobster boat?"

Carson glanced to see if her hand had reached for the door, hoping she wasn't about to open it and bolt.

"No, actually, I bought a Boston Whaler. Just got it Monday." He smiled. "Don't worry. I've been practicing all week. I've taken it out to the island a few times and haven't gotten lost yet."

"That's reassuring." Abby faced the windshield again.

"Good thing the sea is pretty calm." He parked near the boat ramp and turned off the truck before facing her. "By the way, you know anything about boating?"

Abby stared at him, her eyes widened, then narrowed as she arched an eyebrow. "Seriously? Are you trying to scare me? I thought you wanted me to go."

Carson burst out laughing. "Just testing. No, really, I do know how to operate a boat. My family always had one. Most of my boats have been sailboats, but trust me, I am seaworthy."

"Glad to hear it." Abby opened her door and climbed out. He jumped out and met her on her side of the truck.

As they walked down toward the water, he pointed to a boat bobbing alongside the dock. "There she is. Pretty, isn't she?"

Abby glanced at him, her head tilted. "I suppose you could say that. *She* looks new."

When they reached the boat, Carson knelt down to steady it while Abby climbed on board.

"Have a seat." He motioned to the padded bench behind the wheel. "The boat is fairly new. One of the lobstermen bought it for a pleasure boat but decided he didn't need it after all and wanted a bigger lobster boat instead. Gave me a pretty good deal, I think." Carson untied the boat and jumped in. He stood, instead of sitting next to her, giving her space. Taking the wheel, he started the engine and motored away from the dock toward open water.

"So what's her name?"

"Who?" Carson looked around, seeing no other women.

"The boat. You said it was a 'she.'"

"Well, of course. But I don't know what to name her yet. Got any ideas?"

"Island Girl?"

Carson shook his head. "No, too tropical."

"Sojourner?"

"Too serious."

"Sea Princess?"

"Sounds like a cruise ship."

Abby gazed out at the water. "I can't think of anything else."

"Me either. Let's just call her 'Lady' until we think of something better."

Even though "Lady" sounded like a horse or even a famous dog, Carson wouldn't suggest "Abby," like he almost did. That would scare her off for sure. It scared him too. He sneaked a glance at her while she looked out the other side, trying not to stare. She wore a red ball cap over her long brown hair that was pulled into a ponytail and poked through the back of the cap. First time he'd seen her in jeans, which happened to perfectly fit her long, slender legs like a second skin. Good thing she wore them so she could climb around the island without getting bit by bugs or scratched by brambles. Abby kept her hands tucked in the pockets of her zipped-up navy-blue hoodie.

When she turned to face him, he jerked his gaze back to the front of the boat.

"How long does it take to get there?"

"Not long, maybe thirty minutes if the waves stay calm." Part of him wanted the trip to take longer, just to enjoy the ride. But he was even more eager to show her the lighthouse property and share his plans for it.

"It's hard to tell one island apart from the other," Abby said.

"At first, I thought so too. But now, I can see the difference." He pointed to one of the islands in the distance. "That's the one. You see, it's taller than the rest and has more trees."

"Okay, if you say so. Too bad you can't see the lighthouse from here."

"I know, because it faces out toward the ocean and not the harbor, but tell you what. I'll circle around so you can get a look at it from the other side before we pull up to the dock."

Abby leaned forward, peering through the boat's windshield. As they drew closer to Hope Island, Carson slowed the motor. Abby stood, her eyes focused ahead.

As they rounded the evergreen-covered rocks, Carson's pace quickened when the lighthouse came into view. The thrill of seeing his very own lighthouse never dimmed. This was his lifelong dream, and he could hardly believe it had come true. He couldn't wait until the buildings were ready for visitors.

"It needs to be painted," he said, apologizing for the blotched, shabby appearance.

"It's still cute, though." Abby's gaze fixed on the tower. "I'm sure it will look great when you get finished with it."

Cute? That was an adjective he hadn't thought of when describing the lighthouse. "One of the first things we'll do next week is clean the tower and paint it. Next time you see it, you won't even recognize it." *Next* time? He didn't even know if she would come back with him another time. Guess that was getting a little presumptuous.

"I look forward to it," she said, smiling, but didn't take her eyes off the lighthouse.

Carson's heart skipped a beat. Imagine that. He hadn't scared her away. Yet.

"Let's get to the dock and tie up. There's a lot more to see on land."

Chapter Four

Carson offered his hand, and Abby took it to climb out of the boat and onto the dock. He certainly did behave like a gentleman. She straightened and looked up at the lighthouse peeking over the treetops while memories of her childhood visits of exploring the island and the lighthouse ran through her head. Times when life was fun and full of adventure, times of innocence when she believed things would stay as they'd always been.

She took a minute to balance on the floating dock, then followed Carson toward the land. The shoreline was littered with shiny rocks, their wet sheen evidence of a higher tide. He stepped off first and waited for her.

"The path uphill is a little bit of a challenge, so watch your step." He glanced at the steep dirt and rock trail leading up. "I intend to make it safer and more user-friendly."

"I'll be all right. I've climbed some trails around San Diego that were pretty difficult." She'd worn her tennis shoes with the thickest tread just in case.

He looked as if he wanted to ask a question but instead said, "Good. Then let's go. Look out for loose rocks though."

She gave him a wry smile. He certainly was protective. "You first." She nodded toward the incline.

He turned and headed up the trail, and she followed. The rocks wobbled slightly, and thick pine needles disguised the area around the rocks. Once she stepped into the needles and her foot sank several inches, a surprise that almost threw her off balance. She decided to keep her eyes on her feet, glancing up occasionally to see how far they were from the top and how much closer they were to the lighthouse.

Carson stopped ahead of her and turned to look back. "You doing okay?"

"Sure." She gave him a confident smile. She didn't want him to think she was a wimp, even though she was surprised to see how high they'd climbed when she glanced over her shoulder. She'd forgotten how far above the water the lighthouse was. The view must be amazing at the top.

Finally, she scrambled over the last step, practically on her hands and knees. Carson stood ahead, his hand outstretched, and she gladly accepted his help. Once on level ground, she brushed off her hands and scanned the area.

"What would you like to see first—the lighthouse?"

"Sure. You're the tour guide, so lead the way."

Trees had grown up close to the tower, making the lantern room at the top barely visible above them. The lighthouse was not as Abby remembered the last time she'd been on the island. Instead of shining white, it showed signs of neglect: paint peeling on the outside and the metal gallery above rusted.

"Is that a bird's nest up on the roof?" Abby peered up.

"Yes, I'm afraid it is. I think it's empty now, though. At least I hope it is. I really want to get the tower, as well as the roof, painted this week. I think it used to be red."

"Seems like I remember it being red too. Hard to tell now that it's so rusty."

They tramped through tall weeds to the front of the lighthouse. Carson unlocked the padlock and shoved the heavy door, which groaned on its hinges as it opened. Just a few steps inside the round building, the spiral staircase began. Abby stared up at the metal stairs as déjà vu set in.

The last time she'd been there was during high school when her mother and father brought her over. At that time the Coast Guard operated the light but weren't present all the time. Father had asked for permission to see the light, so two guardsmen met them at the island and unlocked the lighthouse for them. Mother had reminisced about living there, telling of childhood adventures. Then as now, Abby wished she had been there when Granny still ran the light.

Musty air filled the hollow building as Abby and Carson climbed to the top, holding the handrail as the metal stairs creaked with each step. "We'll get the rust scraped off these and repainted, then they'll look good as new," Carson said, his voice echoing through the tower. Funny that he seemed to know what she was thinking about as she tried to remember what the steps used to look like. At the top, he pushed open a small hatch.

"You go first," he said. "Reach through and grab the handles to pull yourself up." Abby did as he said and found herself in the lantern room while he climbed up behind her. Despite the trees, the vista before her stretched to the edge of the horizon, with islands and boats strewn across the water.

"Would you like to go outside?" Carson motioned to a small door in the side of the lantern room.

"Is it safe?"

"Oh yes. The inspector said it was still stable—just in need of some TLC like everything else." He opened the door and climbed through to the outside gallery. She hoped the inspector was right as she followed Carson out. A gentle breeze greeted them, refreshing and cool after all the climbing. The peaceful scene made it hard to imagine the sudden dangerous storms that could threaten anyone caught in them. But it was such a storm that took her grandfather from Granny when he was returning from a trip to the mainland. Yet even in her grief, Granny carried on his duties, saying it was her responsibility to do so.

She was deep in thought when Carson tapped her on the arm. "Ready to go back in?"

Abby nodded, and they returned to the inside of the lighthouse and climbed back down.

When they reached the foot of the stairs and stepped back outside, Carson relocked the door, then turned to her. "Let's go see the keeper's house." A small stone building sat between the keeper's house and the lighthouse.

"This is the oil house where they stored the oil for the lantern. I'm not sure what I'll do with it yet."

"It looks like a dollhouse to me." Abby could see Emma having tea parties with her dolls and stuffed animals in the six-foot-square building. "It's cute."

"I wonder if the keepers thought it was cute."

"Probably not. I wonder if it still smells of oil?"

"That and other things. I'll air it out and repaint it too. I might still use it for storage though—yard equipment and stuff like that."

The two-story brick keeper's house was about fifty feet from the lighthouse. Broken windows and a tarp on the roof warned her that the house had suffered from neglect as well. A trickle of fear mingled with sadness as Abby walked toward the building. What would she find inside? Were there any signs of the time Granny and Mom lived there? After all, it'd been over fifty years since they had left.

The grass reached their knees as they walked the unused path. "Next week, I'm going to bring a lawnmower and make this place like a yard again." Carson pointed to some overgrown shrubs. "Looks like those are going to bloom, but I don't know what they are."

Abby's spirit lifted. "Rhododendron. Granny planted them." Granny had often talked about her favorite flower and how she missed them after she left.

"That so? Cool. I'm glad they're still here."

So was Abby, and she breathed a sigh of thanks for that connection to Granny.

As they walked around to the front door, Abby glimpsed hints of blue water through the trees. The view would be wonderful once the trees were cut back. Carson let her into the house, and she walked through the foyer where the stairs began and turned right into the next room, the former parlor, she assumed. She paused as she took in the scene. Not much furniture existed besides a couple of broken wooden chairs. Plaster was coming off the walls in places, revealing the wood framing behind. The brick fireplace sat cold, some of its bricks crumbling on the edges.

"How much of this is original?" Abby asked.

"Not much, except the fireplace and some of the walls. The Coast Guard stayed here a few years and turned one of the downstairs rooms into an office."

"I wonder what happened to the original furniture?"

"Perhaps your grandmother took some of it with her."

"Maybe she did. I don't really know, but Mom probably does."

They surveyed the rest of the downstairs, which included the kitchen, its wood cabinets standing open, and a dusty old stove. A Formica table with chrome legs and matching chairs with cracked vinyl covers stood on the torn linoleum floor, evidence of the era the Coast Guard inhabited the house. Attached to the kitchen was a small enclosed porch that seemed to have been an area for storage. The screen door had been chewed at the bottom by some kind of animals. Abby glanced around to see if any of them were in the house.

"At least the Coast Guard added another bathroom downstairs." He pointed to a door off the kitchen. "It may not be historically correct, but it's nice to have." Opening another door, he revealed an empty room. "This will be the keeper's bedroom, so he will be separate from the upstairs guests. It might even be my room someday."

Abby glanced at him. "You're going to live here?"

"Yes, I plan to. Does that surprise you?"

"A little, I guess. I thought you were going to hire someone to run the bed and breakfast."

"I could, but I intend to run it myself, at least in the beginning." Carson motioned toward the foyer. "Would you like to go upstairs? I think the steps are pretty solid."

From the foyer, they climbed wooden steps up a narrow stairwell with a small landing where the staircase turned before leading up to the second floor. "Up here, there are four bedrooms and another bath. I'd like to add a bath for each room, if possible," Carson said, as they walked down the hall.

Abby peered into each bedroom and saw more walls with patches of plaster missing. She pointed to a dark spot in the ceiling of one room. "Water damage?"

"Probably. I plan to get the roof redone next week. We need to take advantage of the dry weather as long as possible."

As they went back downstairs, Abby noticed a small door beneath the stairs. She walked over, opened it to peer inside, then smiled.

"There's nothing in there, as far as I know." Carson's brow wrinkled. "Why are you smiling?"

"My mother told me she used to sit in the closet under the stairs to read."

"Seems like it'd be rather stuffy in there."

"Maybe so. But what a great place for a child to hide and pretend they were somewhere else."

Carson returned her smile. "Guess it's kind of like having a treehouse, but inside."

"Exactly." A sense of home enveloped Abby, and even in its current state, she could visualize herself being comfortable in this place.

They headed back outside. "So what do you think? Can you picture it as a bed-and-breakfast?"

"Yes, I can. It has great potential, but it'll take a lot of work."

"True, but I'm willing to tackle it."

"Do you know how long it'll take?"

"No, I don't. A few months, depending on weather and available workers. It would be great to have it finished before the tourist season begins."

"That's only two, three months away. Can it be done that quickly?"

"I know it's a stretch, but I prefer to be optimistic. As long as all the subcontractors show up on time, and we don't run into any problems, I think it can be done."

"I'd like to see it when it's finished."

He tilted his head and studied her. She had a feeling he'd wanted her to say something else. But she refrained from offering her help. After all, what could she really do? She had to quit trying to rescue people. Wasn't that what Kevin had said? Besides, Carson was doing fine on his own, and Abby had enough to take care of already with Mom and Emma.

***

She was interested in the restoration. He could see the gleam in her eyes. But he was disappointed she hadn't volunteered to participate in it. Had he been expecting too much? After all, he didn't really know her. Yet he thought he could read her. Or maybe he was seeing what he wanted to see instead—a woman interested in partnering with his dream instead of ridiculing him like his ex-fiancée.

Well, he wouldn't push. He didn't want to risk offending or annoying her. "Want to look around a little more?"

Abby shrugged. "Is there more to see?"

Carson smiled and crooked his finger. "Come this way." He walked down a trail in the opposite direction from the way they'd come up. "This is another steep path, so be careful." He glanced behind himself to see how she was doing, resisting the urge to take her hand. She didn't act like she wanted to be babied. A roof came into view as they continued down. The bottom of the path ended at a small brick building.

He waved his hand toward it. "This was the foghorn house."

She glanced at it and nodded. "I remember this now. What are your plans for it?"

"Come in. I'll show you." He unlocked and pushed open the door, letting her enter first. The one-room building had a window in front facing the sea. "Since the size of this room is large enough for a bedroom, I thought it would be a nice guest suite, maybe even a honeymoon suite, because it's so private." She glanced away as a slight blush appeared on her cheeks. "Of course, I'll have to install a bathroom. But look at this view. Once I get the trees and shrubs in front of it cut back, it'll be wonderful."

Abby crossed her arms as she walked to the window and looked out. What was she thinking? "Sounds like a good idea."

"I thought so." He smiled, hoping she would too.

When she glanced back at him, a smile eased its way across her face. Why was she so reserved? She'd almost relaxed in the keeper's house, but now the invisible wall had returned.

"I wonder what Granny would think."

Granny? Oh, her grandmother, the lighthouse keeper. "She might be surprised the foghorn isn't used anymore."

"And maybe glad. She told me it was a lot of work to keep it going when the fog lasted longer than a day. And noisy. But don't they need it now?"

"No, the battery-operated thing out there that looks like R2D2 from *Star Wars* replaced the foghorns. Plus, there are buoys in the water making noise, and most boats have GPS now to keep them away from the shore."

"Granny said there were times it got so foggy, you couldn't see the water. How frightening that would be, especially if you were in a boat."

"I've come over when it was pretty foggy, and it is rather scary. You feel helpless and lost and hope you're headed the right way. I suppose the key is to not be on the water when it's foggy."

"If you can help it. I remember she also said sometimes the fog rolled in when least expected, even in the middle of the day."

"Didn't they say at the ceremony that she saved some people? I wonder if it was foggy then."

"I never heard her speak of it if she did."

"I'm trying to get my hands on the logbooks. The keepers had to record the weather and anything significant. But those guys weren't very wordy."

"Guys?"

"You know, keepers. Sorry, most of them were men. And the men only wrote what they needed to for the records. The ones I've read were rather boring. And terse. I read one that simply stated, 'Took afternoon off to go to wife's funeral.' That's all. Wouldn't you think he'd say more than that?"

They stood at the window looking out toward the sea that peeked through holes in the foliage, as if playing hide-and-seek. Abby had relaxed again and appeared more comfortable, but her shoulders tensed at his remark. Did he say something wrong?

"I'd like to read a logbook, especially one kept by my grandparents." She faced him with eyebrows lifted. "Do you think you can get one?"

"The National Archives in DC has most of them. You can go there to look at them, or you can request a pdf." Disappointment registered on her face. "But I've put in a request, so we'll see what turns up. I'm pretty sure they'll have the most recent ones from the Coast Guard, but who knows whether they'll have any before that."

"Knowing my granny, I bet she kept very good records. She was pretty meticulous, from what I remember and from what Mom has told me. I sure hope you can get her logbooks."

"Tell you what. I'll follow up on my request first thing Monday morning and let you know." At least he'd have some reason to talk with her again. And now, more than ever, he wanted to get those logbooks.

Chapter Five

Abby couldn't get the island out of her mind. Ever since Carson brought her back, she'd been thinking about the place. It desperately needed restoration, and she was glad Mom hadn't been able to see it. The forlorn buildings would have been devastating for her to witness, so Abby had decided not to tell her just how bad they looked, trying instead to sound optimistic when she told her mother about the visit.

"I can't believe the old house will be a bed-and-breakfast." Mom shook her head. "Did the house still look pretty good?"

"It needs work, but Carson plans to restore it to its original condition, if not better."

"I sure would like to see it again. Just can't imagine myself climbing that hill anymore."

"Carson's going to do what he can to make it easier and safer for people to get to the top. I'm sure his insurance company will require it."

Maybe someday Mom would be able to go there again. Her health was declining every day, so the sooner the better. But did Carson seriously think he could turn the property into a B&B in three months?

On Monday, Abby dropped off Emma at daycare before taking Mom to another doctor's appointment. Since it was her monthly routine checkup for her lungs, the doctor needed to see if she was any better or worse since her last bout with a cold. Abby hated sitting in the waiting room, so she went outside to enjoy some fresh spring air. A couple of doors down from the doctor's office she spotted the sign for Tammy's Fabric Shop, its burgundy-striped awning a departure from the green-striped ones of the other businesses lining the street. When she'd been an interior designer in California, she'd been a frequent visitor at fabric shops. Why not see what kind of selection this store carried?

The bell on the door jingled as she entered, and a voice from the back of the store called out, "Be there in a minute."

Abby strolled through the shop, feeling the various textures and eyeing the colors and designs. The desire to decorate returned, and she realized how much she missed her old job. But leaving it behind was part of starting over here. As her eyes scanned the store's contents, she couldn't help but put things together and coordinate them in her mind.

A woman with graying hair pulled back into a long ponytail and glasses hung by a beaded chain around her neck hurried up to her.

"Hello there." She extended her hand. "I'm Tammy. This is my shop. Can I help you find anything?"

Abby shook her head. "No, thank you. My mother is at the doctor's office, so I thought I'd take a short stroll in the meantime."

"Oh, who's your mother? I might know her." The woman's brow crinkled as she thought.

"Grace—"

"Oh! You're Grace's daughter, Abby. I heard you'd come back to town. So nice to meet you. Actually, I knew you when you were a little girl, but I moved away a while myself." Tammy placed her hand on Abby's arm and looked into her eyes. "Is Grace okay?"

"About the same as usual. She's just having a follow-up appointment."

Abby fingered some crisp maroon-and-green plaid fabric. Wouldn't it be pretty as curtains? And maybe a chair cushion?

"That's a lovely fabric. Wrinkle-free. Are you doing some redecorating?" Tammy picked up the bolt, holding it so the material hung like a drapery.

The question took her aback. "Why no, I'm just admiring your selection. But if I were, I'd find a place to use that fabric." Her mind traveled back to the island and the keeper's house. She could see how the fabric would look on a chair by the fireplace, a matching pillow on the sofa. Before she could stop herself, a vision for the downstairs living room formed in her head. What was she doing? Trying to help someone who hadn't asked for her help?

She glanced at her watch. "I'm sorry, but I need to go back for my mother. You have some very attractive fabric here." She headed to the door and called back over her shoulder, "Nice to meet you."

"You, too, and tell Grace Tammy said hello."

When she returned to the doctor's office, Mom was sitting in the waiting room. "I thought you'd left me. Where'd you go?"

"I just took a little walk. Tammy at the fabric shop said to tell you hello."

"Oh, you met Tammy?"

"Yes, I just stopped in for a moment."

Abby took Mom's elbow and helped her out. She opened the car door and waited for her mother to get in. When Abby got into her seat and started toward home, Mom spoke. "Thinking about decorating again?"

Abby glanced at her. "No, not really. Just killing time. But she did have a nice selection."

"Tammy's is the place to go if you were doing any decorating. But you've got your place fixed up real nice." Mom coughed. "And you've helped spruce up my house too. You're very good at that. Maybe you could start decorating for other folks around here."

"Mom, I don't think Hope Harbor's residents could keep me in business."

"Maybe the B&Bs here in town need some redecorating."

The town only had three main streets, with only a dozen old homes that had been converted into quaint places of lodging. "Maybe so, but I still don't think that's enough places to support a decorating business. Besides, I have a job."

"Which you're missing right now, thanks to babysitting me."

"It's not a problem, Mom. The folks at the daycare understand."

"Well, I'd say you're overqualified for that job."

Abby shrugged. "It's good enough, Mom. It works for me and Emma."

Abby took her mother home then went back to the daycare, trying to forget the conversation. When she left her life in California after Kevin died, she had no intention of trying to recreate that life back home in Maine. The two places were so vastly different. It was as if she became a different person in each of them as well. And the California interior designer did not fit in Hope Harbor, Maine.

That night after she put Emma to bed she started doodling on a sketch pad while listening to but not watching a TV show. When the show ended, she yawned, put down the sketch pad, turned off the light, and went to bed.

***

Carson checked the address. Yes, this must be where the meeting was. He parked his truck and gazed up at the immaculate yellow Victorian with the white gingerbread trim around the large veranda. The sign out front read Sunshine Cottage Bed and Breakfast, but the large house could hardly be called a cottage. From the looks of the place, it must have at least eight bedrooms, if not more. He'd like to know how much they rented their rooms for.

He stepped up on the porch with its antique wicker furniture and knocked on the door before noticing the antique crank doorbell. Maybe it worked. He twisted the knob and, sure enough, heard the unpleasant old-fashioned noise. Steps approached from the other side and the door opened. A friendly faced middle-aged woman stood before him. "Hello. Can I help you?"

"Yes, I'm here for the bed-and-breakfast owners club meeting. Have I got the right place?"

Her eyes widened, but she smiled and stepped aside, revealing a large foyer with a red Persian rug on the floor and a grand walnut hall tree boasting a huge mirror. She motioned for him to enter. "You have. And who might you be?"

"Carson Stevens. I'm renovating the Hope Island lighthouse and turning the keeper's house into a bed-and-breakfast."

She extended her hand. "Mary Warner. I manage this place." She gestured to a room off the large hallway. "The meeting is in there. Some of the others have already arrived."

Carson entered what must have been the parlor. Ornate Victorian furniture filled the space with gilt-framed paintings and velvet-tufted chairs. A massive fireplace dominated one wall, its mantel displaying an antique clock in front of an opulent mirror. When he entered the room, conversation stopped among the people seated in a circle, and all eyes focused on him.

"Everyone, this is Carson Stevens, the one who is turning the lighthouse property into a bed-and-breakfast," Mary said.

Curious looks accompanied forced smiles and mumbled hellos. Not exactly a warm welcome. The others acted as though he were some sort of alien.

"Hello." Carson mustered enthusiasm and a broad smile to reduce the awkwardness.

"Help yourself to the coffee, Mr. Stevens," Mary said, motioning to a silver cart with a silver coffeepot.

"Please call me Carson." He took her up on her offer and poured himself a cup in one of the dainty china cups, remembering to take a saucer like his mother would tell him to do. He could down that small amount of coffee in a heartbeat but restrained himself. However, he didn't restrain himself from taking a couple of the powdered sugar cookies on the tray beside the coffee pot. He hadn't seen cookies like those since his mother hosted a ladies' luncheon at his house when he was a child.

Carson took a seat, balancing his cup and saucer, and nodded to the four others in the room who were sizing him up as he was them. From what he could tell, the others were two couples, probably husbands and wives.

"I'm sorry, I didn't catch your names," Carson said, even though no one had offered a name.

One of the men spoke up. "Joe and Betty Phillips. We run the Rose Lane Bed-and-Breakfast."

The other man followed suit. "Sam and Phyllis Butler. Our bed-

and-breakfast is the Seaview."

Another couple entered the room next, and Carson found out they ran the Blueberry Hill B&B. So far, four of the town's dozen bed-and-breakfasts were represented. So where was everyone else?

Mary came in and sat down beside him. "Well, that's about everyone but Fred, and he's always late."

"Really? With so many B&Bs in town, I thought there'd be more people here," Carson said to her. "I know the season hasn't really started yet, but it's getting close. Are the other owners out of town?"

"No, these are all the owners."

"But there are more B&Bs. Who owns those?"

Mary chuckled. "Fred. He owns most of them."

Carson tried to hide his surprise. Here he'd thought all the lodging establishments were owned by "moms and pops." He'd never expected one person to have a monopoly.

Before he could digest the information, the front door opened, and another man entered.

"Fred, you're just in time," Mary said.

Fred was not at all what Carson had envisioned. He wasn't a large man, just average, in fact, with thinning gray hair and wire-rimmed glasses. And instead of a commanding personality, he seemed rather quiet, but serious, more like a bank teller than a corporation. He nodded to the others then poured himself some coffee before taking the only armchair in the room. Carson wondered if the chair was reserved for him, since no one else had taken it.

"Fred, this is Carson Stevens," Mary said. "He's the one who bought the island and is turning it into a bed-and-breakfast. Carson, this is Fred Harding."

Fred raised an eyebrow. "Nice to meet you, Mr. Stevens." He sipped his coffee. "So you're going to turn that old keeper's house into a B&B? I imagine that'll take quite a bit of work."

"Yes, sir, it will. But my crew is doing a good job on it, and we're making progress. As long as the weather holds out, we'll stay on schedule."

"And when exactly do you expect to be open for guests?" Fred's smile appeared rehearsed and didn't reach his eyes.

"I'm hoping by June or July."

Fred sputtered and acted like he gagged on his coffee. "So soon? You think it'll be ready by then?" Fred glanced around at the others. "Can you imagine?"

The others smiled and shook their heads as if on command.

"Mr. Stevens, you certainly have high hopes," Fred said, sounding somewhat demeaning.

Echoes of his father's voice reverberated through Carson's mind. Always negative and doubtful about Carson's ability, his father had criticized his son's judgment as long as Carson could remember. He stuffed down the bad vibes and kept his composure.

"Yes, sir, I guess I do."

Fred put down his coffee cup on the small table beside him and leaned forward as if Carson were a child sent to the principal's office. "Have you hired someone to run it for you yet?"

"Actually, no. I'm going to do that myself."

More surprised looks circulated through the room.

Fred chuckled. "Now that's interesting."

Oh boy, here it comes.

"Have you ever operated a bed-and-breakfast before?" Fred asked the dreaded question.

Did the man treat everyone like they were total idiots, or was it just Carson's privilege?

"No, sir. I haven't. But I've stayed in some, and I know what good service is."

Fred's smile became a grin. "Well, Mr. Stevens, I go to restaurants, but that doesn't make me a chef." Fred chuckled and scanned the group as their cue to laugh with him.

Carson bit his tongue. Why was this man trying to make him look like a fool? He carefully put his coffee cup down on the table, afraid that if he held it any tighter, he'd break it.

Carson faked a laugh. "Crazy, huh? Well, if I get in over my head,

I'll find someone else to manage the business. But I'm willing to try first."

Fred's face darkened. "I hope you know, Mr. Stevens, our association has very high standards. Even though you're on the island, we expect you to conform to the same standards as the rest of our establishments."

Carson's gut twisted in knots, reminding him of a similar conversation he'd had with his father. *Lord, help me keep my temper from showing in my words.* "I wouldn't expect any less. And I assure you, I intend to not only meet your standards but surpass them."

Fred sat back and rubbed his chin. "Is that so? Then you really do have mighty high expectations."

"As a matter of fact, that's the reason I wanted to join your membership, so I'd be fully acquainted with your standards."

"I think that's a good idea. You can get with Mary after the meeting, and she will fill you in on the dues and so on." He slapped his hands on his knees and looked around. "Now. Shall we get on to business?"

Carson tried to listen to the rest of the meeting as the conversation switched to civic improvements in preparation for the season. Carson prayed his face hadn't turned red from anger. Talk about being on the hot seat. Who was this Fred Harding guy? He acted like he owned the town. And frankly, owning eight B&Bs in a town with twelve might be a good reason. But he didn't have to be rude or give Carson the third degree. Maybe Carson expected the other owners to welcome him to their club and encourage him, but that sure didn't happen.

However, if Fred thought his jabs would discourage Carson, he was wrong. Carson loved a challenge, and as if getting his B&B ready wasn't challenge enough, Fred's remarks increased Carson's resolve even more. Never tell Carson Stevens he couldn't do something. He might look like an idiot, but he would prove Fred Harding wrong. Now he was more determined than ever to succeed in his plans. Hope Island Lighthouse Bed-and-Breakfast was more than a business idea. It was the culmination of a lifelong dream. He had to make it work. He *would* make it work. With or without Fred Harding's support.

***

Carson peered up at the top of the lighthouse, watching a workman climb a ladder to the roof. The man reached for the bird nest.

"Is it empty?" Carson called out.

The man gave him a thumbs-up, removed the nest, and climbed back down. He leaned over the gallery railing. "You want it?"

Carson shrugged. "Sure. Toss it down."

The nest floated to the ground. From the size of it, Carson could tell it had held a pretty big bird. Bits of feathers were stuck in the nest, as well as the remnants of the bird's meals—skeletons of fish and bones of small animals. Hopefully, the bird wouldn't come back.

Today was demo day. While the lighthouse was being sanded and scraped, other men would be inside the keeper's house tearing out everything that needed to be replaced, such as old wood and carpet. One of the contractors turned on the generator to start sandblasting the lighthouse, and the loud drone dominated every other noise around. Carson watched the men work and felt guilty standing there doing nothing. He walked over to the keeper's house to see how he could lend a hand.

Stepping inside the front door, he found men with masks prying old carpet off the floorboards. He sure hoped the original wood floors were in good shape. Nick looked up and walked over.

He lifted his mask to speak. "Did you want something, Mr. Stevens?"

Carson motioned to the other workers. "Please. It's Carson. I'd like to help. What can I do?" He needed to get his hands dirty, to prove to all the doubters his dream was achievable.

"First, you have to put on a mask. Probably asbestos in here, so we wear them as a safety precaution."

Carson took the mask Nick handed him and put the straps over his ears. Nick motioned for him to follow, and they headed to the kitchen.

"You can help in here. We need to pull these counters and cabinets off first." He handed Carson a hammer. "Knock that counter loose from this end. I'll go over to the other end and do the same, then we'll lift it."

Carson went to work, banging away at the countertop from the bottom. After a while, it gave way, and he and Nick lifted it and carried it out the back door. Years of dirt and grime were revealed as they removed each thing from the kitchen. The cabinets were tackled next. Once they were taken down, the men took a lunch break.

"You gonna put a modern kitchen in here?" Nick asked.

"Yes, we need to function by twenty-first-century standards."

"We'll have to check the plumbing and electrical once we get everything out. You'll probably need some new pipes and rewiring."

Carson saw dollar signs, but he wasn't surprised to hear the information. No one had lived there for thirty years, and the place had to be brought up to code before it was habitable. He was certain the investment would be worth it once the place was ready for guests. Even if he was the only one who ever lived there, he'd like to have an updated kitchen.

He'd stayed in a few other lighthouses that had been converted to bed-and-breakfast inns—two in Michigan and one in Oregon. Each of them had their own personality and unique setting, and the owners told him they stayed booked pretty much year-round. But they were in remote, difficult to reach locations, even though they were on the mainland. Carson felt he'd have the advantage of being close to the mainland but unique in being on an island, even if he had to provide the transportation himself. And even if he had no experience as an innkeeper.

As the sun dropped toward the trees, the men packed up to go. Carson's back ached from all the manual work he'd done that day. A desk job didn't get you in shape for this kind of work, and although he enjoyed hiking, he hadn't done much of it lately. When he moved to Maine, he'd quit going to a gym. Surely there was one around here somewhere. Although at the moment what he really wanted was a massage and a hot tub. Unfortunately, the family inn where he was staying didn't provide such things.

At least he had Wi-Fi at the inn so he could do his computer work. He'd have to get service on the island, too, if he was going to continue to work his other job. He didn't know how long it would take to make a profit with the B&B. The ones in town were only booked a maximum of six months, with the majority of them closed during the winter months when no one visited the area. He hadn't decided yet if he would close or not. Just how bad could it be to stay out there during the winter?

Chapter Six

"Mom, do you have any furniture that belonged to Granny?" Abby scanned her mother's living room.

"A few things. Why?" Mom sat in the recliner stroking Hercules, who was wedged between her and the side of the chair.

"Just wondering how the keeper's house looked when you lived there."

"Well, that rocking chair over there was hers." She nodded at the familiar chair.

Abby studied the primitive wood rocker that she thought had always been at her mother's house. "Is this the same chair she rocked you in when you were a baby?"

Mom nodded. "Same one. Of course, I don't remember. But I rocked you in it when you were a baby."

Emma went over and climbed up in the chair. "Did you rock me in it when I was a baby, too, Momma?"

"No, honey. We didn't live here when you were a baby."

Emma's eyes drooped. "You didn't rock me?"

"Of course I did, just not in that chair."

"Then rock me in it now!" Emma reached for Abby.

Abby smiled. "All right. But you're not a baby anymore." Abby picked up Emma, put the child in her lap, then proceeded to rock. The chair creaked, showing its advanced age. "I think we may be too heavy for the chair." She tickled Emma, making her giggle and slide off.

Abby stood. "Now you can say you were rocked in that chair too." She looked around. "That's all, Mom? Just the chair?"

Mom frowned and twisted her lip. "And that big ole Bible." She nodded to a huge book resting on the top of the small bookcase.

Abby walked across the room and lifted the book with both hands before carrying it to the dining table. The massive Bible must've weighed ten pounds. Emma climbed back into the rocking chair and began rocking her bear and singing to it. Abby sat down and opened the old book to the yellowed page that read "Presented to" then, handwritten, "Charles and Abigail Martin, June 18, 1920, on their wedding day from Thomas and Mary Martin." Abby turned the pages to the center of the Bible where a stiffer paper was titled "Family History" then a page for Marriages, Births, and Deaths.

On the announcement page for births, she found listed "Charles Martin II, Born July 12,1931, Died July 15, 1931." Below it, "Thomas Martin, Born October 8, 1933, Died November 2, 1933." Next was "Baby Girl Martin, born March 10, 1935, Died March 10, 1935." Apparently, the little girl hadn't lived long enough to name. The entries tugged at Abby's heart. Finally, the last entry was "Grace Abigail Martin, born April 22, 1944?"

"Mom, I had no idea Granny had lost so many children before you were born. How sad."

Mom nodded. "She told me she'd given up on having children until I came along. The others were all born prematurely, and since they had to go to town to get a doctor, by the time she needed one, it was too late to fetch him."

"You were born several years after the others. She must have been thrilled to finally have a healthy child. Wonder why there's a question mark after your date? Do you think she entered the date later and wasn't sure?"

Abby's mother smiled. "I doubt she was sure I'd survive. The question mark probably represents her wonder if she'd be writing the date of death. She always called me her surprise child. Not only did I survive, but it was a surprise she had a child so late in life. But when I had you at age 42, it seemed like we Martin women had babies later than most. Of course, you were only 30 when Emma was born."

Abby shook her head. "Strange that there were so many years between you and the previous baby."

"Mother might have had more miscarriages that weren't written in that Bible. But she always said I was a strong baby. Too bad I'm not strong now."

"You're much older now, Mom."

"Yes, but your granny lived to be 90, and she always seemed to be in good health, even then. I think it was all the work she had to do at the lighthouse after my father died, climbing up and down the steps, carrying oil, doing yardwork, fixing things—everything. The lighthouse board planned to give her an assistant, but she rejected the idea. I think she wanted to prove she could do it herself."

"But she assisted your father, didn't she?"

"Yes, she did. That's how she knew what to do."

"Seems like she'd want an assistant then. Especially since she was taking care of a small child too."

"It does, doesn't it? But your granny was fiercely independent and wasn't interested in sharing the home with a stranger. Of course, as I got older, I helped as much as I could. But until then, when I was too small to help, she did it all herself. The Coast Guard didn't push, since Father died during the war while men were in short supply here, most off fighting somewhere."

Abby turned the page and the next one read "Deaths." The only death listed was that of her grandfather—"Charles Martin, Drowned March 3, 1945."

"I guess you don't remember your father much, since you were just over a year when he died."

"No, not really. He smoked a pipe, and sometimes when I'm around another person smoking one, the aroma reminds me of him. I think he had a deep laugh, but I'm not sure if I remember it or if Mother told me and I imagined it."

Abby glanced at the framed black-and-white photo her mother had on the mantel of her grandparents standing in front of the lighthouse. Sure enough, her grandfather, dressed in his lightkeeper's uniform, had a pipe in his mouth, arms crossed over his chest. Her grandmother stood proudly beside him, a slight smile on her face as if she found something amusing. Abby could almost see Granny's eyes twinkling the way she remembered them. How had her grandmother remained so happy after all she'd been through?

Abby closed the Bible and rested her hands on top of it. How she wished she could talk to Granny now.

"You sure are interested in your grandmother today." Mom coughed a few times, then caught her breath. "Must be because you went to the island."

Abby nodded. "Yes, I think so. When I was a little girl and heard Granny talking about the lighthouse, I thought the stories were interesting, almost like fairy tales. But now that I'm an adult, I appreciate the reality of her life."

"Don't forget I lived there for seventeen years while I was growing up, so I know a bit about it myself." Mom coughed again, and Abby went to the kitchen to get her a glass of water.

"Grandma, who did you play with when you were little? Did you have a bear like mine?" Emma asked from the rocking chair, her long dark curls framing her little face.

"Well, Emma, I didn't have a bear just like yours, but I did have a teddy bear. I had a couple of dolls, too, so I played with them. But there weren't any other children on the island."

"And you had Hercules," Emma said.

Mom chuckled. "I didn't have Hercules back then, but we did have some barn cats."

"No playmates for you, and no companionship for Granny. I just keep thinking about how she managed after her husband died, how she raised a child all alone out there," Abby said.

Mom shrugged. "I never gave it much thought myself because she just did. Granny was resilient, and she did what had to be done. She didn't have anyone else to depend on."

Abby shook her head. "I don't know. She just strikes me as a woman with supernatural strength. I can't imagine doing what she did."

Mom glanced at Emma as she rocked and sang a song to her Wonder Woman bear, then looked back at Abby. "But Abby, you're doing the same thing."

"No, Mom. My life is easy compared to Granny's, although it feels hard to me." Abby remembered her conversation with Carson. "Mom, did you ever see the logbooks Granny kept?"

"I remember seeing her write in them, but that's all. She had to record temperatures, wind, rain or ice, you know, the weather. Nothing too exciting."

"Carson said some of the female lighthouse keepers kept more detailed records than the men. Did Granny, by any chance, keep one of her old logbooks and leave it to you?"

Mom shook her head. "Not that I can recall. You can look through her old trunk if you'd like. But I figured all that official stuff would've been turned over to the Coast Guard. Why would she keep it?"

"According to Carson, a lot of logbooks are at the National Archives now, and he's requesting the ones for Hope Harbor."

"I didn't know you could do that. Or even if the books still existed. If he gets his hands on them, maybe he'll let you see them."

"He said he would." And she assumed he would do as he said. But then again, maybe she assumed too much. It was, after all, his property, just like the lighthouse and the other buildings. She'd been careful not to show too much interest in the renovation, not wanting to overstep her bounds and not sure she wanted to be involved anyway. Yet she thought he wanted her to be. Why else would he ask her to go there? But if it was information he was looking for, he wouldn't get much from her because she didn't know anything.

But now that she'd been to the island and learned a little more about her grandmother from the old Bible, she was being drawn back. Was there something she needed to discover? Something that would reveal the clue to her grandmother's strength, some insight Abby hadn't yet grasped?

***

Carson cupped his coffee in his hands, letting the warmth penetrate his fingers and crawl up his arm. Work on the island had to stop when a storm rolled in, drenching the crew while they scrambled to the boat. Still shivering from the rain, Carson couldn't shake the chill even though he'd changed clothes. The storm seemed to have come out of nowhere, and the choppy ride back while waves crashed over the side of the boat was enough to make even a seasoned mariner pray for safe return.

Thankful for Mo's, Carson hoped to catch up on some of his paying work at the coffee shop. Waiting for a document to open, he gazed outside as rain streamed down the windows. When Abby Baker rushed inside, the surprise startled him out of his trance. She wore a bright green raincoat with a hood that practically hid her face and hair, but when their eyes made contact, her smile registered instant recognition.

Why his heart raced like it did when he saw her was beyond him, but he couldn't deny he welcomed the sight. He waved her over.

"Care to join me?"

"Sure. Let me get my coffee and I'll be right back." She unclasped her coat and hung it on the back of the chair across from him at the tall bistro table. She shook her long hair loose before heading to the counter. Should he have offered to get her coffee for her? Why didn't he think of that before she walked away? Good thing they were just friends, or he'd be guilty of being a bad date.

She came back to the table with a cup twice as big as his.

"Guess you need the Most Joe today." He smiled and nodded at her cup.

She shrugged. "Rainy days make me sleepy. In fact, I dropped off Emma at Mom's after preschool and she went right to sleep, so maybe the weather has the same effect on her."

"Yeah, me too. But I need to do some work."

"Oh, then I don't mean to interfere." She started to get up.

He reached out his hand, placing it on top of hers, sending a warm current up his arm. "No, please stay. This can wait. I was kind of daydreaming anyway."

She nodded toward the laptop. "What kind of work do you do?"

He shrugged. "I design websites. Plus, I have a couple of corporate clients whose websites I manage for them. The kind of work I can do anywhere and almost any time."

"So you could work from the island too?"

"If I have Wi-Fi. That's one thing I have to guarantee."

She glanced outside the window. "I guess you couldn't do any construction work on the island today."

"Well, actually, we started this morning when it was just overcast. But the storm whipped up right after noon, and we had to make a dash for the boats."

"Hope everything's all right, you know, with the rain and all."

"I think so. We have everything covered. At least we were able to get a coat of paint on the lighthouse this week. Glad we got that done. It sure looks better." He stopped himself from saying she should see it, in case she didn't want to.

"That's good. How's the house coming?"

He couldn't prevent the smile that hit his mouth at her interest. "All right, I guess. We had to stop doing anything to the plaster walls so we could run new electrical and plumbing. I think the original wood floors will be good once we get them cleaned up and polished. Don't know why people would cover them up with carpet." He watched her response for a sign of interest.

"I guess at the time, carpet was the latest thing and thought to be easier to maintain than wood. Maybe it even helped keep the house warmer. Some of the houses I worked on had beautiful wood floors beneath the old carpets."

"You worked on houses?" Carson looked at Abby's delicate hands, amazed that she had used them for manual labor.

"Well, I didn't actually work *on* the houses like you are, you know, construction. I'm an interior designer, or at least I used to be."

"Oh. I didn't know that." The idea came to his mind to ask, but he held back. "So you don't do that anymore, I guess."

"Not since I moved back, no. I don't see much use for that here in Hope Harbor." She glanced down at her coffee and focused on stroking it with the stir stick and rearranging the pretty heart the barista had designed on the top. She sighed and looked back up at him. "I used to live in San Diego, which is completely different than here."

"Yes, I'd say you're right about that." He took a swallow of coffee. "In fact, I'd say the only thing California and Maine have in common is that they're both on oceans."

She smiled and her shoulders relaxed a little. Then a tiny crease appeared in her brow. "Did you hear anything about the logbooks?"

He shook his head, sorry to have to tell her he hadn't. "No, not yet."

As he'd expected, disappointment showed on her face. "I asked my mother if she had one, by any chance. She didn't. Said they were government property so Granny wouldn't have kept them."

"So far, the most interesting thing we've found is old newspaper stuffed behind the plaster. In the past, they used it for insulation."

Her eyes widened. "Have you read any of it? Do you know what year it was from?"

"Yes, I looked at some of it. The paper I saw was dated in the 1940s, probably around the time of World War II. Lots of stuff about rationing and salvaging. Pretty interesting, actually."

"Did you save it? I'd love to see it. My mother was born in 1944, so she was born during the war."

He had a sudden urge to rush to the island. "I'll save any of it that's still readable and make sure you get to see it. I'm sorry, I didn't think you'd be that interested in it."

She fixed him with a determined gaze. "I don't know why, but I've got this deep desire to learn all I can about my grandmother. Ever since I went to the island, that desire has grown even stronger. So anything that tells me more about her and her life is important to me, including those old newspapers."

Her passion to find out so much about her grandmother caught him off guard. Up to now, she'd shown little emotion about anything, but this enthusiasm of hers was exciting and revealed a different side of her personality.

"First thing tomorrow, if the storm is gone, we'll go back out, and

I'll try to find the newspaper for you. We'll probably remove all we can without tearing out all the walls before we blow some real insulation in. I'm not sure, at this point, how much more plaster will have to come out—it depends on the plumbing and electrical."

"I wish I could go with you. I would like to help with the renovation."

He almost choked on his coffee. "You do? I mean, you're welcome to come, you know."

"I appreciate that, but I do have a job. At Emma's preschool. It wouldn't be right of me to just take off."

"Of course. I completely understand. Just let me know if you can."

"I will. I'll try to work something out. I really want to go back to the island." Her gaze dropped to her cup again, then she glanced back up. "You might think I'm strange, but I feel like the island is calling me back."

The longing in her eyes made him want to do whatever he could to satisfy it.

He placed his hand on her wrist and focused on her beautiful face. "I don't think you're strange at all. Or maybe I'm just as strange because I feel the same way."

She arched an eyebrow, then smiled. He'd take her kind of strange any day.

Chapter Seven

How would she have time to go to the island? What was she thinking? She couldn't just go off and leave the staff at the preschool short a person. It wasn't as if she needed the money as long as she got her widow's pension, but she liked staying busy and felt like she was helping others at the same time. She shouldn't have told Carson she wanted to go with him. What an irresponsible thing to do. He must really think she was crazy.

She could go when she got off at 2:00, but how would she get there? She didn't know anyone else going out at that time. Most of the lobstermen had come back in with their day's catch by then. She needed to leave when Carson did, in the morning. One thing she liked about the interior design business was the flexible hours, but the preschool wasn't like that. Everything started and stopped at the same time every day.

After she left Mo's, she went back to her mother's house to get Emma. A wonderful aroma hit her when she entered the door.

"What are you cooking, Mom?"

"Chicken and broccoli casserole, your favorite."

"It smells great." Abby didn't remember ever declaring the dish as her favorite, but Mom and Emma both liked it, so Abby was content with not having to cook dinner. She'd lost her desire to cook meals anymore, especially for just her and Emma. "Mom, you're spoiling me, you know."

"That's my job, isn't it?" Mom coughed as she shuffled through the kitchen. "Besides, it's just a casserole. No trouble."

Mom always loved casseroles. Abby believed it was a comfort food for her, something Granny had created out of whatever they had.

Throw it all in one dish, sprinkle some cheese on top, and bake it. Voila! Dinner. When Abby was growing up, she was suspicious of the contents of the mysterious dish that always looked the same but never tasted the same. But Dad had liked casseroles too. Abby didn't think she'd ever eaten a meal with separate components until she went to college and found out she could. But she wouldn't complain. It had to be better than fast food. Coffee and salad—they were her mainstays, but life wasn't all about what she wanted. It hadn't been for a long time.

Emma skipped into the room. "Hi, Mommy. Did you go for a run?"

Abby scooped her up in her arms. "No, honey, not today. It's been raining all afternoon."

"Where'd you go? Shopping?"

"I picked up a couple of things, then I went to Mo's."

"You could've had coffee here," Mom said, handing Abby the plates.

"I know, Mom. I just wanted one of their special coffees. They're really good on rainy days like this."

"Oh, that *fancy* coffee." Mom waved her hand as if to dismiss the idea.

"I ran into Carson there."

"Carson. The young man that bought the lighthouse? He's right nice-looking."

Abby's face warmed, but she couldn't disagree.

"I suppose they couldn't do any work over there in this weather."

"No, they had to leave around noon, he said."

"Sometimes it's safer to stay on the island instead of ride the storm back to the mainland. Lots of folks have made that mistake and regretted it." Mom motioned to the casserole dish sitting on top of the oven. "Would you please carry that over to the table and dish it out? I think I need to sit a minute and catch my breath."

"Sure, Mom." Abby brought the dish and put some of it on each plate while Hercules wove between her legs, reminding her of his presence. Then she poured herself and her mother some water and

Emma some milk and brought it to the table. "Emma, would you please get the napkins and forks?"

Emma scrambled to get the items, standing on tiptoe to reach the forks. When she brought them back, she put them by each place, then climbed up on her chair and reached out for the two adults' hands on each side of her. "God is great. God is good. Let us thank Him for our food. Amen."

"Thank you, Emma," her mother said before turning her attention to Abby. "So did Carson tell you how things were going?"

"Well, he did say they'd painted the lighthouse."

"That's good. It sure is pretty when it's freshly painted."

Abby tilted her head, noting the sound of affection in Mom's voice when she spoke of the lighthouse.

"That's about all he said they'd done besides tear out old carpet and cabinets and such in the house. He said the place needed to be rewired and new plumbing put in before they could patch the walls."

Mom nodded. "I'm sure it needs it, what with being vacant all these years."

"Mom, he said the walls were stuffed with old newspapers for insulation. Did you know that?"

She shook her head. "No, I wasn't aware of that."

"He said some of the papers dated back to 1945."

"My goodness, I was just a toddler. That was during the war, you know."

"That's right. I wish you could tell me what it was like on the island then, but you were too young to remember."

"Just what my mother told me. She used to talk to me about rationing, saving every piece of everything. She stayed like that all her life, even after the war was over. Never threw one piece of foil away."

Abby smiled but didn't remind her mother that she had the same habit as well.

"Do you know, back in the war, they used the lighthouse to look for German subs?"

"They did? Our lighthouse?"

Mom nodded. "Yep. You know the Nazi subs were up and down our coast."

"I wasn't aware of that. I didn't know they got that close."

"Oh yes, some even came ashore as spies over on Long Island and off the coast of Florida. They were caught, but I heard stories of German subs coming up and buying the fish off local fisherman. The government tried to keep that information a secret from the public. Guess they didn't want them to get scared."

"That's amazing. Do you think Granny was ever in danger on the island?"

Mom shrugged. "Don't know. She said the Coast Guard would come use the lighthouse for a lookout tower, so I guess we were all right when they were there. They were my 'uncles,' Mother said. I didn't know until I got older that I really didn't have any uncles. You know it was common practice back then for parents to call their friends 'aunt' or 'uncle' when speaking to their children. I remember how nice and friendly the Coast Guard men were to me. Sometimes three or four would come by, but other times just one, Uncle Michael. He was the nicest, and I liked the funny way he talked."

"But if you'd been in real danger, surely they'd have made you move to the mainland."

"Seems likely. I know the military took over some of the islands off the coast, the ones real far out. Some folks weren't too happy about being booted off their own property, but you know, it was wartime."

"I'd really like to see the newspapers they found in the walls. There might be interesting stories about this area during the war."

"Probably so. You think Carson will let you see them?"

"He said he would, but he wasn't sure they were still readable or if they'd been thrown away." Abby stirred her food idly.

"Why don't you go over there and see if you can help?"

Abby put her fork down. "Mom, we've been over this. I can't leave my job to go there. The school needs me."

Mom pointed her fork at Abby. "You know what? At the hairdresser yesterday, Ruth said her daughter, Kristen, is looking for a job. She has a six-month-old and wants to work somewhere she can take the baby with her. Couldn't she take the child to the nursery at the preschool while she's at work? Maybe you and she could share the job—you work two or three days and she works the others. What do you think about that idea?"

"She could definitely take the baby with her. Several of the ladies who work there have babies as well as preschoolers. But I don't know this person, Mom. I can't recommend her if I don't know her."

"She's a good girl. Husband's a lobsterman, of course. I'm sure the folks at the preschool know her anyway, even if you don't. Most people around here know everyone else."

"That's for sure." Abby's pulse quickened. "I'll talk to them tomorrow at the school and see what they think." Hopefully, they would agree to the suggestion. One never knew what information Mom would pick up at the hairdresser.

***

The phone buzzed in Carson's pocket. What now? Was a supplier calling to tell him a material wasn't available or else cost an extra arm and a leg? He'd had enough of that news so far in his quest to renovate the keeper's house.

Before he grumbled hello, he glanced at the number. Abby? His heart rate sped up, and his senses peaked on high alert. He blew out a breath and tried to sound calm.

"Hi, Abby."

A pause on the other end before the voice. Was she surprised that he knew it was her, or was she reconsidering the call?

"Hi, Carson. I wanted to tell you I'll be able to go to the island with you tomorrow. I've worked things out with another girl so I can be free three days a week. Is this too short a notice?"

Was it okay? Steadying himself and trying to sound cool, he said, "No problem. What time would you be able to go?"

"I can drop Emma off at the preschool at 7:30, then meet you at the docks. Is that early enough?"

"That'll be fine. See you tomorrow morning."

"May I pack a lunch? I'll bring enough for both of us, okay?"

"Sounds great. Bye." He shut off the call and stared at the phone. Wow. What a surprise. When she said she'd try to find a way to go, he didn't really think she would. This was one time he didn't mind being wrong. He ran through the list of things that needed to be worked on the next day, choosing what tasks he could assign to her. He didn't know her well, but she said she wanted to help, so he wanted something for her to do. This much he did know: she wanted to be useful and not just watch, much less get in the way. She wasn't a pampered princess like … He needed to push away those comparisons to Jennifer.

Today had been another wasted day as far as work on the island was concerned since the rain had hung around, so he was anxious to get back and see if there had been any damage. He was especially hopeful the newspapers they'd taken out of the wall weren't in the trash heap. So far, tomorrow's forecast appeared favorable, and with Abby along, the day already looked brighter.

The next day, Abby's car was in the parking lot when he pulled up. At least she hadn't changed her mind. She gave him a little wave and a smile that competed with the sight of the early morning sun as she climbed out of her car. She retrieved a backpack from behind her seat and pulled it over her shoulders. Her baseball cap was in place to hold her long ponytail, a look that was so right for her, along with her skinny jeans and hoodie.

He tore his eyes away from her long enough to climb out of his truck and grab a sack full of supplies he'd bought at the hardware store the day before. "You ready?" he said as he turned to face her.

"You betcha."

Standing there with her hands on her hips and feet spread, her ponytail blowing in the wind, she indeed looked like she was ready. What was it about that stance? Ah, he knew it. Wonder Woman. He could see the character prepared for battle. He chuckled.

She tilted her head. "What's so funny?"

"Oh, nothing." Maybe she wouldn't be amused. "Let's go." He

motioned toward the dock.

She raised an eyebrow, then turned and started walking down to the boat. He hurried to catch up with her.

"Skies are clear today, thank God. No rain showing in the forecast either, so we should have several days of good weather."

On the way to the island, Abby told him how she was able to get off work. "How convenient that the other lady wanted to work part-time and free you up," he said.

"I know. Mom says it's a 'God thing' and that He worked it out because He wanted me to be able to go to the island."

Carson raised his eyebrows. "Why would He want you to go to the island?"

She shrugged. "I'm not sure He did. That's Mom's belief. She sees divine direction in most things."

"Even in bad things?"

Abby shook her head and gazed away. "I don't know, maybe just in good things. But I really don't know why God allows some things to happen."

"I don't either. I figure someday I'll have a chance to ask Him in person."

They tied up at the island dock, grabbed their things, and started walking. Two other boats were already there.

"They get here early, don't they?" Abby asked as they walked past the other boats.

"As soon as it's daylight. There's a lot to do, especially with the rain delay yesterday."

Abby glanced up while walking to the top of the hill. "I can see the red roof of the lighthouse. It looks so new."

Carson looked up as well. "Amazing what some fresh paint will do. We cleared a few trees out around it as well, so now you can see the lighthouse from farther away."

She smiled as if pleased by the change. "Nice."

He couldn't agree more.

Chapter Eight

A bby loved the rich scent of the conifers that covered the island. She took a deep whiff and smiled. What a perfect day. The sky was clear azure and the previous days' storms had freshly watered the grass and trees, turning them a brilliant green in the morning sunshine. How invigorating. Abby embraced the freedom of knowing she didn't have to be anywhere else right now.

Men's voices and hammers pounding rang out above them as they climbed up. When they reached the top and stepped into the yard, Abby saw evidence of how much work had been done already. Old boards and other debris lay in piles. Men on the roof peeled off time-worn shingles and threw them down below while others hammered new shingles in place.

Carson stopped beside the keeper's house and looked up at the roofers. "How does it look?"

One of the men gave a thumbs-up. "Coming along. Had to replace some of the decking, but nothing damaged underneath. We're putting new flashing around the chimney too."

"Sounds good." Carson returned the thumbs-up.

"So maybe the bad decking was the reason for the water leak," she said.

Carson glanced at her with a surprised look. "Yes, hopefully there won't be any more leaks."

The change inside the house was a shock. Everything had been removed, and parts of the lath beneath the walls was exposed.

"Looks a little different than the last time you were here, doesn't it?" Carson asked.

"Quite a bit." The only thing in the main room that looked the same was the fireplace. "What are you planning to do to the fireplace?"

"Just make sure it works and patch the mortar where there's cracks so it doesn't leak smoke into the house."

"Are you going to leave it the original brick or paint it?"

His brow creased. "Paint it? No way. I like the red brick. Don't you?"

She nodded. "Yes, I do, especially here. It's more authentic that way."

As Abby studied the fireplace, she visualized Granny's rocking chair beside it. Was that where it had been? She would've been warmed by the fire and also given some light from its glow. Abby scanned the room, imagining curtains made of material she'd admired at the fabric shop hanging on the windows. She shook her head. Why was she decorating the place when it wasn't hers to decorate? But she couldn't help it. Her former career had trained her to look for ways to improve home interiors, yet she wouldn't tell Carson her ideas. He probably had some concept of his own about how he wanted to decorate it.

"Excuse me," Carson said. "I need to see what's going on in the other rooms." He stepped into the kitchen area where she heard him talking to a couple of men. Above her, the hammers pounded a muted rhythm from the roofers, even though there was a second floor between. Abby walked over to the fireplace and ran her hand down the rough brick. "If only you could talk," she said.

Carson returned. "The plumbers and electricians are trying to coordinate their work. It's kind of like the chicken and the egg." He smiled.

"What comes first, you mean?" She spread her hands out and glanced around. "So how can I help?"

"I've got just the job for you." He reached into the sack he'd brought and pulled out a scraper. "You can scrape the paint off the windows and windowsills. When you're finished with that, there's sandpaper in here and you can start sanding." He gazed at her almost apologetically. "Are you okay with that?"

Abby took the scraper and sack from him. "Of course. I can do that."

"Good. I'll be upstairs working if you need me."

Abby carried the scraper over to the window where the paint was peeling on the trim and the sill. She began scraping, listening to the sounds of work going on around her. What would Granny think, seeing all this being done to her house?

She finished one window and rested, letting her eyes roam around the room. Spotting the places in the wall that were exposed, she remembered the newspapers Carson had told her about. He hadn't mentioned them today and she forgot to ask. Was there any more old newspaper in there? She walked over to the wall and looked down into the dark recess. Should she put her hand in there, not knowing what she might touch?

Remembering the flashlight on her phone, she pulled it from her pocket, turned it on, and held it over the opening. Sure enough, crumpled up newspaper was between the lath and the wall. She gingerly reached down and grabbed a piece, hoping she wouldn't also touch a critter of some type.

Pulling the piece out, she laid it down on the floor and knelt beside it to smooth out the creases. The date at the top was March 10, 1945. Abby had heard a little about rationing during the war, but the number of ads promoting it surprised her. There was an ad for saving paper by writing on both sides. Another ad featured a cartoon of a woman flying a bomber with a caption that read "You can bomb Hitler by saving your grease." Still another ad showed a woman canning that read "Canning at home for victory." It seemed like every part of one's life could aid the war effort.

An article listed what to do and what not to do in a blackout. Next to it was a short article about people who had been fined or ticketed for not obeying the blackout orders. One person failed to drive without shields over their car lights, and another was fined for smoking outside. Her grandparents wouldn't have to worry about car lights, but maybe her grandfather refrained from striking a match to light his pipe outside. And they probably had to cover their windows as well. How dark and lonely it must have been on top of the island with no light anywhere around.

She glanced at the date again. March 10, 1945. Her grandfather had died the week before. And Granny was left alone with a baby barely a year old. Abby's eyes moistened as she imagined the grief her grandmother must have felt. How did she cope with the loneliness? No parents to turn to, no neighbors for company, plus the shadow of war looming over the country.

Abby scanned the rest of the page before turning it over to the other side where she found more ads showing how to be patriotic and salvage. An article listed servicemen missing, injured, or dead from the county. Granny didn't have to worry about Grandpa being on that list, yet he died in service to his country anyway, just not in the war. Most of the other articles listed various civic clubs and how they were helping the war effort by rolling bandages or planting victory gardens.

She didn't realize Carson had returned to the room until he spoke. "I see you found some of the newspaper."

Startled, she glanced up. "Yes, in the wall there." She pointed.

"Pretty interesting stuff." Carson studied her face. "You all right?"

She swiped her eyes with the back of her hand. "I'm fine. Just reading about what was going on around here during the war and the fact that my grandmother was in the middle of it is rather overwhelming."

"Wasn't your grandfather here too?"

Abby shook her head. "He was for most of the war, but he drowned just before this paper was published. So she was by herself until the war ended."

"Do you think she stayed here? I heard that some of the keepers had to leave because the Coast Guard moved in for surveillance during the war."

Abby twisted her lips. "Mother said they stayed here. I don't know where else she would've gone. By that time, their parents had all died. And Granny didn't have any sisters or brothers. But Mom said the Coast Guard came by occasionally."

"Hmm. Perhaps we could contact the Coast Guard station nearby and find out what happened here."

"Yes, I'd like to know that." Abby looked around. "I'm sorry. I'm supposed to be helping. I finished that one window, then got sidetracked."

"That's okay. I came in here to see if you're ready for lunch."

Abby checked her phone for the time. "Already? That was fast."

Carson shrugged, smiling. "Yeah, I know what you mean. When you get here, it almost feels like you've entered a time portal."

Abby nodded. She truly had. "You're right. I felt like I was back in 1945 for a while."

"So, let's take a break and reconnect with this year." He looked around. "Did you say you brought lunch?"

She jumped to her feet. "Yes, I did." She grabbed her backpack.

"Let's find a nice place outside where we can see the water."

"May I make a suggestion?"

"Sure." Then he grinned. "I bet I know what you're thinking."

"You think so? What?"

"The lighthouse. You want to sit at the top of the lighthouse."

"You guessed it. Is it possible or is the paint still wet? Or do you not want to do that?"

"The paint's been dry for days, and we haven't painted any of the interior yet. And yes, I'd love to have lunch at the top. It's the best place to be on the island. We can sit on the gallery, or if it's too windy out there, we can sit in the lantern room."

"Great," Abby said and followed him. She glanced over her shoulder and almost said, "Be back later," then realized there was no one else in the room. At least no one from this century.

***

Carson was glad to find the other workers had left the lighthouse so he and Abby could have it to themselves. As they climbed the stairs, he tamped down his excitement about spending the time with her, hoping he didn't act like an adolescent boy with his first crush. *Get a grip, Carson.* The door to the gallery was partly ajar, bringing fresh air, sunshine, and a hint of new paint into the old tower. He followed her outside where a gentle spring breeze blew through the trees.

For a few moments, they simply stood at the railing gazing out at the view. Some of the lobster boats were already heading back to the harbor after having caught their day's work. He waved his hand in case one of the captains looked up at the lighthouse.

"How do you know they're looking up here?" Abby asked.

A horn sounded in response and he chuckled. "Guess they're admiring our new paint job."

Abby's cute laugh tickled him to the core. "I'm glad they noticed. I wonder if they usually look at the lighthouse or did so today because of its new bright-red color."

"What would you do?"

"I'd look at it every time I passed. But I'm a bit biased."

"What I'm told is that all the local people keep an eye on the island and the lighthouse. They're rather possessive of it. If something doesn't look right, they report it to the Coast Guard. Thanks to them, vandalism has been kept to a minimum."

"That's good to know. I wonder if it's always been that way." Abby gazed at the water.

"You mean when your grandparents were here? I'd venture a guess that it was the same back then too." Carson's stomach growled. "Hey, I'm hungry. Let's sit over there out of the wind. Sound all right with you?"

Abby glanced where he pointed. "Sure." She moved over to the side of gallery and sat down cross-legged, her back leaning against the lantern room.

Carson sat down beside her, anxious to find out what his lunch would be. She unzipped her backpack and removed several containers, placing them beside her, then showed him two Ziplock bags with sandwiches.

"Turkey or roast beef?" she said. "It's organic, good quality, I promise."

He chuckled. "Roast beef."

She handed him one of the sandwiches. "I thought so."

"Why? I look like a roast beef guy?"

She grinned. "You look like a guy, and in my experience, most guys prefer roast beef over turkey."

"Well, I'm glad I look like a guy at least. And I do like roast beef."

She pointed to the containers. "Pickles in this one, carrots and celery sticks in this one, cookies in that one." Reaching into her backpack again, she pulled out a bag of chips. "Oh, and chips. Hope you like multigrain."

"Are you trying to make me healthy?"

"Couldn't hurt," she said. "Actually, I just brought what I like, since I really don't know what you like. I guessed about the roast beef."

He picked up the cookies and tried to see through the opaque container. "Good thing you made cookies. Not sure my system can handle so much healthy food."

"Actually, I can't take credit for those. My mother made them. She loves making sweets."

"Good. Because I love eating them."

"I forgot. I brought some water too." She withdrew a bottle from her bag and handed it to him.

He took a bite of the sandwich, inwardly moaning at the delicious taste. "This is quite a spread." He swigged some water. "Thank you so much. Next time you come, lunch will be on me."

Abby nodded, mid-chew. "Deal," she said after she swallowed.

For the next few minutes, they didn't talk, focusing on their lunch instead. Carson couldn't remember the last time he'd enjoyed someone's company so much. Abby was easy to be around, unpretentious and undemanding, so unlike his former high-maintenance fiancée. With Abby, he didn't sense the pressure to fill expectations but could just be himself. Perhaps if they were a couple, there would be more demands, but he didn't think so. Abby was completely different than Jennifer.

"I forgot to tell you," he said, remembering the one thing she'd wanted him to do. "I heard back from the Archives."

She jerked her head toward him. "You did? What did you find out? Will they give you the logbooks?"

"Yes. And no. They won't let me have the originals, but they will copy pages and send them." He shrugged and lifted his hands. "Better than nothing, right?"

"Sure. I just want to read them, but it would be nice to have one to show your guests, wouldn't it?"

"Yes, but I have to work with the system. Problem is, I have to be pretty specific about what I want copied. Are there any particular dates you'd like to see?"

Abby stared into space as she pondered the question. "I'll have to think about that a bit and let you know. Is there a limit to how much you can copy?"

"Since the service isn't free, there might be a financial limit."

"Oh, it's expensive?"

"Depends on how many pages you want." Carson cut his eyes at her. "Or there's another option. We could go to Washington, DC and look at the logbooks in person."

She twisted her lips. Was it because he said "we"?

"I don't think that's possible."

"Didn't think so. So let's pick a year or so you'd like to see, then find out if they have those for this lighthouse. Then maybe narrow it down to months and days."

"All right. I'd like to see a book with my grandfather's entries and also one with my grandmother's entries."

"Is there one year that would have both?"

She nodded. "1945."

Chapter Nine

When Abby got back to her mother's, she was tired from the work but energized by being involved in the process. Even though there was still so much to do, seeing partial progress was exciting.

Emma came running, arms outstretched. "Mommy! I missed you!"

Abby laid the old newspaper on the kitchen table, picked up her daughter, and gave her a squeeze. "I missed you, too, Emma." She turned her head toward her mother who was coming into the room, Hercules on her heels.

"Kristin brought her home, so I didn't have to go get her. Wasn't that nice?"

"Yes, very." Abby didn't mention that she and Kristin had worked that out the day before. "Mother, look at this."

Mother came over to the table and plopped down in a chair, out of breath as if she'd walked a mile or more. "What do you have here?"

Abby pointed to the top of the page. "Look at the date."

"March 10, 1945. You got this from the old house?"

"Yes, it was in the wall. Remember, Carson said that years ago they used newspaper for insulation."

Mother scanned the paper. "My goodness. Look at all this about rationing and saving things. Mother told me about it when I was older, but I didn't realize how many things they salvaged."

"What gets me is saving grease for bombs. I didn't know cooking grease could be used for bombs," Abby said, pointing to the ad about it. "Carson said grease had glycerin in it, and glycerin was an ingredient in bombs. Can you imagine?"

"I don't know how Mother could have cooperated even if she'd wanted to. This ad says to take the pound of grease you've saved to the butcher. She wouldn't have gone all the way to shore to turn in her grease, I don't think."

"Seems like she was already helping the war effort just by being a lighthouse keeper during the war."

"It does, doesn't it? And she had to use ration books just like everyone too. I used to have one of her old books."

Emma pointed to a picture on the newspaper. "Is this you, Grandma?"

Mom chuckled. "No, I wasn't that old when this paper was printed. In fact, I was just a baby." She poked Emma in the tummy, sending the girl into a giggle fit.

Abby went to the living room and picked up the photo of Granny and Grandpa. She carried it back to the kitchen, studying it as she walked. "Do you know when this photo was taken?"

"It's probably on the back."

"I guess it was taken before you were born, since you're not in the picture."

"Probably so."

Abby carefully unfastened the back of the frame and removed it to reveal the flipside of the photo. Scrawled in cursive handwriting was Hope Island Light, April 5, 1944. "So you weren't born yet."

"No, I wasn't, since my birthday is April 22, 1944."

Abby examined the photo. "What is that building off to the side behind the lighthouse?"

Mom took the photo and studied it. "Oh, that was the barn. It's gone now."

"You had a barn? Did you have farm animals?"

"We had a milk cow, and I think at one time we had chickens. But Mother said a mink ate the chickens, so she gave up on them. We had a garden too. We grew tomatoes, corn, potatoes, onions, and green beans. When you can't run to the store easily, you take care of yourself the best way you can. Seems like we always had plenty of food. Mother canned vegetables and made jam out of wild blueberries. There's also an apple tree on the island, so we had dried apples when they weren't in season and a number of foods made with apples."

"I wonder if Carson knows where the barn was." Abby held the photo up and studied it. What was it about that photo that bothered her? She just couldn't put her finger on it.

Mother laughed and pointed to an ad in the newspaper. "Look at this. Maybe you need this kind of job. 'Wanted: Intelligent Women for Challenging Laboratory Jobs. These jobs are for women of intelligence who want to make something important to help the war effort. You will be trained, and the wages are excellent. Apply at Harvey Radio Laboratories, Cambridge, Mass.'"

"Wonder if you had to take an IQ test to apply?" Abby said and both of them laughed, which brought on another choking fit for her mother.

After Mom recovered, she pointed to a photo with two women. "Bet you don't know what they're doing."

Abby studied the photo. "Drawing lines on the back of their legs?"

Mom chuckled. "Yes, that's what they're doing. During the war, the women were asked to turn in their nylon stockings to be reused to make parachutes. So since they didn't have stockings, they drew lines on their legs to look like seams."

"Seams?"

"You can be thankful you never had to wear hosiery. The stockings had seams that ran down the back of the legs. They were a pain to keep straight, too, let me tell you."

"You're right. I'm glad women don't wear those anymore."

Mom looked up from the newspaper. "So, tell me about today."

Abby recounted the day's events at the island while her mother nodded, but her gaze was far away. Abby wondered if her mother was really listening. "Mom?"

"Hmm? I was remembering when I was a child and used to go up the lighthouse and stand on the gallery. I felt like I was on top of the world."

"Did you wave to the boats?"

"I sure did. All the lobster boats honked their horn when they saw me up there. I thought I was pretty special. I'd pretend I was the queen, and everyone below had to obey me."

Abby smiled at the thought of her mother as a little girl standing on the gallery, waving to all the boats.

"I enjoyed being out there today too. It was nice."

Mother studied her. "And how was the company? Was he nice too?"

Abby's face heated. "Mom, Carson is a nice guy, easy to be with. Quit trying to make something out of it. We're getting to be friends, and that's all I want."

"Is that all he wants?" Mom lifted an eyebrow.

"All I know he wants is to get the work done so he can be open for business."

"Well, I'm glad there's something you can do to help him."

"I've done a little remodeling before, sanding and painting. Nothing too big."

"So you're going back to the island tomorrow?"

"No, Kristen has Thursday and Friday off, so I have to work tomorrow. I won't be able to go back to the island until next Monday." Even as she spoke the words, Abby longed to return.

The next two days, Abby thought about the island almost all the time. She wanted to know what was going on, what they had done while she was gone. Several times, she pulled out her phone and looked at Carson's number, but she just couldn't make herself call him. She didn't want to be a pest. Besides, if he wanted to talk to her, he'd call her. Yet it bothered her that he didn't call. Didn't he know she was interested in what was going on? Wasn't he aware of how much she wanted to be there? It probably never crossed his mind. Yet, there had been a few times she'd caught him looking at her in a way that sent a warm sensation through her. Was Mom right? Was he attracted to her? She shook her head. It didn't matter. They were just friends.

***

Carson's finger stopped midair as he held his phone. He couldn't wait to talk to Abby again, but should he hold off until next week, when she could come back? He had enjoyed having her there with him that one day, but he couldn't call just to chat. But now, he had something to tell her he thought she'd want to know.

He looked at the package lying on the table beside him, National Archives in the return address. He'd paid extra to have it express-shipped. Why? He had no idea. But probably because Abby was so interested, he wanted to get it as soon as possible. He'd scanned the documents briefly, but he hoped to go over them again with Abby. However, now it was Friday afternoon. Maybe Abby had a date that night or something. He didn't think she was seeing anyone, but maybe she was. Was this a bad time to call?

Suck it up, chicken. Just go ahead and call her.

He punched in the number, clearing his throat before she answered. What if she didn't? Guess he'd just leave a message.

"Hello." Her voice had never sounded better.

"Hi, Abby, it's Carson. Are you busy?"

"Hi, Carson. No, not at all. What's up?"

He blew out a sigh of relief. "The copies of the logbooks I ordered came today. I thought you might like to see them."

"Already? Well, yes, I would, but when?"

"Um, are you doing anything tonight?" Did that sound like he was asking her for a date? "I mean, I guess you already have plans. Sorry for the short notice. I got kind of excited when I saw the mail."

"No, I don't have any plans. Just hanging out with Mom and Emma."

"Hey, I've got an idea. Do you like pizza? Why don't I pick up a pizza and bring it over to your mom's, then we can all look at the copies together."

Silence. Had he lost the call? Then she said, "All right. Sounds good. I'm sure Mom would like to see them too. What time?"

He almost dropped the phone. "Is seven too late? I need to jump in the shower, just got back from the island a few minutes ago."

"Okay. We'll see you then."

"Hey, wait. What kind of pizza do you like?"

"I like thin crust, veggie, but Emma likes pepperoni and cheese, so I usually get half and half. But really, whatever you want is fine. We're flexible."

"Emma and I can share the pepperoni and cheese. Will your mother eat some too?"

"She might have one piece. Any kind is fine with her."

"Got it. See you in about an hour," he said.

He pressed end, his heart racing. He never thought he'd get so excited about such an ordinary evening. But he wanted to share the logbook copies. Sure. He wanted to see Abby. Plus, he liked her mom and little girl. They kind of felt like family, even though he barely knew them. They were simple, real people, not trying to impress anyone, unlike the people he'd known in the corporate world.

Fifty minutes later, he pulled into Grace's driveway. He grabbed the two pizza boxes from the car seat and the package of copies then walked to the front door. He raised his hand to knock, but the door opened before he could.

"Hi, Mr. Carson!" Emma stood in the doorway holding the dressed-up bear as Abby walked up behind her.

"Hi, Carson." Abby held the door open wide. "Come on in." She sniffed the air. "Pizza smells good. Why don't you put it on the kitchen counter?" She nodded toward the kitchen. "Can I carry that package for you?"

"Hello, ladies." He handed her the bulky envelope he carried in one hand, holding the pizza boxes in the other. A large cat sat nearby, eyeing him suspiciously as he entered.

Grace was already seated at the table. "Hello, Carson. Good to see you again." Her smile was as genuine as her greeting, lighting her otherwise tired face. "Emma, why don't you get some paper plates for us?"

"That's a big cat." Carson nodded toward the animal who had followed them into the kitchen.

"That's Hercules," Emma said.

Carson lifted an eyebrow. "Hercules? I'd say he's appropriately named."

Grace chuckled. "You wouldn't have thought so when Abby first brought him home, one of her first rescues. She saved him from certain death when she found him half-frozen near a dumpster. He was such a tiny creature, my husband named him Hercules as a joke. But he had amazing strength for such a little thing and fought his way to health. He lived up to his name."

"I guess he did." Carson leaned over and rubbed the cat behind its ears. "Hello, fella." Hercules meowed in response.

"I'll pour the drinks," Abby said. "Carson, we have soda, if you'd like."

"Sure, anything is fine," he said.

"Do you like root beer? I like it," Emma announced, standing beside him and peering up in his face.

"I love root beer. Will you share some with me?" Carson winked at the little girl.

"You can have your own." Turning away, she said, "Mommy, Mr. Carson wants root beer too."

"Coming right up."

Carson opened the pizza box on the counter while Abby fixed the drinks, handing Carson his before serving her mother and Emma. "Carson, why don't you sit over here?" Grace pointed to the chair beside her. He took his seat, and Abby handed each of them a plate with pizza. Before anyone could eat, Emma grabbed his hand on one side and her mother's on the other, so Carson took Grace's hand while Emma prayed the "God is Great" blessing for them.

Grace and Abby wanted to be brought up to date on the latest progress at the island, so he told them all about it while they ate their pizza. When they were finished, Abby cleared the table.

"So let's see what you have," Abby said, hands on her hips.

Carson withdrew the stack of papers from the envelope and put them in the center of the table.

Abby picked up the top sheet and began reading. "Keepers' Log.

Hope Island Light Station. Charles Martin, Keeper." She read across the page that was divided into columns. "March 1, 1945. Cloudy. Winds NNW. Temp. 39, Sea choppy." The next entry read "Light breeze, SE." The next, "Light Breeze with Rain," the next, "Maintenance crew came to work on fog bell mechanism," then the rest of the page noted more weather and sea conditions.

"Not too exciting, is it?" Grace asked. "Father was a man of few words."

Carson rifled through the stack. "Here's one that might be more interesting. It's titled 'Journal of Shipwrecks in the vicinity of Hope Island Light Station.'"

Abby leaned over to see, her shoulder against his, the contact sending a surge of warmth through him. "September 15, 1940, American Schooner struck rocks in strong gale. Called Coast Guard in Bar Harbor. Rendered assistance by launching station boat and getting close enough to toss life buoy rope to crew members. Two managed to get to boat. Others rescued by Coast Guard. Six on board, all saved and brought back to keeper's house for coffee and warmth."

"Wow. That's exciting!" Carson said. "Much more interesting than the regular logbook."

"My father did that? I had no idea," Grace said.

Abby was spellbound as she read the rest of the entries about shipwrecks near the lighthouse. Just seeing her excitement elevated his own.

"Carson, thank you so much for getting these. I never expected you to get them so quickly. It's so cool to read my grandfather's own writing. I appreciate what he went through so much more." Her response was worth everything it cost him to overnight the package.

"I didn't request any records from earlier dates, but there are some that go back into the 1800's. I'm sure they're very interesting, too, but your grandparents weren't there then."

"I think my mother and father served at Hope Island Light from just after they got married in 1920 until Mother left in 1960. That's a long time," Grace said.

"It sure is. They were the lucky ones, getting to stay so long. So many other keepers were dismissed not long after the Coast Guard took over management of the lights in 1939 and started automating them." Carson had studied enough about lighthouses to know how rare it was that the Martins had managed to keep their positions as lightkeepers, especially after Mr. Martin died.

"They must've trusted Mother's ability," Grace said, a proud smile on her face.

"Guess so," Carson said. "Or they really liked her."

"Did Granny ever rescue anyone?" Abby asked.

"Yes, she did," Grace said. "I remember her bringing some folks to the keeper's house to dry them off and warm them up. When I was a teenager, she rescued some boys who had gone out fishing and their boat capsized in rough water. She hopped in the station boat, rowed out to them, pulled them into the boat, and then brought them back to the keeper's house. I remember how shook up they were, shivering for all it's worth. Mother and I gave them some hot chocolate."

Emma pretended to shiver, hugging her bear tight.

"Emma, you're not cold, are you?"

She nodded. "Can I have some hot chocolate?"

Catching on to her ruse, they all laughed.

"You silly goose," Abby said, grinning. She glanced at the wall clock. "Time for this goose to go to bed."

"No, Mommy. I want to hear more stories about hot chocolate."

"Another time." Abby stood and reached for Emma's hand. Looking over her shoulder, she said, "Please excuse us, Carson." Turning to Emma, she said, "Tell Mr. Carson good night."

Carson leaned back and started to push away from the table. "Do you need to leave? I'm sorry if I've stayed too late."

"It's okay. She has a bed here. I'll take her home after a while."

Emma let go of Abby's hand and ran to Carson, reaching out to him with both arms. He leaned over and hugged her. "Good night, Emma. Thank you for the hug."

He released her to her mother, wishing Abby would give him a hug too when he said good night to her later.

After they left the room, Grace turned to Carson. "Son, don't let Abby scare you off. She's still getting over her husband's death."

Chapter Ten

The news hit him in the gut. He assumed she'd been divorced. "I'm sorry. Was it recent?"

"Two years. He was a marine. Killed when his helicopter was shot down in the Middle East."

Carson shook his head. He wanted to kick himself. He had been so selfish, hoping Abby was interested in him. "Must be tough for her."

"It was. She's doing better now. I think moving back here from California was a good thing for her to do."

"I hope I haven't been too pushy."

Grace reached across the table and patted his arm. "Don't you worry about it. You had nothing to do with what happened. Abby has to deal with it herself. But let me tell you, getting her interested in your work on the island has put a new spark in her. She seems more interested in that than anything else I've seen since she's been back. So I'm glad you asked her."

"Well, thank you for telling me. And I've really enjoyed Abby's involvement with the work."

"I thought you should know. Abby might not tell you herself."

A door closed softly in another room, signaling Abby's return.

"Already asleep?" Grace asked, looking up at her daughter.

"Yes, she wanted me to read to her, but I only made it past the first two pages before she nodded off."

"Must be nice to go to sleep so easily," Carson said.

"I know." Abby slid into her chair at the table, then glanced at him. "Can I get you anything else?"

"No, I'd love some coffee, but then I really wouldn't be able to go to sleep."

"Carson, I want to ask you something." Abby got up from the table and came back with a photo. "These are my grandparents, Mom's parents."

Carson took the photo and studied it. "Those lightkeeper's uniforms were pretty sharp." He pointed to the man's suit. "Snazzy double-breasted coat and look at the K for keeper patch on the lapels."

"I like the cap." Abby eyed the picture. "What's that insignia on the front?"

"It's the lighthouse emblem with U.S.C.G. underneath. Look. There's a star on his sleeve. Wonder what that's for?" Carson noted.

"Twenty-five years of service," Grace said. "Mother told me this picture was taken right after he got it. He was pretty proud of it."

"Carson, do you see that barn back there? I didn't see it when we were there. Do you know where it might have been?"

He peered closely at the photograph. "Hmm. Not sure. It's certainly not there now." He looked up at Grace. "Do you remember it?"

"I remember we had one. I'd have to go there and figure out where. Maybe I can do that someday."

"Sure. As soon as we get it ready up there, we'll take you over."

Grace forced a tired smile. "That would be nice, Carson."

"I'd like to take Emma, too, when it's safe enough, you know, when all the debris is gone," Abby said.

"They hauled off a lot of stuff today. It's more manageable when we clear it as we go instead of trying to take one huge load. I think it's pretty safe now, too, because there are no holes to fall through, but you would be the best judge of that."

Abby twisted her lips as she tossed her hair back over her shoulders. "I'm not sure. I wouldn't want to put her in danger."

"Tell you what. Why don't we take her on a little boat ride tomorrow? We can take a little picnic and get close enough to the island to show her. But let's wait until everything is finished before we take her up there. At least she can see the lighthouse from the water. Okay?"

"Do you have a child's life vest?"

"I'll get one first thing tomorrow."

Abby glanced at Grace. "I think that'll be all right. Don't you, Mother?"

Grace nodded. "If the water's calm, a boat ride would be nice. Just hold on to her in case you hit some big waves."

"Okay, Carson. As long as the weather's good for boating."

"I'll check the marine forecast before we go. If the wind is too high, we won't take the boat out."

Abby nodded. "Yes, let's do that. If you promise to help me keep an eye on her."

"I promise." He wouldn't let the child out of his sight.

***

Abby held Emma around the waist as she sat next to Carson on the seat of the boat. He'd started out standing behind the wheel, but Emma wanted him to sit down by her, so he'd obliged. Now the three of them were snugly behind the windshield. A brief thought of family togetherness passed through her mind, but she quickly pushed it aside. If there was any family resemblance, it was more like brother-sister. Her granny might have referred to Carson as "Uncle Carson," like she did the Coast Guardsmen Mom remembered. She smiled at the thought. Wonder how Carson would like Emma calling him "Uncle"?

Emma loved riding in the boat. She giggled every time they hit a wave and bounced, especially when the water sprayed them. No doubt the trip was like an amusement park ride for her daughter. True to his word, Carson had bought her a child's life vest. He really was a nice man, and she was thankful to have him for a friend.

"Hold on to your bear," Carson said when they hit a wave.

"I am. She needs a vest too," Emma said.

"I didn't see any that small, or I would've gotten one."

Abby wouldn't have been surprised if he had. He and Emma got along quite well.

"Do you have a little girl, Carson?" Emma asked, looking up at him.

Carson glanced at her with raised eyebrows. "No, Emma, I'm afraid

I don't. I do have two nephews though. They're my sister's children. But she's going to have another baby soon and maybe it will be a girl."

"I hope not." Emma looked down at her bear and smoothed its skirt.

"Emma! Why would you say that?" Abby said.

"So I can be his only girl." Emma stuck her lips out.

Abby's face flamed. What on earth?

"Well, you're my only girl now," Carson said, winking at Emma. "And you're definitely my only Emma."

Emma beamed, satisfied with his answer. Abby didn't know what to say. Maybe he *would* end up being called "Uncle."

Carson glanced back down at Emma. "What's your bear wearing?"

Emma frowned at him. "It's Wonder Woman. You don't know who Wonder Woman is?"

He nodded his head. "Ah, I should have known. I've just never seen a bear with a Wonder Woman outfit. Is Wonder Woman your favorite character? Is that why you got her the outfit?"

Oh dear, Abby dreaded what was coming.

"My daddy gave it to me. He called my mommy Wonder Woman, so he got the outfit for my bear."

Carson lifted an eyebrow and glanced over Emma's head at Abby. "Is that right?"

Abby could see his mind churning as he tried to figure out why she was called Wonder Woman. She'd have to tell him the story about her bittersweet title. "I'll explain later," she said.

As they neared the island, Carson pointed ahead. "There it is, Emma. That's the island where your grandmother and great-grandmother lived."

Her eyes widened as she took in the view.

Carson slowed the boat as they got closer and began a slow circle of the island. When they reached the other side, he pointed to the lighthouse, its red roof dominating the top of the island.

"Look up there, Emma. Do you see the lighthouse?"

Emma's mouth gaped, staring. "How do you get there?"

"You have to go up the trail to the top of the island."

"Can we go now?"

Carson and Abby exchanged glances. Abby shook her head.

"Not today, I'm afraid. But as soon as we get it all fixed up, we'll bring you back and you can go to the lighthouse in person. All right?"

Emma nodded. "Okay."

Abby was thankful he respected her wishes. After circling the island, Carson headed to some of the other islands where he did the same.

"I'm getting hungry. Are you ladies ready for lunch?" Carson glanced at Abby.

"Yes," Emma said.

"Great. I know a park by the water where we can tie up and get out."

Carson motored toward one of the larger islands where picnic tables were visible near a dock. He tied the boat to one of the cleats on the dock, grabbed the picnic supplies, and placed them on the dock before helping the others out.

As they walked toward the shore, Abby said, "Emma, why don't you go find a table for us?"

When they stepped on land, Emma ran to one of the tables. "Here's one!"

Abby and Carson followed with the food. After they'd laid everything out, they enjoyed a nice lunch while watching other boats pass by. Soon Emma finished and ran to the nearby swing set where other children were swinging. "Mommy, push me, please!"

Abby stood to heed her child's request, but Carson held out his hand. "Let me."

She lifted her eyebrow. "Sure. She'd like that. I'll clean up here."

Carson joined Emma, and soon the child was flying high on the swing. Abby packed everything up, then paused to observe. The joy on her daughter's face warmed Abby's heart. *Thank you, God.* If only for today, Carson was filling the void left by Kevin. But Abby didn't want to get Emma's hopes up if she thought Carson would really become her daddy. Would the child be satisfied as long as he was just a friend?

Chapter Eleven

M onday morning brought a brisk wind, producing a choppy sea. Carson eyed Abby who was bundled up in her hoodie with a windbreaker over it. She didn't protest when he'd suggested she sit on the bench beside him to get out of the wind.

Her body touched his, warming him like another jacket. She'd stopped at Mo's on the way to the boat launch and brought them each a thermos cup full of hot coffee, but sipping it during the boat ride proved difficult, no matter how badly he wanted to drink something warm.

"It'll take longer to get there today, since the wind is blowing against us."

She nodded. "At least it's sunny. I'd hate to be out here if it were overcast or foggy."

Carson relaxed and decided there was no need to hurry, even if he was anxious to get to the island and get started. "So what's the story about the Wonder Woman teddy bear?"

Abby glanced at him, a surprised look on her face.

"You said you would tell me later. Remember?"

She released a sigh. "Yes, I did. You see, I met Abby's father, Kevin, when we were running a superhero race out in California. He was dressed as Superman, and I was dressed as Wonder Woman. So the name stuck."

"And you called him Superman?" Carson offered a smile.

"Not often. However, he called me Wonder Woman as much as he did my real name." Abby's pained expression conveyed some angst about the nickname.

Carson laughed, and Abby frowned. "I guess that is pretty funny to some people."

"No, it's not that. But the other day, something about the way you stood reminded me of a Wonder Woman poster I've seen."

"What did I do?" She didn't seem to find the conversation humorous.

"Nothing really. It was just the way you were standing." Did he have to tell her what he was really thinking?

"I hope you don't start calling me Wonder Woman now."

"No. I'll have to come up with my own nickname for you."

"You think I need one?"

"Maybe. One might pop into my head." He tried hard to get her to smile, and a laugh would be a bonus.

"I'm fine with just Abby." She picked some lint off her sleeve.

"I kind of like Abby too. It suits you." Actually, he was quite content with her name, perhaps because he especially liked the person it referred to.

Once they got to the island and tied up, they grabbed their supplies and joined some other workers who arrived at the same time. Abby brought their lunch again today, and he couldn't wait to find out what kind of healthy food she'd packed this time. But lunch would have to wait because they had a lot of work to do first.

Abby returned to her job from last week, sanding the woodwork on the windows. She should be able to finish it so they could start painting today. Of course, she wasn't on the clock, so he couldn't force her to work. If she found more newspapers she wanted to read, she had that right.

Two brick masons showed up to start working on the chimney. The inside had been cleaned out last week, and the flue was checked and found safe. Carson left Abby downstairs in the living room with the masons while he went upstairs to work.

***

Abby resumed her sanding, tuning out the men who scraped and pounded the brick fireplace in the room with her. Images of Saturday's outing came to mind. Had Granny and Grandpa ever had picnics outside? She tried to envision them with her mother as a baby sitting on a quilt in the sunshine. But she soon let that scene go. They weren't here on a Saturday outing like she had been. This was their life, their work.

She had read back over the logbook copies showing her grandfather's handwriting. The cursive letters were beautifully formed and consistent, evidence of the penmanship people used to be taught. He would be appalled if he saw her own handwriting. A combination of cursive and print, she was glad no one else had to see it. After all, isn't that why God invented keyboards? She chuckled to herself at her own joke.

Wonder Woman. What a misnomer. She was anything but, and when Kevin called her by that nickname, more often than not, he was making fun of her. After all, Wonder Woman was strong and brave, courageous and independent. She was assertive and knew what she wanted—characteristics Abby wished she possessed. Kevin used the name to tease her when she wanted to help people too. He accused her of trying to rescue everything and everyone, from animals to people, as if she had some sort of grandiose ideas of her own self-worth. Far from it, especially with Kevin's ridicule.

Abby's attention was drawn to the men in the room. The noise they'd been making had stopped, and now they were talking. She listened, then glanced over.

"This one's barely sitting in here. The mortar is completely loose," one of the men said, jiggling a brick on the fireplace.

The other man looked on, touching an adjacent brick. "This one's loose too."

"Did we ever have an earthquake around here?"

"Not that I know of. No, I think someone moved these on purpose."

"Why would someone do that?"

The first man pulled several loose bricks out. "Hmm." He scanned the whole fireplace. "Wonder if any others are this loose?"

The other man reached into the hole. "Hey, I feel something in here."

Abby stood and took a few steps toward the fireplace to see what the men had found.

"Feels like a book. A pretty big one. My hands are too big to reach in there and pull it out."

"Here. Let me try." One man stepped back and the other reached in. "Yeah. I can feel it. But I can't get it out either."

"Maybe I can help," Abby volunteered. "My hands are smaller than yours."

They looked around at her and moved away. "It's in there. You have to reach in and down a little. It might be heavy."

Abby reached into the space and felt around until her hand landed on the book. She grabbed hold of the thickness and lifted. It was hefty, but more awkward to lift out than anything else. Her arm scraped the rough edges of the opening as she grasped the book and pulled. Just as she thought it was coming, it hit the side and she lost her grip and dropped it. Her heart beat frantically as she tried again and again. She wouldn't give up though. Whatever the thing was, she had to get it. There was a reason it was hidden. Someone had put it there. But who? And why?

She tried several more times, sweat popping out on her brow. Her arm burned from the scratches, but she was determined to get the book out, as she was pretty sure by now it was a book. Carson's voice came from the doorway. "What's going on in here?"

The men filled him in, and Carson appeared beside her. "Can I help?"

Abby pulled out her arm and brushed it off, noticing the red marks streaking it.

"No. I can get it. I know I can." She took a deep breath, exhaled, and then stuck her arm back in. This time, she got a good grip on the book and slowly lifted it and tugged it toward her. When the dark volume emerged from its hiding place, Carson helped to pull it out the rest of the way. He blew the dust off the top, then wiped it with his hand.

The two of them studied the cover of the old leather-bound volume.

Abby ran her finger over an embossed emblem. "What is this?"

Carson carried it to the window. "It's the symbol of the US Lighthouse Service." His eyes met Abby's.

He carefully opened the book, its yellowed pages dry and brittle. On the inside front page, he read, "Lighthouse Keepers Logbook," then glanced up at Abby. "Abby, it's the real deal."

He turned another page and across the top was printed *Journal of Light House Station at Hope Island Lighthouse*, the latter written in cursive. Printed next, *Keeper's name*. In cursive, the blank was filled in as Abigail Martin.

Abby's breath caught. Her grandmother's logbook.

Carson placed it in her hands. "I believe this belongs to you, Abby."

She stared at him. "Are you really going to let me have it?"

He nodded. "If you want to keep it, you may. If not, I'll keep it here. I'm not turning it over to the Archives. I know you want to spend some time reading it, so go ahead and take it."

Her eyes moistened. "Thank you, Carson. This means the world to me."

"I know. Do you want to look at it now? We really don't have a good place to see it except by the window."

"If you don't mind, I would love to see what's in it. Not to read all of it at once, however. I want to relish every word when I have time."

"Go ahead then. You can tell me about it later." He turned her arm over to look at her scratches. "You need to wash that off before it gets infected. Use some water from my water bottle. There's a first aid kit in my backpack. I'll go get it."

He left the room before she could respond and hurried back with the water and kit. "Let's go outside and do this. We have to take care of you first."

She clutched the book against her chest as she followed him outside. He took the book and placed it on one of the fold-up chairs set outside. "Stretch out your arms." When she did, he poured some cool water over them. Pain seared through her at the contact, and she saw how scraped up her arms really were. Carson then dabbed a bit of antiseptic cream on the injuries, which calmed the irritation down. "I don't have any Band-Aids large enough, so just keep your arms away from everything."

"Thank you, Doctor Stevens." She waved her arms trying to cool them.

Carson picked up the book and handed it back to her. "Why don't I bring that chair inside, and you can sit by the window to look at the book?"

"That would be nice."

After he set up the chair in the living room, Abby sat down with the logbook on her lap.

Chapter Twelve

Abby opened the book and gingerly turned to the first page.
March 10, 1945

Today marks the first day I assume responsibilities as the keeper of this lighthouse. Charles, my husband, drowned last month when his boat overturned during a gale. He was on his way back to the lighthouse after going to town for provisions. It is so ironic that he saved others but could not save himself. Last year, he tried to save that young couple, but the man drowned trying to save the woman and the woman almost drowned trying to save the baby, then did die not long after Charles brought her ashore. He was so upset about not being able to save them.

I have not heard officially from the Coast Guard if I will be able to take my husband's place, but in the meantime, I will continue his duties, handling them as well as I can without him, if only to do so in his honor. Charles always tried to be the best keeper he could be in his twenty-five years of service and won several lighthouse pennants during that time.

I began to keep the log the day after he drowned, but I want to write more than the logbook allows, more intimate thoughts which I do not wish to share with anyone else. So I'm using this extra logbook for that and will keep it hidden someplace no one knows about but myself. And God.

It is difficult to express the ache inside of me, the hole in my heart that losing Charles created. We've been married twenty-five years, so he was my whole life until Grace arrived. I am thankful to have her company, but she does not replace my husband. I don't want to dwell on Charles' death, but it hurts to think of his final moments. I'm sure he tried to fight the swells, though strong as he was, he lost the battle.

As I was told at the funeral, so many times, I'll see him again in heaven. That fact gives me some small comfort. I feel guilty admitting that, right now, that comfort is not enough. I want him here, now. I want to touch him. I want his big, strong arms around me. I want to hear him chuckle. I even hold his uniform coat to my face and breathe in the aroma of pipe smoke it still carries. His presence was so large. His death left a huge gap in our home, in our lives.

He was a good husband, the best. He loved me and appreciated me, never failing to give me a compliment on something I'd done. Although I am not a pretty woman, he made me feel beautiful and worthwhile, and he was proud to be my husband, as I was his wife. No one can take his place. The thought of marrying again is beyond my ability to comprehend, even though Charles would encourage me to do so. He was firmly convinced that a woman needed a husband to depend on and would not want me to remain alone. Especially raising a child.

Grace doesn't understand that he is gone. They were just getting to know each other, so I feel almost as bad for her as I do for myself. She's a bright child and growing quickly, and she loved for Charles to read to her, trying to recite the words herself. I think she'll learn to read early, or else will have all the books committed to memory. We haven't received a new library box since the war started so we've been through all of the books we have. The Coast Guard has much more important things to concern themselves with than a library box.

Speaking of the Coast Guard, they have been so considerate since Charles died. Every day, they switch crews to perform lookout duties here. Charles didn't like their intrusion in our lives when they first arrived, but he eventually accepted it as a way to do his patriotic duty. I, for one, am glad he didn't have to leave for some foreign country to fight this long, dreadful war. How ironic to think I didn't want him to go fight lest he be killed, when he was killed while performing everyday duties here, just going to the mainland for supplies.

I talk to God about this frequently. Although I did not lose a husband to the war, I lost him just the same. So, like many who are left behind, I want to know why. Why did this happen? Why here? Why now? I'm afraid to admit that I'm angry, but at whom? I want to be angry with God, but I know it's not right to be. He has blessed us and answered so many of my prayers. He gave me Grace when I had given up all hope of having a child. So why did He allow her to lose her father before she had a chance to know him? I probably shouldn't ask God why I suffered this loss because I have so much to be thankful for.

I feel so tired, as if I'm dragging a weight around. It would be easy for me to just go to bed all day so I wouldn't have to think or face another day without Charles. But I have a duty to perform and a child to care for. If I didn't have Grace, I might not have a reason to go on. Someone told me once that the miserable thoughts I have grieve God. I'm sorry if they do. I do not mean to offend God, who is my only hope now.

I am trying to read my Bible more. I want to find answers, and it's the only way I know to hear God when I ask Him questions. The Psalms have always been my favorite verses and have comforted me all my life. I need those words now to comfort this dark soul of mine. I do not wish to be morose around others, especially dear little Grace. I've tried to hide my tears from her and keep up a good front. She is such a happy, cheerful child, and I do not want her to feel my despondency. I wonder if she can tell something's not right. She thinks Charles is coming back home. When she sees the guardsmen, she says, "Papa?" and it pierces my heart. I know I should not let her keep on hoping he'll return, but I just haven't been able to find the right words to tell her. Is that lying? God forgive me if it is. I do not need to add another sin to my list.

Someday when she's older, I'll tell her. But what does a toddler know about these things? Parents are supposed to protect children from such tragedy, and this poor child has had too much in her short life. Times like these it would be nice to have a family to lean on. But both my parents and Charles' passed away years ago. I had no brothers or sisters either, and Charles' only brother was killed in Italy, early in the war.

I am thankful, though, for the good people of Hope Harbor. People like Mr. Reynolds who brings the mail and offered to bring groceries from the mainland since I lost Charles. A couple of the lobstermen who couldn't join the military have stopped by to bring me a lobster like they did when Charles was here. He sure did love lobsters and really appreciated it when they gave us some.

With the guardsmen coming and going, I shouldn't be lonely. I suppose I do feel safer, even though it's hard to believe a Nazi sub would appear near here. But I heard they've been spotted along the coast in other areas and have even sunk some of our ships, so I suppose there really is a danger. All the guardsmen are polite, timid young men mostly. They come in groups of four for twelve-hour shifts. They bring their sandwiches from the Coast Guard station mess hall, but we've always made coffee available for them.

Their superior, the station commander, drops by to check on the crews but doesn't usually stay long, since he has other crews to oversee on other islands. His name is Michael O'Brien and he is quite jovial. He's a nice-looking man with auburn hair and a ruddy complexion, and he always greets me with a beaming smile, bringing a small ray of light into my gloom. Since Charles' death, he has stayed longer and visited me, checking to see how I'm doing. He's such a considerate man, older than the others, probably about the same age as myself. In fact, he told me he was due to retire, since he's already put in his twenty years, but the war required him to stay in service.

He always brings Grace a treat when he comes, usually a peppermint stick, which I break up and dole out over the week. She gets so excited to see him, but I don't think it's just because of the treat, but maybe because he pays her attention and plays horsey with her, bouncing her on his knee. Charles liked him too, said he was a good man. Mr. O'Brien had only been here three or four months before Charles died, but they became friends, even telling Grace to call him Uncle Michael. He doesn't come here every day, usually once a week while Charles was alive, but he has been here twice a week since, helping to relieve my loneliness.

I doubt he'll be able to come as often on a regular basis, but it has been nice to see him and have another adult to talk to. It is selfish of me to want him to visit when he has much more important responsibilities. I must learn to stand on my own two feet now, and I pray God will help me do it.

I'm new to this role of being the primary lighthouse keeper, and almost as new to being a mother at my age. But somehow, we'll find a way to do both. Lord, I need your strength.

***

Tears streamed down Abby's face. She wiped them with the back of her hand to keep from dripping on the page.

Granny's words had reawakened the pit in her own stomach that came from losing Kevin. She and Granny shared the same pain, the same loss, the same loneliness from their husband's sudden death.

Carson had left her alone to read the journal, but he returned and stood beside her. Abby sniffed, and Carson laid his hand on her shoulder.

"Sorry, Abby. Was there something you read in the logbook that upset you?"

She glanced up at him. "It's not a logbook. I mean, it's a personal journal she kept. She expresses her feelings about things. In fact, when I read how she felt after Grandpa died, I could really *feel* her loss." She didn't really want to talk to him about its reminder of Kevin though. Grief could be hard to explain unless you'd been through it yourself, which is why she understood how Granny felt.

His hazel eyes softened, showing compassion and tenderness. He must have made the connection between her grandpa's death and Kevin's. Hopefully, he wouldn't ask her about it.

"It's not a keeper's journal? So, it's like a diary?"

Abby nodded. "Yes. And she mentioned the Coast Guard being here doing surveillance during the war. I believe she was grateful to have their company after Grandpa died. She mentioned one man by name, Michael O'Brien. He was the commander of the nearest Coast Guard station. Apparently, she knew him better than the others because he stopped to talk with her when he was here."

"Michael O'Brien? Maybe we can check with the station and find out more about him."

"That's a good idea."

"I guess none of those guys are still around anymore. They'd have to be in their nineties if they are."

"And I don't think Michael O'Brien would be, because Granny said he was the same age she was."

Carson motioned to the book. "Are you going to let Grace read it?"

Abby nodded. "She'll probably want me to read it to her because she wouldn't be able to see well enough."

"It will be a trip down memory lane for her, no doubt."

"She was just a toddler in 1945, but she does remember a little. She's always had a good memory, better than mine, in fact."

"Wonder if she'll remember that O'Brien guy?"

"I think she might. She told me there was one man in the Coast Guard she really liked, and I bet he was the same man."

"Well, when you get finished reading it today, let's wrap it up really well so it won't get wet when we go back. Do you plan to read more now?"

"No, not yet. I want to take my time to read it and share it with Mom."

"I can't believe we found that journal. I wonder why she hid it?"

"I don't know, but for some reason, she wanted to keep it private. I wonder why she didn't bring it with her when she left the island?"

"Maybe she forgot it."

"Or maybe she wanted to leave the past behind." Abby's gaze drifted off. "And I believe I was meant to find it."

Chapter Thirteen

Carson couldn't believe they'd discovered Abigail Martin's personal journal. How timely that Abby was at the keeper's house when they found it. Was this more than a coincidence like Abby thought? And after all these years, the journal had been hiding there. And if they hadn't found it when they did, it would've been sealed up in the fireplace.

He didn't ask to read it, just relied on what Abby told him. Since the journal belonged to her grandmother, it seemed like he would be intruding on personal family information. If she decided to let him read it when she finished, he was content to wait. Seeing those tears glistening on her cheeks had wrenched his heart. She said the reason was empathy for her grandmother, but based on what she said, she probably related to the death of a husband too.

He never expected to meet a member of the Martins when he bought the lighthouse property, and he was thrilled when he found out Abby was one of them. Yet despite her connection, he had been attracted to her the first moment he saw her arrive at the memorial ceremony with her little girl. He still was, but she had no interest in a relationship with him, and now that he knew about her husband's death, he was certain of it. He'd just have to accept that fact and enjoy being her friend. It was a small price to pay to be able to spend time with her.

He chuckled to himself. Wonder Woman indeed. She was definitely a wonder to him. Not like a cartoon character but a real person—a caring, sensitive person. However, today when he caught her crying, she'd appeared so vulnerable, so unlike Wonder Woman.

When he arrived home that day, he found another package from the National Archives in the mail. He opened it and read a note attached to some papers. "Mr. Stevens, we found some more entries from a logbook for the Hope Island Lighthouse from the year 1945 and thought you would like to have them."

Carson looked at the next page, which was a copy of a logbook page. The name next to Keeper was Abigail Martin. The page was similar to the logbook page her husband had written.

Light breezy, sea light chop.

Gale from the north, very cold.

Foggy, turned on fog bell.

Supply boat came and delivered supplies.

Postman came today and brought newspapers and magazines.

Commander O'Brien inspected lighthouse property today. Reported it to be in excellent condition.

Abigail's entries were a bit more detailed than her husband's. But apparently, she kept the most details in the logbook that had been hidden, the one she had used as a personal journal. Of course, Abby would be interested in seeing these pages too, and comparing them to the other records they had.

***

Mom marveled at the journal, running her hand across the cover. "You say this was hidden in the fireplace?"

"Yes. I guess she didn't want any officials to mistake it for the legitimate journal and read her personal information."

"You know, I saw Mother writing in journals my whole life but just assumed it was lighthouse business. I had no idea she kept two separate ones. Have you read any of it yet?"

"Just the first entry." Abby pointed to the pages she'd read. "Would you like to read it?"

Mom scrutinized the book. "My goodness, I can't read that. Mother had nice handwriting, but it all runs together for me. You'll have to read it for me."

Abby read the section she'd already read. When she was finished, her mother's eyes brimmed with tears. "Bless her heart. I can just imagine how hard it was for her to take over when Father died. It's bad enough to lose someone you love without having to assume their role. I guess you and I can understand her grief, can't we?"

Mother peered into Abby's eyes, then patted her hand.

Abby tried to hold it together but couldn't stop the tear that ran down her cheek. "Yes, we can." She sniffed and grabbed a tissue from the counter. "Mom, are we Martin women doomed to live without our husbands?"

"No, honey. My parents were married twenty-five years before my father died, and your father and I were married fifty years. Unfortunately, you and Kevin weren't married that long."

"But it still hurts to lose them, however long you've been together."

"That it does. It's like you've lost part of yourself."

Abby just nodded, glad that Emma was in the other room watching *Frozen*, her favorite movie.

"Do you want me to read any more, Mom?"

"No, I'm tired and need to go to bed. Go ahead and take it home with you. You can let me know what else it says another time."

Abby and her mother had never really talked about their mutual feelings of loss, neither of them wanting to bring up sad memories. But there was a common bond they had and discussing it had strengthened their relationship.

Abby took the journal, then retrieved Emma, who protested the interruption, even though she'd watched the same movie at least fifty times already. She even had an Elsa outfit for her bear, but she only wore it for special occasions, like going to church.

After they got back to their apartment, Abby gave Emma her bath and read her a book when she put her to bed. Then they said their nighttime prayers, and she kissed Emma good night and turned out the light as her daughter fell fast asleep.

The journal beckoned, and Abby couldn't wait to read more, so she made herself a cup of decaf coffee. She settled into a comfy chair big enough for her to tuck her feet under herself and opened the book.

March 20, 1945

Mr. Reynolds, the postman to the islands, came today bringing newspapers and the latest Life *magazine. He stayed for a good while and had coffee. We talked about the war, what was going on where, and what the news was from town. Seems everyone has a relative in the war, and every day, the townsfolk wait for news of their loved ones, praying they are not one of the casualties. Mr. Reynolds says the war in Europe should be over soon, that we have the Nazis on the run now. Thank God for that.*

News isn't so good from the Pacific though. Who knows when that will end? Stories of terrible treatment of our soldiers in prison camps over there are in the news. And all I can do here is pray for those poor men. It makes me wonder how much good it does them for us to ration sugar when they're not even given food? I don't have a car, so I'm not saving any gasoline, and I don't have any scrap rubber or metal to donate. Seems like I'm not doing much at all to help our boys. We've always had a garden, so that's not new to us, but we can call it our Victory Garden, I suppose. And I've always canned what we grow so it will last the winter, because we can't always rely on the supply boat to bring our food when the weather is too bad for it to come.

To be honest, I think we've had it better here than they have on the mainland. The Coast Guard has shared some of their meat with us, knowing how difficult it is for us to get any. Charles loved a good pot roast, so Mr. O'Brien still brings us one sometimes. The rest of the time, we have fish or lobster. Thank God, we still have Angel, our cow, so we have milk for little Grace. I have to laugh when I remember how we got Angel up here after Charles built the barn. We brought her over in a boat, but she was too afraid to get out of it. So we had to rig up a pulley and lift her up. You never heard a cow make such noise! Charles named her Angel because she "flew" to the top of the island. She's still an angel to me because she keeps us supplied with milk, and so we have butter too.

About rationing, I wonder if those movie stars who look so happy advertising rationing do it themselves. Do they, too, go without like the rest of the country? I find that hard to believe. At any rate, I think it's easier for us to abide by the rationing and shortages because we never had much to begin with and have had to make do with what we had. But I'm very thankful when I can get some canned peaches in our provisions from the store because Grace really likes them.

Just when I thought spring was on its way, it's cold here again. Started yesterday with a gale that blew so hard, it was hard to walk between the house, the lighthouse, and the barn. I wondered if I might get blown off the island, heaven forbid. I stuffed old newspapers in the cracks around the windows here at the house because I could feel the air blow right through. It's been hard to keep the house warm, and I keep Grace bundled up all the time, so the poor little thing won't freeze. I'm knitting her another sweater and cap now since she's outgrown the ones I made her as a baby.

Thank God, Mr. O'Brien came by this morning and made sure we had enough wood and a good fire in the fireplace. I must admit I look forward to his company. Of course, I look forward to visits from anyone on the mainland, but his visits are the most special. He has a way of making me laugh, and that's good for Grace too. Today, he hoisted her up on his shoulders and danced around the living room singing, "When Irish Eyes are Smiling." And what a beautiful voice he has! Grace was delighted and giggled so hard! Ever since he left, she's been trying to sing that song. I'll have to ask him to teach her.

He told me he's from Michigan, somewhere near the Great Lakes. I've never been there, but from what he says, the lakes look like the ocean, because they're so large you can't see the other side. Imagine that. He also told me his wife is still in Michigan, that when he received the station assignment in Maine, she stayed behind because this station is what they call a stag station—men only. I'm sure she must miss him. He also told me he has two grown sons. Both were in the navy, but one died at Pearl Harbor. I could see the pain in his eyes when he mentioned his dead son, and my heart went out to him.

He doesn't talk much about the war, unlike Mr. Reynolds. I don't think Mr. O'Brien is supposed to share much information with me. Not that I'm a threat or a spy, but it's wartime and he has to keep military business with the military. I asked him if he'd seen any German subs in our area, and he didn't exactly answer. But he did say the lighthouses on islands farther out were more likely to spot them. Mr. Reynolds told me one of "their" subs had surfaced near West Quoddy and startled some fishermen nearby. Even offered to buy their fish. Apparently, the poor fishermen were scared out of their wits and turned over their entire day's catch. Wonder if they had American money to pay with? If they did, where did they get it? I asked Mr. O'Brien about the submarine story, and he just laughed and said the stories he heard were quite amusing. He acted like the story about the fishermen wasn't true, but what if it was? If the Germans are so bold to approach an ordinary fisherman, why wouldn't they stop at an island like ours? When I hear stories like that, I'm so grateful to have the guardsmen here.

Well, I must end this now. I need to mend Grace's clothes. She has a tear in her coat, and I also need to make her another dress, a warmer one. Her old ones are worn out, and too thin for this weather. I have some fabric left over from the last skirt I made myself that should be enough to make something for her. I wish I could buy her a pretty store-bought dress, but then where would she wear it? We're not leaving the island until I know the weather is much warmer. I should take her to church so she can be christened, but I'm going to wait until she gets older. I do not wish to take the boat all the way to the mainland with just her and myself, at least not yet. I suppose I could ask Mr. Reynolds or even the Coast Guard to take me, but I don't want to put them out either. I might even forget how to act around the townspeople by the time I get back. If not for the people who come here, I'd be a complete hermit.

A hermit? Abby had thought of herself as one when she'd moved to Maine. Even though she was around a few people every day, she wasn't in the company of nearly the number of people as she was in California. Her old friends there thought she was crazy, that she'd get bored and come back. But they didn't know the Maine Abby, the one who'd come from a small town and was content to be only known for being Grace's daughter, not a successful careerwoman. Here, she was just a daughter and a mom.

Abby glanced around for something to mark her place and saw her sketch pad lying nearby. She could tear a corner off one of the pages. But when she picked it up, she was startled to see the sketch she'd done over a week ago. She'd drawn a design for the interior of the keeper's house, complete with furnishings laid out. She didn't even remember making the sketch, but as she studied it, she could see the house designed that way. She wondered if Granny would like her ideas for decorating the house. Perhaps she'd show it to Mom and see what she thought.

Would Carson like it? But if she showed it to him, he might think she was being presumptuous. Was she guilty of trying to help someone again?

Chapter Fourteen

Carson got up early and made a trip to the hardware store before he met Abby. Nick had called to tell him the plumber was missing two wrenches, so Carson needed to replace them, at least until the others were found. Seemed like every day someone lost something. Either he had some very forgetful workers or one of them was a thief. But Nick said most of the guys were friends and had worked together before. Carson had a hard time believing one would steal from another. But who else would have taken them?

The store clerk pointed to the aisle where the wrenches were. Carson rounded the corner, glancing down at the note where he'd written what sizes to get. As he stepped into the aisle, he bumped into a man whose back was to him.

"Oh, excuse me."

The man turned around with a frown. Fred Harding. The last person Carson wanted to see, much less run into.

"In a hurry, Mr. Stevens?" Harding glanced at the other man whom Carson recognized as the store manager and smirked. "Guess you need to catch the tide right so you can get to your island."

Carson bit back a retort and faked a laugh instead. "Good one, Mr. Harding. Just getting some tools so I can get an early start." Carson reached over to a wrench hanging on the display.

"You know which end of that thing to hold?" Harding grinned, and the other man smiled with him.

"Not quite, but you know, I have some excellent workers who do. Good thing, huh?"

Harding crossed his arms. "Well, you need some good workers if you expect to finish that place this year."

Was his face red? Carson could control his tongue, but not his gut reactions.

"Yes, sir. I'm very thankful to have a capable crew." He turned his attention to the wrenches and quickly grabbed the ones he needed. "If you'll excuse me, sirs, I need to get going." He wanted to say something about not having time to stand around and talk like they did but restrained himself.

As he left the aisle, he said, "Good day, gentlemen."

Harding nodded. "You stay safe out there, Mr. Stevens."

Carson quickly paid at the front counter and hurried out. So far, this day wasn't getting off to a great start. And what did Harding mean by staying safe?

***

Abby talked about the journal from the time she met Carson the next morning until she got off the boat at the island. It didn't occur to her at the time that he wasn't listening, but now she realized that he seemed distracted. Had she been having a conversation by herself? She thought he'd been focused on steering the boat, but now worried that his silence meant he wasn't interested in what she had to say. Was he bored with all her talk about the journal? She fought embarrassment when she considered his lack of responses. And to think, she wasn't usually a talkative person.

He helped her off at the dock as usual and they climbed the hill, this time in silence because she quit talking. Did he even notice? What if he was bored with *her* and not just her obsession with the journals. She shrugged it off. Why did it matter? They were simply working on a project together.

When they reached the top, the men were standing around talking instead of working.

"What's going on?" Carson asked as he scanned their faces.

"Some of the guys couldn't make it today. They said they were called off to another job."

"Another job? I thought this *was* their job," Carson said, planting his hands on his hips.

"Well, sir, no. I mean, they work for more than one contractor, and the other job took priority."

"Fine. So why are you guys standing around?"

"Waiting for supplies. They should've been here by now."

Abby had never seen Carson's face so red. He was obviously angry but kept his composure. From the kitchen, noise indicated somebody was working. Carson stepped into the room. The plumber poked his head out, and Carson handed him the wrenches.

"Everything else all right in here?"

"Pretty good, but I could use a little help. My assistant was under the weather today."

"Of course he was," Carson muttered under his breath. He called out over his shoulder. "Any of you guys got plumbing experience or want to lend a helping hand?"

Two of the men stepped forward. "Sure, boss. What do you want us to do?"

"Help him." Carson motioned to the other man.

To the other men, he said, "Look around here and see what else you can do until the materials get here. I'm not paying you to stand still."

Who was this Carson? Abby had never seen him so serious. Things weren't going well today for him. Had something happened to upset him before they got here?

"Would you like me to continue where I left off?"

Carson glanced toward her in surprise, as if he'd forgotten she was there.

"Sure. Sorry. I got a little sidetracked."

"That's okay. Looks like you've got your hands full."

"Um-hmm."

"Carson? Is there something going on? I mean, you act kind of distracted."

He shrugged and stuck his hands in his pockets. "It's nothing. You go ahead and take care of the windows. I'm going to take some guys down to the dock and wait for supplies."

"Of course. Don't let me stop you." Not that he would. But somehow, she knew his "nothing" was really something—something that wasn't good.

Chapter Fifteen

Well, he should have expected there'd be some problems. What construction site didn't have its share? Had he overreacted because he was still ticked off by Harding's comments? True, every time he remembered the insinuations the man had made about Carson's inability—no, his naiveté—his blood began to boil. Still, he shouldn't have been so short with Abby. He just didn't want to share the scene with her. In fact, even reliving the conversation in his own mind made him feel stupid.

He'd tried to stay busy to keep from mulling over the experience and completely forgot about Abby. How was that possible? But when he saw her eating lunch by herself outside on the grass, he was filled with guilt. He owed her an apology. He took a deep breath, exhaled, and then strode over to where she sat reading one of the old newspapers laid out beside her.

Carson cleared his throat. "Finding anything interesting?"

She looked up and shielded her eyes. "I think so."

"Sorry I forgot about lunch."

"You were busy. Besides, I'm okay eating by myself."

Carson gulped. Did she mean since she was a widow or didn't want his company? "Of course. But I fully intended to eat with you. I guess I just didn't get hungry. Too busy, you know."

Abby gestured to the ground beside her. "It's not too late, is it? I brought enough to share."

He plopped down on the ground and accepted the sandwich she handed him. "Thanks."

"Did you get your supplies?"

"No, but I talked to the supplier. He apologized and said there was a mix-up, and he'd have them out first thing tomorrow."

"That's good."

"Yes, those things happen."

She tossed him a bottle of water. He unscrewed it and gulped some down.

"What about your workers? Will you be short?"

"I've contacted the contractor, and he assures me we'll be covered tomorrow."

"Glad things worked out. I knew you were upset about it."

He swigged some more water. "Actually, you were right. I did have something else on my mind."

She faced him, her elbow propped on one knee, a look of concern etched on her lovely face. "You don't have to tell me about it. I don't have to know all your business."

"No, it's fine. Last week I went to the meeting of the Hope Harbor Bed-and-Breakfast Association. Let's just say I didn't get the warm welcome I'd hoped for, especially from one man in particular."

Abby frowned. "They were rude to you?"

Carson shook his head. "Not so much 'they.' Mainly just the one guy who was pretty condescending, and I guess he hurt my ego. I ran into him this morning at the hardware store."

Her eyes widened. "Who is he? Not that I would know him, but Mom probably does."

"You really don't need to tell her about it. His name is Fred Harding, and he owns most of the bed-and-breakfasts in town. So I guess he's pretty important. At least he thinks so."

She flipped her ponytail behind her head. "So you think he doesn't want competition from you?"

"I doubt it. How could he consider me a threat to his business when he challenged my ability to run a B&B? Actually, I think he just likes to push his weight around, show off his power to impress others. But he did succeed in getting under my skin. If I weren't a Christian, I might've said something ugly."

"I'm glad you didn't. It wouldn't have helped the situation. It never does."

What a strange thing for her to say. Surely, she wasn't talking about herself. He couldn't imagine her ever losing her temper that much.

"Yeah, I'm glad I didn't too. I'd rather regret what I didn't say instead of what I said."

She studied him a moment. "So I guess getting bad news this morning when we got here just added to your frustration."

"Yep. Guess it did. It's like everything changed for the worse since meeting him. Which is ridiculous, of course."

"I know how you feel. Bad news comes in threes, right? So maybe now you're due for good stuff again."

"You're right. No more bad news." Carson finished his sandwich and downed the rest of his water. Talking with Abby had really helped. He brushed off his hands and hopped up. "Are you finished?"

"Yes, I am." He pulled her to her feet a little too hard, and she almost fell against him. She smiled as she got her balance. "Still working that frustration out?"

His face heated. "Sorry about that."

She laughed. "Not a problem." She picked up the paper and stuffed the other things in her backpack before straightening. "I'm finished in the living room. May I start on the windows in another room?"

"That'd be great. Why don't you go upstairs to the bedrooms? I think the kitchen is too crowded for you to work in right now."

"Will do."

"Oh, I forgot to tell you I got some more copies from the National Archives. They're copies of pages from the logbook when your grandmother was the keeper."

"That's great. When did you get them?"

"Yesterday. I'm sorry, I meant to tell you sooner but got sidetracked. When would you like to see them?"

"Call me when you get back tomorrow and maybe you can bring them by if it's not too late."

It hit him that she wouldn't be with him the next day, and he didn't like the empty feeling that knowledge gave him.

***

Mom was tired, so Abby didn't stay long when she picked up Emma and headed for her apartment. Much as she wanted to see the copies Carson had received, she needed some time alone. Not that she didn't enjoy being with him. On the contrary, she did, but maybe she was spending too much time with him. That morning when he didn't talk to her and sort of ignored her, her feelings got a little bruised, sending up a red flag. Of course, it was stupid to let his lack of attention bother her. Why should he have to confide in her anyway?

She had to admit she was relieved when he finally did share what was on his mind, but she didn't want him to think he owed her any explanation. He didn't owe her anything, and she shouldn't expect anything. Maybe she needed to define for herself what being friends meant. After all, she'd never been friends with a guy. She'd had friends who were girls, but she dated guys. And married one. And wasn't that supposed to be the ultimate friendship? But, she wasn't sure she could say Kevin had been her best friend. No, her and Carson's relationship was nothing like her and Kevin's, nor did she want it to be.

Emma wanted to play on the lawn in the middle of the four apartment buildings when they got home, so Abby played chase with her until it got dark. She didn't have time for a run, so she might as well get some exercise too. The activity also helped use up some of Emma's energy from sitting at Mom's that afternoon and would assure an easy bedtime. Abby waved to one of her neighbors sitting out on her balcony. She didn't know the lady's name but knew she managed one of the gift shops downtown. Abby hadn't met everyone in the apartment complex but recognized most of the tenants.

That was one of the benefits of living in a small town like Hope Harbor. She was safe there, and so was her daughter, unlike living in a big city like she had before. Strange that she had felt safe when Kevin was alive, even when he was deployed. Just knowing he would protect her if he were there, or maybe the fact that others knew she was his wife made her feel safer. But after he died, that safety net—or the illusion of it—disappeared. The stalker incident had made her paranoid, extra sensitive to any stranger lurking near her or Emma. And after reading about child abductions, she was even more distrustful. A visit back to Maine had shown her how much Mom's health had declined, and she'd decided to leave California and come back home. Back where life was safe.

Abby fixed Emma and herself a salad with rotisserie chicken she'd picked up at the grocery store. Thank goodness Emma liked salads. Their town wasn't big enough for a major fast food chain, so she didn't have to give in to Emma's begging to go to one. After dinner, Abby bathed Emma and read to her until she fell asleep, which didn't take long.

Then Abby took a long overdue shower herself. She put on her yoga pants and a T-shirt and opened the balcony door, ready to sit and unwind. Cool air greeted her, reminding her that Maine wasn't ready to start summer yet and making her crave something hot. She decided on a cup of herbal tea, and after she made it, she threw on her hoodie then went back outside, propping her feet up on the railing after she sat down on the patio chair. Holding the warm cup with both hands, she scanned the scene, noticing the illuminated windows of the apartments, reminding her she wasn't alone.

Mom thought Abby would be lonely in an apartment. Funny thing was, she could feel lonely in a roomful of people. Yet here in Hope Harbor, she was beginning to enjoy being by herself, yet still part of the community. Abby's thoughts drifted back to the island and Granny, who didn't have the comfort of a community isolated out on the island. Did she ever want to quit and move to town? Abby went back inside and sat down on a bar stool at the counter, then opened the journal.

April 15, 1945

The last two weeks have been dreary. Fog and mist every day, as if the country is in mourning for our president, Franklin Roosevelt, who died just three days ago. Could the timing be any worse, with us in a war? His vice president, Harry Truman, has taken over. What big shoes he has to fill after his predecessor's four terms in office. I would hate to be him right now. Mrs.

Roosevelt must be in shock, as I well know about, of having her husband die so suddenly.

The mournful sound of the foghorn blowing out into the haze sounded so ominous. I'm thankful the Coast Guard has managed the horn and I haven't had to. Even little Grace covered her ears and shook her head to say, "Stop." I tried to explain what the noise was, but I don't think she understood. I put some cotton in her ears, and I think it helped because she quit holding her hands over them.

What is it about fog that's so depressing? I suppose dark should be the opposite of light, but I believe fog is really the opposite of light. At least it's the opposite of sunshine. I don't know why I feel so much happier when the sun is shining. Maybe it's because I can see better. I can see colors—the deep blue of the sea, the green of the trees, the bright blue sky. I can see the red roof of the lighthouse and the white tower beneath, when only twenty feet away in the fog, the tower disappears. There's an eerie sense that we are in a world of our own, apart from civilization. Even if I wanted to go down to the dock, I wouldn't be able to see the mainland. Like everything else around us, it would have vanished as if it never existed.

I can't imagine the fellows from the Coast Guard can see anything from the top of the lighthouse in the fog, even with their binoculars. How could they spot an enemy submarine in this kind of soup? Seems like a sub could be right under their nose, and they wouldn't see it. I shudder to think one could be so close, but Mr. Reynolds says they are and that we have boats called subchasers looking for them. It's so hard to imagine all that wartime activity happening so close. But I have to admit I get a little spooked when I see the guardsmen appear out of the fog as if they just materialized, like ghosts. Or should I say angels? Perhaps if I think of them as angels, I would feel less fearful and remember the good Lord is watching over us.

Besides my own complaints, Grace needs to get out into the sunshine too. She doesn't seem as happy as usual, but maybe she's reflecting my own mood, even though I try to pretend I'm fine and make her laugh. But I do believe she needs some fresh air instead of the dank air in our house. I even made cookies today to cheer her up. Of course, I shared some of them with the Coast Guard men too. They really appreciated them. With our limited *ration of sugar, I don't bake often, but the men told me they'd bring me extra sugar if I promised to make more cookies. These boys must miss their mothers. They don't seem old enough to have wives. But it's nice to have company, even though we don't converse much. Their presence helps me not think so much about being alone.*

Much as I want to stay here and take care of the light as Charles would have, there are some days I'd like to have neighbors, especially other women, and "talk over the fence" as they say. I wonder what it would be like to have neighbors. I keep reading my Bible and repeating the verses that say, "You are not alone. The Lord is with you." And I know He is, even if it doesn't feel like it sometimes. I think women may be more melancholy than men. At least that's what Charles said, and he could've been right.

I must break off now. Someone's at the door.

So, just when I was writing about being lonely, who should come to my door but Michael O'Brien! Grace and I were delighted to see him. She was standing and holding on to the sofa when he walked in with his big smile, greeting her with, "How's my little darlin'?" like he always does. She let go of the sofa and tried to go to him. She even took three steps before she plopped down on her bottom, arms reaching for him.

Her first steps! I'm sorry Charles wasn't here to see it. But Michael was, and we celebrated with lots of applause and hugs. I'm glad he was here to witness her milestone. It's as if God knew how lonely I was and sent Michael to keep us company. And to top it off, Michael brought some strawberries! He said they were first of the season on the mainland. Grace tasted one for the first time and loved it. I will make her some strawberries and cream later, maybe even bake a little cake, and we can put the strawberries on top of it.

I found Michael staring at Grace when I came back from the kitchen with coffee for both of us. He kept glancing from me to her, and I wondered what he was thinking. When he finally said, "Grace must take after her father," I knew he was looking for family resemblance and saw none. Well, many children don't look like their parents. Even siblings don't always look similar.

Of course, Grace's frame is small, and mine is large. So was Charles'.

However, I did have a cousin with a small frame. Perhaps Michael's remark shouldn't have rattled me so, but it did, and I didn't know what to say. So I lied and said, "She does." Of course, Michael knew Charles before he died, so he knew what Charles looked like. But perhaps now that he can't compare characteristics face to face, he'll accept my lie as truth. Am I beginning to make lying a habit? The Bible says God hates lying. Lord, forgive me.

Michael also brought Grace a special gift, a Golden Book, The Poky Little Puppy. As soon as he pulled it out of his coat, Grace reached for it and pointed for Michael to sit down. Michael did just that, and Grace climbed up on his lap, making him open the book so he could read to her. That child sure does love to be read to! Michael and I laughed at how bossy she was, as if she were ordering him around. Well, I guess she was at that. I'm sure no one else can get away with bossing him around, since he tells everyone else what to do. Of course, he has superiors somewhere, but not around here.

He talked a lot about Ireland today, his home country. He told me many of our men have been sent to bases there and said he hoped to go there, too, some day after the war. I think he was sorry he couldn't be sent, but the Coast Guard doesn't go overseas because they guard our own coast. I told him I would love to go to Ireland, too, and for a moment I wondered what it would be like to go with him, shocking myself. Why would I even think such a thing, he being a married man? I guess I just forgot for a moment that he was and thought about how much fun such a trip would be with him. Lord, I'm so sorry to have such an adulterous thought. Obviously, I miss Charles more than I even believed. I hope Michael couldn't read my mind. I would be so embarrassed.

He's so easy to be around, I sometimes forget he's here on official business and not just visiting. He feels like a good friend, and I'm thankful to know him. I told him I was afraid that when Grace really started walking, she might get away from me. When I said, "If only I had a fence around the house to keep her from wandering off," he said, "We'll build you one. Just tell me what you want."

I couldn't believe he even offered! I told him I'd love a white picket fence and had always dreamed of having one around my house, and he said he'd make sure the fence was just like I wanted. I questioned if there was anything wrong with his men making the fence, but he just laughed that warm laugh of his and said the lighthouse property was government property, and his men worked for the government. I do believe Michael is spoiling me and Grace, but he is such a great comfort at this time in my life.

I honestly think Michael is a gift from God, like Grace is. They both arrived when I needed them the most. After so many years of trying to have a child, God gave me Grace. I had long given up, much like Sarah or Hannah in the Bible. They were both older when they had their long-awaited child. Sometimes I wonder if I'm too old to raise a child, but at least I'm not ninety like Sarah was! I promised I'd raise her the best I could, and I want to teach her to be a godly person. I pray I can be a good example of one.

I'm thankful Michael is a godly man. I've never heard him use coarse language or lose his temper with his men, even when they did something that would warrant his anger. I think he's kind of like a father to them because they're such young men. But they truly look up to him, as they should. In some ways, he's like Charles—his professionalism, his commitment to a job well done, his character. But Michael's more jovial, with a personality that makes you think his life isn't as serious and important as it is. I'm sure he knows so much more about what's going on in the war and around us than he is able to tell. For example, it was Mr. Reynolds who told me about the mines they put in Casco Bay to block the German subs. I asked Michael for confirmation, but he just shrugged and said that area was not his jurisdiction, so I didn't press him.

I just want him to know he can talk to me as a friend if he needs one, much as I want to talk to him as one. But I guess that wouldn't be possible. I wonder if he ever gets to talk to his wife on the phone. Surely, she is lonely without him. But he said they have family near her, so maybe she doesn't get as lonely as I do. I suppose I shouldn't worry about his business. Charles used to tell me not to waste my brain on things that didn't concern me. So much time alone has given me too much time to think. I would read a book if I had a new one, so I'll ask Mr. Reynolds to bring me one from the town *library next time he comes.*

I need to be prepared to be independent when the war is over, and the Coast Guard will not be here all the time like they are now. I cannot rely on someone else for company or consolation besides God and, to some extent, Grace. I must pray for strength to carry on. I must be strong for Grace. When she and I are all alone, only God will remain to protect us and look out for our needs. He always has and He always will.

Chapter Sixteen

The next morning as Abby was putting Emma into her car seat, the neighbor she'd waved to the night before walked over.

"Good morning," she said. "I'm Robin Fletcher. I live in 4D."

"Good morning," Abby said, straightening and turning to face the woman. "I'm Abby Baker. I live in 3C."

"Yes, I've seen you and your little girl." She bent down and smiled at Emma, then stood up. "I manage The Brass Lobster. You know, the tourist season is almost here, and I could use some part-time help. Would you be interested?"

"Thank you, but I have a job at Emma's daycare."

"Yes, I knew you did, but I thought you might like to have some extra hours. I really need some help." She held up her hand, and Abby noticed the woman wore a black wrist brace. "Tendinitis. It really limits me, and I need to put our new stock out."

"Oh, I'm sorry. I'm sure it does. I wish I could help, but I don't have the time now."

"That's all right. I was just hoping. It's hard to find employees here during the summer. The young people want to work in the more exciting tourist areas like Bar Harbor or with the water sports instead of in a gift store."

"I'll keep an eye out for anyone looking for a job." Abby closed the car door and walked to the driver's side.

"Thank you," Robin said and waved goodbye before walking to her own car.

The poor woman. It was too bad she couldn't find help. But Abby already had her hands full between the daycare and the lighthouse. And it wasn't like she was really needed at the lighthouse. She just wanted to be there. If she didn't go, the work would get done without her. Maybe she could work one day a week at the gift shop. Carson probably wouldn't care. Would he?

***

Carson closed the door to his room and headed for his truck when the owner of the inn hailed him.

"Mr. Stevens, glad I caught you." The older man hurried over.

"Yes?"

"Well, you see, when we rented your room to you, we didn't know how long you'd be staying. The tourist season is about to start, and we've already got reservations for your room. We have some regulars who rent it every year." The man was out of breath by the time he finished his explanation.

"So, you're telling me I need to leave?" Was he being kicked out?

"Well, sir, yes. These folks have been coming here for years, and you know there isn't another place like ours in town. I'm sorry."

"Do you have any suggestions for another place I can stay? I'll be here a while, at least until the house is ready on the island."

"Maybe there's a vacant apartment in town. Or maybe you can rent a room in a house somewhere. But you better hurry because some folks rent their whole house out for the season and get a good price for it."

"When do I need to get out?"

"By the end of the month, please."

Carson's gut tightened. "That's two weeks away."

"Yes, sir, that's right. Please don't be offended. You've been a good guest."

"Don't worry. I understand business is business. I'll be out in time for your seasonal guests." Carson walked to his truck, trying not to show his irritation. He climbed in and started the engine, blowing out a breath of hot air. Of course, he understood. His business wasn't as important as the seasonal guests who probably paid top dollar to stay in the same room. But a little more notice would've been nice. Now where would he go? He'd have to start asking around. Maybe the workers on the island would know of something. But from what he'd heard, most of them didn't live in Hope Harbor but in other towns in the area. Carson realized he might not be able to find something else in town.

If only the keeper's house was ready. But he was already pushing to get it ready during the summer. Any more problems like he had yesterday could really throw him off schedule. Why did it seem like things had just turned around for him? Everything had been progressing smoothly up till now. If he believed in curses, he'd think Harding had put one on him. Carson drove to Mo's to get a Big Joe. Maybe someone there would know of something.

He parked the truck out front and went inside, finding a line waiting to get coffee while man-bun and tattoo-girl scurried behind the counter to wait on customers both inside and at the drive-thru window. When did Mo's get so busy? Carson looked at his watch and noticed he was later than normal, having been delayed by his conversation with the inn owner. He crossed his arms and tried to be patient. Maybe he could skip the coffee. No, definitely not. Today especially.

A child's voice called out. "Hi, Mr. Carson!"

Carson glanced around for the child but didn't see one.

"Over here."

The woman standing in line in front of him pointed to the drive-thru window where Abby and Emma waved. A welcome sight couldn't be timelier. He smiled and waved back, then remembered Abby wouldn't be coming to the island today. Too bad she didn't come inside for her coffee so he could talk to her. But they were both in a hurry. He held up his phone and pointed to it. She nodded and smiled while the barista handed her coffee, then she drove off. He texted her.

I'LL COME BY WITH THE LOGBOOK COPIES TONIGHT. OKAY?

While he was getting his coffee, his phone chirped.

OKAY. CALL FIRST TO SEE WHERE I AM.

At least he had something good to look forward to later.

***

"Robin Fletcher? Yes, I know who she is. She runs that gift shop downtown, The Gold Lobster or something." Mom handed Abby the grocery list she'd stopped by after work to get.

"The Brass Lobster." Abby studied the list. "Is this all you need?"

"Oh, and I need two of my prescriptions refilled. I called the pharmacy, so they should be ready."

Did Mom really need so many different medications? Abby often questioned her mother's doctors about the drugs, afraid of them prescribing more than was necessary for an older woman, and worried that one drug might interfere with another. Two ibuprofens were enough to knock Abby out, and she was much stronger than Mom.

"Why did you ask about Robin Fletcher?"

"She lives in my apartment building and asked me this morning if I'd be interested in working in her shop part-time. She's having problems with tendinitis and needs help with tourist season coming. I wish I could help her."

"What did you tell her?"

"Mom, you know I don't have time. I've already given some of my days at the daycare to Kristin so I can go to the island and work on the restoration."

"Is Carson paying you for that?"

"Of course he's not. I just wanted to help."

Mom shrugged. "Well, seems to me that since he doesn't really need your help and she does, maybe you don't need to go to the island so much, and you could get paid doing something else."

Her mother was right, and Abby had already considered the same idea. "Maybe I can just go there once a week and work in the shop once a week. She's having a hard time finding employees."

"Maybe I could work for her," Mom said, followed by a cough. "Come season, the local businesses will take anybody who's able, even someone old like me."

"Seriously, Mom?" She wasn't too old to work in a gift shop, but was she able?

"If I felt a little better, I could."

Abby smiled. "I wish you could, too. You'd enjoy meeting people."

"I know I would." Mom shook her head. "I'd like to be useful."

Abby leaned over and hugged her mother. "You help me so much with Emma, and I appreciate you tons."

"That's not work at all. That's a blessing for me."

"And you're a blessing to us."

"I love my girls." Mom glanced into the living room. "Are you going to leave her here with me while you're at the store?"

Abby's gaze followed her mother's where Emma sat on the floor in front of the TV. "Sure. I'll be back before she even knows I'm gone." But Abby went to kiss her daughter goodbye anyway. She never wanted to leave without telling her loved ones goodbye, in case it was the last time she ever saw them. Losing someone unexpectedly created certain phobias. "Bye, honey. Be back in a few minutes. I have to pick up some things for Grandma. Love you!"

Emma hugged her bear. "Love you, too, Mommy." Abby didn't think she even took her eyes off the television screen.

While Abby shopped, she mulled over her conversation with Mom about being blessings to each other. Granny had written about Grace and Michael being blessings to her—Grace, the long-awaited child, and Michael, the Coast Guard officer who took a special interest in her and Grace. It must have been a great comfort to her after Grandfather died. But how hard was it for her when the Coast Guard left the island? That must have felt like experiencing another loss, a different kind of loss.

Abby's phone rang, and Carson's name popped up on it. "Hello?"

"Hi, Abby. It's Carson. I just got back from the island. Are you home?"

"No, I'm at the store getting some things for Mom. When I get finished, I'll take the things to her and pick up Emma. I should be home in about thirty minutes."

"Sounds good. Gives me time to shower and grab a bite to eat. Hey, have you eaten?"

"No, not yet. I was going to fix something when I got home."

"Why don't I pick up some food for us? Pizza again or something else?"

"Do you like BLTs? I've got a craving for one, with avocado. Can I make you one too?"

"Sure, if you don't mind. But you can leave the avocado off mine. Sounds too healthy."

Abby laughed. She didn't know very many men who liked avocado. But bacon—who didn't like it?

"All right. I'll leave the avocado off. But you don't know what you're missing!"

"So, where do you live?"

"Spruce Hill Apartments, apartment 3C. Just go out Seaview Street to the church and turn left on Church Street. You'll see the apartments on the right. We're in building three, second floor."

"Sounds good. I'll see you in thirty."

***

Carson pulled into the parking lot of Abby's apartment and sat in his truck a few minutes to take in the scene. The apartments were aptly named, as spruce trees rimmed the property and dotted the well-manicured lawn. The buildings were vintage mid-century, with shuttered windows and painted white wood siding. An inviting place like this would probably not have any vacancies.

He grabbed the copies, climbed out of the truck, and walked over to the stairs that separated the buildings and led to the second floor. The aroma of bacon wafted from the door marked 3C, confirming he'd arrived in the right place. He knocked, happy to see Abby open the door, looking prettier than ever. How did she manage to be so gorgeous, yet so natural? Her long, silky brown hair fell over her shoulders and down her back, giving him the urge to touch it and see if it was as soft as it looked. The warmth glimmering in her green eyes invited him in and even gave a hint that she was happy to see him.

"Come in." Abby stepped back as Emma ran up beside her.

"Hi, Mr. Carson." The little girl grinned at him.

"Hi, Emma, Abby." Carson stepped into a tastefully decorated room with bright colors mixed with soft ones.

"What a lovely place you have here."

"Thank you. We like it."

"I can see why. And is that a balcony out there?"

"Yes, it is. Not a very large one, but it's big enough for a couple of people to sit on and have coffee."

"It looks inviting."

She motioned him to follow. "I'll show it to you."

They stepped out the sliding doors to the small balcony that overlooked the center green and faced the balconies and patios of the other apartments in the other three buildings. A couple of fir trees shaded the lawn, and a fountain sat in the center of a small brick square with benches on either side.

"Nice space."

"I think so. It gives Emma some room to run around."

Carson leaned his elbows on the railing. "Do you know your neighbors?"

"Not personally, but I know what each of them looks like."

"Seems like a quiet place."

"It is. Many of these people have lived here a long time, and they don't like a lot of noise."

"Are there any other apartment complexes like this in town?" He looked over at her, optimistic.

"No, just this one. Hope Harbor hasn't grown much over the years. And I think the town wants to stay that way. They like the tourists for the extra income, but they don't want them to stay."

"Looks like I need to find another place to live for the time being. I'm getting kicked out of the inn." He straightened and faced her.

"You are? What did you do? Hold a wild party?" Her eyes twinkled and his heart melted.

"Apparently, I overstayed my welcome. Seems the inn has some long-standing reservations from regular guests during the summer, and I'm in the way."

"Oh, I'm so sorry. Where will you go? Do you have any ideas?"

He shook his head. "I just found out this morning I need to leave, so I haven't had much time to look."

"Mommy, I'm hungry." Emma pulled on Abby's shirt.

"All right, honey. Go wash your hands and set the table for us."

Emma ran off, and Abby and Carson went back inside. "I really love what you've done with the place. Your decorating skill is evident."

"Thank you. I'm kind of a minimalist, so I don't use a lot of items."

"But you use just enough."

Carson noticed the pink flush in her cheeks. He followed her into the small kitchen. "How can I help?"

"I hope you like chowder. The deli in the grocery store makes a good one, and I thought it'd be good with the sandwiches." She stirred the chowder in a pot on the stove.

"May I put these on the table?" Carson picked up the plates holding sandwiches.

"Sure. Thanks." Abby dipped up the soup and brought it to the table where Emma was meticulously placing the silverware at each place.

When she finished, she climbed up onto her chair.

"Have a seat, Carson." Abby motioned. He waited for her to slide into hers before he sat down.

Emma reached for each of their hands, bowed her head, then said her "God is Great" blessing.

"Yum! This sandwich is great." Carson couldn't remember the last time he'd had a homemade BLT.

"Glad you like it. It's even better with the avocado," Abby teased, her eyes sparkling. "How do you like the chowder?"

Carson took a spoonful and nodded. "Perfect. I haven't had any clam chowder since the last time I was in Boston."

Warmth filled him, not only from the soup, but from the company. He was so comfortable, and the situation was so family-like, it was hard to believe he'd only known Abby a short while. But he didn't really know her. He just liked being with her and really hoped she enjoyed his company as well. Even though she'd invited him over, he had no delusions about the reason. She wanted to see the logbook copies. Of course, she didn't have to offer him dinner, but she probably felt like she should repay him for getting them for her.

After an enjoyable dinnertime conversing with Abby and Emma, Carson helped Abby clean up.

"Coffee?" Abby held up a cup.

"Sure, if you're having some."

Abby made them coffee, and they returned to the table where he laid down the copies. Abby put a coloring book and a box of crayons on the table to keep Emma busy while she and Carson read over the logbook entries.

He'd scanned them already, so he drank his coffee while Abby read.

She glanced up at him. "They're not too interesting, are they?"

Carson shrugged. "I'd say they're a little more detailed about the weather than your grandfather's were."

"I suppose you're right. I'm so glad we found the journal to know the real story."

"Interesting, is it?" Carson set his cup down.

"It's amazing. She shares so much about her feelings. I've always thought of my Granny as someone with almost superhuman qualities, but her journal makes her more real, more human."

"Not a superwoman after all?"

"Mommy, was your granny a Wonder Woman too?"

Carson laughed and Abby did, too, her face turning pink.

"Emma, she kind of was, but not like the Wonder Woman you know. She was just a very strong and courageous woman. Remember she was a lighthouse keeper?"

Emma nodded and refocused on her artwork.

Abby glanced at Emma, then back to Carson, a message he took to mean she needed to be careful what she shared in Emma's presence.

"She did have her doubts, but she persevered. I think she was stronger than she thought she was."

"I think that's a common feeling, don't you? I mean, don't you sometimes surprise yourself with what you have done?"

Abby studied him a moment. "I've never really thought anything like that."

"But other people have commented on things you've accomplished, I bet."

Her eyes showed surprise. "I guess they have. But I never did anything as difficult as what Granny did."

He raised his eyebrows. "Oh, yeah? Well, you might not think so, but believe me, you have. And I don't know all you've done, but I know enough to be impressed."

This time, her face really reddened. She abruptly changed the subject. "You haven't told me how things went today on the island. Any new problems?"

He took the hint and switched to his day's activities. "Supplies arrived, and so did the workers, although not all the ones we started with. The plumber thought he was missing some things, but then he realized he'd left them in his truck on the mainland."

"So no surprises?"

"Other than finding out I'm homeless, no."

"Oh, I forgot about that. Where will you go?"

"I have no idea. I was hoping you could make some suggestions. It sure would be nice to find a place like this." He glanced around the room.

"Unfortunately, there aren't any more like this in town. I was lucky to find this apartment."

"I don't suppose anyone is moving out?"

She shook her head. "Not that I've heard. But I can ask around."

"Thanks. I appreciate it. If the keeper's house was ready, I'd move out there. But we have a way to go before anyone could live there."

"Do you have any idea when it'll be finished?"

"If we don't have any more delays, it could be ready in two months."

"Right in the middle of the tourist season."

"Exactly. Not the best timing, but maybe we could offer sightseeing trips out there if it's too late for reservations."

"That's a great idea."

"Maybe if you work really hard, we can get it finished earlier." He gave her a wink.

She looked stricken.

"What's the matter? You know I'm just kidding, right?"

"No, it's not that. But I think I'll quit going over there three days a week. I've been asked to help at one of the gift shops in town. They're really short-handed, you know. So, I plan to accept and work at the gift shop at least one day a week, maybe more when the season starts. Kristin can keep her workdays at the daycare, and I'll pick up a day at the shop. It pays pretty well, I hear."

Of course, it made perfect sense for Abby to work at the gift shop and make money. He wasn't paying her for her help at the island, nor could he afford to. But reasonable or not, why did he feel like he'd just gotten strike three?

Chapter Seventeen

A bby wanted to help Carson. She really did. But she couldn't offer him her couch to sleep on. Well, maybe if he were truly desperate, she could. But that would be awkward, and people would get the wrong idea. Truth was, Mom would probably take him in. She had an extra bedroom, but that would be awkward too. Hopefully, he'd find something soon, and it wouldn't be completely up to her to find a place for him to live.

Why was she always trying to help someone else? Kevin had ridiculed her for being that way. She winced at the memory. Why had he always tried to make her feel bad about doing something good? He'd teased her about rescuing people like animals. He even questioned her motives. In fact, he questioned so many things she did. She never had understood why he seemed to take pleasure in belittling her. And when she asked him about it, he just laughed and said he was kidding. She never thought his remarks were funny, though, because they stung and made her doubt herself. Abby shook her head, trying to make the thoughts go away. Besides, now she didn't need Kevin's approval.

She flagged Robin the next morning on her way to the car and told her she could work one day a week for her, if that would help.

Robin's eyes lit up. "Honey, any help is better than none. Maybe we can get enough done when you're there that there won't be much the rest of the week."

"I hope so. What day is best? I have Monday, Tuesday, or Wednesday."

"Monday would be great. We can price and stock any merchandise that came in over the weekend. Can you start next week?"

"Sure. I can be there after I drop my daughter off at daycare, say, around eight? Is that too early?"

"Oh no. That's perfect. We don't open until ten, so that gives us time before any customers come in."

"I'll see you Monday then."

The smile on Robin's face stirred Abby's heart. Maybe that was why she liked to help others. It made them happy, which made her happy. What was wrong with that?

Unfortunately, from the look on Carson's face when she told him, the news did not make him happy. She couldn't imagine her work at the keeper's house being that important, but maybe with all the other problems he'd had lately, she was just one more inconvenience. She'd try to be more useful and work harder next time she went to the island and quit spending so much time daydreaming.

On Monday, Abby scanned the shelves of The Brass Lobster and listened to Robin's instructions.

"So here in the computer, you key in the product code, the description, and the price listed on the invoice. The computer will automatically mark it up accordingly. Put in the quantity received, then hit print, and the price tags will come out printed on one sheet, unless there's way too many. But I doubt that will happen. There are quite a few price tags per page. Does that make sense?"

"Sounds easy enough." Abby counted the brass bottle openers in the shape of a lobster that were in the box nearest her. "May I try?"

"Go right ahead." Robin stepped back from the computer to let Abby use it.

After she put in all the numbers, a page printed out. She took it out of the printer and showed it to Robin.

"Does this look right?"

"Perfect. You catch on fast."

"I try."

"Okay, now's the fun part. Peel one of those price tags off for each of these little guys and stick them on the bottom, underneath the tail."

When Abby finished with the bottle openers, she moved on to brass lobster magnets and repeated the steps. Next was a box full of lobster earrings, more than one design. As she completed placing the stickers on the objects, Robin arranged them on the shelves, showing Abby where to store backup stock.

"You certainly ordered a lot of merchandise."

"And when the season is in full swing, those things you just priced will fly out of here!"

"I didn't realize there were so many items with lobsters."

Robin laughed. "Oh, we've only just begun. The storeroom is stacked to the ceiling." Robin patted Abby on the arm. "I'm so glad you're here to help me. I guess you can see what a disadvantage I have with this tendinitis."

"I'm glad I could work it in."

Abby noticed a couple peeking in the front window. Robin followed her gaze, then checked her watch. "It's time to unlock the doors. Keep working but move these boxes out of the aisles so people can walk."

Robin opened the doors, and Abby straightened the area around her. The couple were obviously tourists because they didn't look familiar and they examined all the merchandise. The woman oohed and aahed over several items while the man responded with "Hmph." Robin stood behind the counter near the computer, ready to ring up their sales. When the man carried a pile of items over to the counter for his wife, Robin asked, "Where are you people from?"

"South Carolina." The woman's southern drawl was charming.

"Is that right? Where are you staying?"

"We brought our RV. It's in an RV park just out of town," the man said.

"It's so pretty here." The wife beamed. "Except that it's a little colder than I expected. Is this temperature normal for y'all?"

"Yes, it's normal. We have sweatshirts, too, if you'd like to look at them." Robin nodded toward a corner.

"I'll show them." Abby walked over to the sweatshirts. "What size do you wear?"

Leaving her other items at the counter, the woman hurried over to

Abby. "John, come look at these. I think we're going to need them at night."

The rest of the day continued in similar fashion with Robin and Abby either handling customers or stocking merchandise. When there was a break between customers, Abby said, "And I thought working in the daycare was busy."

Robin chuckled. "This is just the beginning. I'll have a couple of teenagers start part-time after school ends. They have more stamina than I do."

The door opened and another couple sauntered in, examining the display of moose keychains. Abby noticed the designer purse and massive ring the woman was wearing and the expensive sunglasses atop the man's perfect haircut, doubting they'd find anything in the store suitable for their refined taste. They both wore linen, his white shorts and white shirt, and hers, white capris and tan shirt with upturned collar. Abby glanced at Robin who mouthed "yacht people."

"Can I help you find anything?" Robin asked, approaching the couple.

The woman smiled. "Do you have anything, you know, a little nicer than these?"

"Yes, I have some gold and diamond jewelry in the case. Would you like to see it?"

"Yes, please." The woman followed Robin to the counter, and Abby returned to her item pricing. The man ambled over to the counter, peering into the glass beside his wife. The two asked Robin to show them several things, discussing the quality of each.

Abby knew the type. Some had been her clients in California. She opened a small box that contained small packages of necklaces with several nautical designs. The quality of the gold jewelry was lovely, and she especially liked the lighthouse pendant with a diamond as the light. Perhaps the jewelry would appeal to the couple as well. Abby picked up a few pieces and turned toward Robin.

"These just came in. You might want to look at them." Abby carried them to the counter and gave them to Robin who laid them down in front of the couple.

The woman briefly glanced up at Abby, then back down at the jewelry. But a look of surprise crossed the man's face before he returned his gaze to the counter.

Abby stepped back to the area where she was working, a little unsettled by the man's reaction. For a moment, she thought he recognized her. Had she ever seen him before? She searched her brain and couldn't remember him or his wife. He didn't ask her who she was, so he must've decided he didn't know her either. Based on the conversation between them and Robin, they had sailed from Bar Harbor and arrived at Hope Harbor that morning. They would be in town just a few days before sailing on to the next stop of their journey to Nova Scotia. They inquired about the best restaurant in town and what other attractions there might be. Since Hope Harbor didn't have much of either, Abby doubted they'd be in town long.

"I think Lily will like this one. She likes lighthouses." The woman held up the lighthouse necklace.

"Will that be all?" Robin asked.

"Do you want one too?" The man picked up another one of the necklaces.

"I do like that one." She pointed to one in his hand that was the symbol of a ship's wheel with a diamond in the center.

"All right then. We'll take these." He pulled out his wallet and purchased the two items.

As they were leaving the store, the man glanced back at Abby, a questioning look on his face. Why did he look at her like that? After they left, she went over to Robin.

"Do you know who those people were?"

Robin looked at the charge receipt. "K. E. Lawrence. Why?"

"I don't know. He just looked at me strangely. I thought maybe we'd met before, but I don't remember anyone with the name Lawrence."

"You're an attractive woman. Maybe he was just admiring you."

Abby shook her head. "It wasn't that kind of look. Anyway, it's not important."

"From what they said, they live somewhere Down East, south of Bar Harbor."

"I'll ask Mom if she knows anyone by that name."

***

But her mother wasn't familiar with the name either. "Abby, I think you're just overreacting. I'm sure the man meant nothing by his actions."

"Maybe you're right." Abby dropped into a kitchen chair. "I am pooped. I didn't realize it could get so busy at that little store."

"And the season isn't even in full swing now. Just imagine what it will be like in a few weeks."

"I can't."

"I thought you might be tired, so I made some supper for you and Emma."

Abby glanced over at the counter where the slow cooker sat. "Pot roast?"

"Yes, ma'am. You go ahead and fix your plates." Mom went into a coughing fit.

Abby always worried when her mother couldn't catch her breath. "Thanks. I'll fix you one too."

Mom sighed and waved her off. "I'm not very hungry."

"But you have to eat too. You need some nourishment."

"All right. Just a little bit."

Her mother picked at her food. It was obvious that the coughing wore her out, leaving no energy to eat. The doctor had suggested she carry an oxygen tank, but Mom had refused, since it was expensive, and her insurance wouldn't completely cover it. Somehow, Abby needed to figure out how to get it for her because she had so much trouble breathing.

"Have you heard from Carson?"

"No, not since he came by the other night." Abby sat upright. "Mom, I forgot to ask you. Carson has to move out of the inn and needs a place to live until he can move out to the island. Do you know any place he can rent?"

Mom stared at the table a while. "Maybe Mrs. Norton's garage apartment is available. You can check with her." She shook her head. "Everybody else is going to rent what they have to the tourists and get top dollar. I wish him luck."

"So do I. Who knows when he can move out to the island? He's had some problems lately, ever since he met the B&B members."

"They're giving him problems? How?"

"I don't think they really are, but coincidentally, he started having problems after he went to one of their meetings."

"Well, I know all those people, and they're pretty nice, for the most part."

"He said Mr. Harding wasn't very nice."

"Fred?" Mom frowned. "He can be a horse's behind sometimes. Likes to push his weight around like a bigwig or something."

"Carson says he owns most of the B&Bs in town, so he must be pretty important."

"I guess he is, sort of. But what kind of trouble is Carson having?"

"Just delays and problems with materials, and some of the crew went to another job."

"Hmm. That's too bad. Well, I hope it gets worked out."

"I do too. I've tried to be some help to him, but I'm afraid I haven't done very much."

Mom reached across the table toward Abby's hand. "I'm sure you've been a big help."

"If only I could find him an apartment. There aren't any vacancies in my complex."

"Well, tell him to check with Mrs. Norton, or maybe you could even check for him, since he's gone most the day."

"All right. I'll do that."

Her mother started coughing and wheezing.

"Mom, I'm calling the doctor first thing tomorrow. You're not getting any better."

Her mother nodded as she caught her breath, too tired to protest.

"Go lie down. Do you need help getting to the bed?"

Mom waved her off. "No, you go on." With great effort, she pushed up out of the chair. Abby went to her side anyway and assisted her back to the bedroom.

"I'll clean up the kitchen before we leave."

Mom lay back and closed her eyes as Hercules jumped onto the bed and took his position at the foot. Abby pulled off her mother's shoes, then laid a light blanket over her. What else could she do to help her?

When Abby finished in the kitchen, she went back to check on her mother and found her sound asleep and breathing normally. As she left the house, a pang of guilt pricked Abby. Was she wrong to leave her mother alone? Should she move back in? *Lord, what should I do?*

***

Carson keyed in Abby's number. He needed to confirm that she was going to the island with him the next day. Wasn't that a good excuse to call?

"Hi, Carson." Her greeting caught him off guard, and he paused before speaking.

"Hi, Abby. How did things go today at the store?"

"Much busier than I expected. But we did get a lot of work done."

"Are you still going to the island tomorrow?" Why was he holding his breath?

"Yes, I'd like to, but I need to check on Mom first, then drop off Emma at daycare. And I'd like to call Mom's doctor while I have cell service. I hate to delay you."

"No problem. I need to go by the hardware store anyway. Do you want to give me a call when you're finished with your errands?"

"Sure, if you don't mind. So how did today go? Did you make any progress?"

"Yes, we did. We finished patching the chimney and the hearth. We also framed out the new bathroom downstairs, so it'll be finished soon." He left out the part about the missing air compressor that had prevented them from doing anything until another one could be sent out. She didn't need to hear his problems right now.

"That's good news."

"Yes, but you said you wanted to check on your mother first thing. Is Grace all right?"

"I'm not sure. She seems to be getting weaker, and I want the doctor to know. He might demand that she get on oxygen, which she has refused to do so far."

He could envision her twisting a piece of her hair while she talked.

"Okay. Look, if you want to stay here, it's okay."

"I'll let you know, if you don't mind waiting for me. Hopefully, it won't take long."

"Call me when you decide."

"I will."

Was he selfish to want her to go to the island when her mother wasn't well? He probably should have just told her to stay and take care of things. He was beginning to doubt himself about everything these days. Maybe he shouldn't have bought Hope Island and had taken on a bigger goal than he could accomplish with his limited knowledge of construction. Maybe he should've bought a lighthouse B&B already established. Maybe he should leave Abby alone since she had more important things to take care of, like a mother and a daughter.

Why was he having these doubts now? He had been so enthusiastic that he hadn't foreseen any problems. It was as if Fred Harding had put a curse on him. Now everything that didn't go as he expected reminded him of what the man had said or insinuated about Carson's ability. Carson shook his head. He had to get those thoughts out of his mind. Blaming his problems on Harding was ridiculous. The man didn't control his life, even if he did have control on the other B&Bs in town.

Chapter Eighteen

Kristen picked Emma up for daycare in the morning, happy to return a favor to Abby for helping her get the job. Once Emma left, Abby packed her backpack for the day, throwing in some shorts in case she had time to run.

She'd left a message on the doctor's answering machine the night before, which she didn't expect anyone to get until the office opened. After throwing her things into the car, she drove to her mother's. Abby still had her own key, so she let herself in and was surprised to find Mom sitting at the table with a cup of coffee and the newspaper in front of her.

"You're up."

"Well, of course I am. It's already 7:30."

Mom was up all right, but she still looked tired and pale as she struggled to get her words out.

"Mom, you worried me last night. Did you sleep well?"

"Far as I know. Aren't you supposed to be somewhere?"

It took so much effort for Mom to speak that Abby felt guilty making her talk.

"I'm meeting Carson in about an hour." Abby debated whether she should tell her she was waiting to talk to the doctor, knowing her mother's stubbornness.

"Did you talk to Mrs. Norton about the apartment?"

"Not yet. I forgot last night. I'll call her this morning."

"She's in the next block. You could go in person."

"That's a great idea. I need to go for a short run anyway. Do you think it's too early?"

Mom shrugged, probably because she was too tired to discuss the matter or didn't care.

"Tell you what. I'll run downtown and make a circle back to her house, so it'll be after eight when I get there."

"Carson?"

Reading her mother's mind, Abby said, "It's okay. He had some errands to take care of too."

Abby changed into her shorts and swigged some water before heading out. "Can I get you anything?"

Mom shook her head.

"Okay, be back in a few," she said after giving her mother a kiss on the cheek.

Abby took off sprinting toward town. She didn't have time for a long run, so she cut her route short. With only a few city streets, it wouldn't take long to circle the town. Instead of crossing over to the park, she stayed on the sidewalk in front of the shops on Main Street. Running past The Brass Lobster, she noticed it was still dark inside. Robin would probably get there soon to get ready for the day.

Abby ran to the end of the block, then turned the corner to go up Seaview Drive. On the opposite corner, Bagels and Breakfast was already busy. A quick glance at the restaurant and she recognized the couple coming out the door. Mr. and Mrs. Lawrence. Before she could look away, Mr. Lawrence made eye contact with her and nodded. Abby forced a little smile and turned away. She knew he was watching her as she ran because her spine tingled with his stare. Why did she have to see them today?

She continued down the street before making another turn at the Episcopal church, glad to finally be out of the man's sight. Her phone rang, and it was the doctor's office. She slowed to a walk so she could talk. After Abby explained her concern about her mother's condition, the doctor told her to bring Grace in as soon as possible. Abby agreed, then ended the call. Now she had to let Carson know she couldn't make it today. But first, she'd go check on the apartment. Maybe she could give him some good news too.

She ran to the address her mother had given her. A white picket fence surrounded the small yard and old craftsman house, reminding Abby of the fence her grandmother had wanted. She'd have to ask Mom if she remembered it. A one-car driveway ran the length of the house, ending in a garage with a second story and a staircase going up to it.

Abby climbed the concrete steps to the front porch and knocked on the door but didn't hear a sound inside. She knocked again. Still no answer.

"Are you looking for me?"

Abby spun around at the voice and found a short woman peering up at her. Gray hair sneaked out from under the woman's straw hat. She wore gardening gloves and held a basket with cut flowers.

"Yes, if you're Mrs. Norton."

"I am. And you are..."

"Abby Baker. Grace Pearson's daughter. I came by to inquire about your garage apartment. Is it available?"

"Grace's daughter, yes, of course, I know you. But aren't you living in the Spruce Hill apartments?"

"I am. I'm not looking for myself but for a friend, Carson Stevens. He's been staying at the inn and has to move out because tourists had already reserved his room for the season."

"Your boyfriend? I don't allow any hanky-panky here."

"Oh goodness, no. He's not my boyfriend. He's restoring the lighthouse and keeper's house on Hope Island. The island is all we have in common." Was that really all? Somehow, saying that felt wrong.

"I've heard of him. Well, to be honest, I have a tenant in the apartment now." Abby's heart sank for Carson. "However, he's moving out in a couple of weeks, so it'll be available when he leaves. Tell your friend he needs to come by and sign a lease and pay a deposit, and I'll hold it for him. Apartments are scarce as hen's teeth around here."

"Yes, I know. I'll tell him. Thank you."

Abby headed back to her mother's house, punching in Carson's number as she walked.

"Hi, Carson. I've got some good news and some bad news."

"The bad news is you can't go to the island today. Right? So what's the good news?"

"I believe I found you an apartment."

"That is good news. Where?"

"It's a garage apartment a block from Mom's. The lady has a tenant there now, but they're moving out in two weeks. You need to go by and pay a deposit so she'll hold it for you."

"Sounds good. I'll do that if you give me the address. But I'm sorry you can't come to the island today. It's your mother, isn't it?"

"Yes, the doctor wants me to bring her in as soon as possible, so I have to."

"I understand. Don't worry, you have to take care of your mother. But I will miss you."

"I hope to be able to go tomorrow."

"Great."

Abby gave him Mrs. Norton's address and said goodbye. She sure hoped it would work out for him. When Abby got back to Mom's, she was lying down on the sofa.

"Mom, I know you're tired, but your doctor wants to see you. I'll help you up."

Mom took Abby's hand and allowed herself to be pulled up without protest. Abby helped her get to the car, then drove to the doctor's office, worried that Mom was so weak.

"Are you going to the island?"

"No, I told Carson to go on without me."

"I'm sorry. It's my fault."

"No, it's not. The island isn't going any place, and I'll get another chance to go."

Mom reached over and patted Abby's arm.

***

The doctor told Abby's mother exactly what Abby thought he would. Mom needed to start using oxygen. Mom shook her head. Outside, the doctor told Abby privately that if she didn't get the equipment at home, her mother would end up in the hospital.

After Abby took her back to her house, her mother sank into the recliner and promptly fell asleep. Abby stayed a while longer, waiting until it was time to pick Emma up. She listened to Mom's breathing, praying for a way to get the oxygen she so desperately needed. Abby thumbed through a magazine while Mom napped. After about twenty minutes, she woke up.

"What did Mrs. Norton say?"

Abby jolted at her mother's voice. "She said the apartment will be available in two weeks and for Carson to come by and put down a deposit. Do you feel better now?"

Mom gave a nod. "Much. I'm glad he'll have a place. I thought about offering him my other bedroom."

Mom's house was small, but it had been big enough for her, Dad, and Abby. Cozy, you might say. But taking in Carson? Abby wasn't sure she wanted him that close to her personal life.

"I'm glad you didn't have to, although it's nice of you to consider. I believe he'll have more privacy in the other apartment."

"Probably so."

Abby pictured the Norton house. "Mom, was there ever a picket fence around the keeper's house on the island?"

Mom's eyes brightened and she smiled. "There sure was. Mother called it my corral. I'm sure it came in handy until I was big enough to learn how to get out of it."

"Did you know the Coast Guard built it for her?"

"No, I didn't know that. Did you read that in her journal?"

"Yes, seems that Mr. O'Brien was very helpful to her."

"I don't doubt it. I know we both looked forward to his visits."

"You know, the fence isn't there anymore."

"You're right. It wasn't there last time I saw it. Do you think Carson will put it back?"

"I don't even know if he knew there had been one."

"Made the place real homey, and I knew where my boundaries were. I imagine it gave her great relief about my safety too."

"If I lived there alone with Emma, I'd certainly want a fence."

Mom looked at the mantel clock. "Speaking of Emma, shouldn't you be getting her?"

Abby glanced at the clock and jumped up when she realized the time. "Yes! I better be going. Do you have something to eat for supper?"

"Yep. Leftovers. Got some canned soup too. I'm not too hungry though."

"I can fix you something before I go." Abby had a hunch her mother wouldn't eat after Abby left.

Mom shook her head. "No. I'm feeling better now and can help myself. You go on now."

"All right then." Abby kissed her mom on the forehead. "I'll call you later or you call me if you need anything."

"Yes, nurse, I will."

***

At the daycare, Kristin greeted Abby. "How's your mother?"

"Better, thank you. And thanks for taking care of Emma for me."

"My pleasure. Any time you need me to, call me."

"I will. Ready to go, Emma?"

Emma ran and got her backpack, and Abby helped her put it on. Abby needed to go by the grocery store on the way and noticed a few unfamiliar faces there. More tourists, she imagined, probably from the campground outside of town. When they were getting out of the car at home, Robin pulled up alongside.

"How'd it go today?" Abby asked, taking two grocery bags from the trunk.

"I missed you. My other lady came in, but she's a little slow. She's retired, but likes to work here to help me during the season, so I let her. She can't work more than four hours a day, though, or she gets tired, plus I think she's limited to how many hours she can work and still get her Social Security."

Emma ran ahead as Abby and Robin walked toward the apartments. "Mom thought she could work, too, but she's in no condition to work."

"I'm sorry she's not well," Robin said. "Oh, that man came back into the store today, you know, that Mr. Lawrence."

Abby's heart skipped a beat. "He did? Did he buy more jewelry?"

"No, he just looked around. Said his wife was getting her nails done over at the hair salon. But the strange thing is, he asked about you."

"Me?" Abby's throat tightened. "Why?"

Robin shrugged. "He said you reminded him of someone from another place and asked if your family was from here. I told him you were, as far as I know."

"I guess that's why he's been looking at me funny."

"Where else did you see him?"

"This morning on my run I went by Bagels and Breakfast, and he and his wife were coming out. We saw each other, and I felt like he was staring at me after I passed. He's been kind of creeping me out."

"Well, don't worry. I think the person he knew wasn't from here, so it was just a coincidence."

"Yes, probably so."

Abby followed Emma up the stairs to their unit, telling herself to relax. But she couldn't shake the fear that threatened to take over. Of course, the whole situation was just a coincidence, but it still bothered her that a stranger was asking about her. Whom did she remind him of? She went inside and double-locked the door. She was probably being foolish because the man wouldn't follow her home once he knew she wasn't the person he thought she was. She glanced at her balcony with the drapes wide open, then hurried over to close them. Foolish or not, she wanted to prevent the possibility of anyone looking in.

Just when she was feeling safe about Hope Harbor, her security was shaken. Her memory flashed back to the last time she'd been stalked. She'd volunteered at a homeless shelter, and one of the men had started following her around. Kevin had blasted her when he found out and told her she was an idiot to put herself and their daughter in danger from derelicts. Maybe he was right. Maybe she shouldn't have worked in that place. And now helping Robin had opened a crack in her new armor. Wasn't there any place she was safe?

Chapter Nineteen

Carson studied the craftsman house with the garage apartment at the end of the drive before he approached the porch. He hadn't seen garage apartments in years, and from the looks of this place, it had been around a while. Hopefully, it was clean and serviceable. Whatever, he'd have to tolerate it for a little while because he had no choice.

A couple of knocks on the door brought a diminutive woman to it.

"Excuse me, Mrs. Norton? I'm Carson Stevens. Abby Baker talked to you earlier about my renting your apartment."

The little lady squinted as she looked up at him. "So you're the man renovating Hope Island? I heard about you."

Carson forced a smile. "Well, I hope whatever you heard was good. Yes, I'm the guy renovating the keeper's house to be a bed-and-breakfast."

She opened her screen door but didn't invite him in.

"Hmm. Do you really think folks want to go all the way out there to stay someplace?"

Note to self: arrange transportation for guests. "Yes, ma'am, I do. I've stayed in several lighthouse B&Bs myself and have thoroughly enjoyed the experience."

"You don't say. When is it going to be finished?"

"I'm shooting for first of July, if all goes well."

"So you're going to move out there when it's finished?"

"Yes, ma'am. I need to be there for the guests." Was that going to be a problem? "Perhaps *you* can be one of our guests." He hoped his attempt at charm would help get the apartment.

The woman chuckled and waved her hand. "No, thank you. I'm fine right here. But I guess that means you won't be able to sign a year's lease on the apartment."

"Yes, ma'am. I mean, no, ma'am, I can't do that. I hope you'll let me go on a month-to-month contract."

"Hmm, well, if you pay up front, I guess I'll do that. Come on in, and we'll take care of business." She opened the door all the way and let him in.

When he finished paying her and signing the paperwork, he swung by Mo's. He had lots of work to catch up on tonight and needed the liquid energy. When he went inside, he hoped he'd coincidentally run into Abby again. He'd missed her today but had a guilty pang when he remembered why she couldn't come. How was Grace doing?

He pushed her name on his phone to ask while he waited in line.

"Hi, Carson."

"Hi, Abby. How's your mother?"

"A little better. The doctor still insists she needs oxygen for her COPD, if we can just figure out how to get the equipment. Thank you for asking."

"Glad to hear she's feeling better."

"Are you at Mo's? The jazz music in the background sounds familiar."

"Guilty. I just got back and need coffee. I have a lot of work to do tonight."

"I can almost smell it. I love the aroma of fresh coffee there."

"Can I bring you a cup?"

"What? I thought you had work to do."

"I do, but I have time to drop a cup of coffee off at your place. I won't stay long."

"Are you sure? I mean, I don't want to put you out any."

"Seriously, Abby, you're barely a mile away. Do you want me to get your usual, or do you want decaf?"

"I guess I'll have decaf. I'll probably have a hard enough time getting to sleep tonight."

"Okay, got it. See you soon."

He ended the call and pondered what she said. Why would she

have a hard time going to sleep? Concern for her mother?

When he arrived at her apartment a few minutes later with coffee in hand, he knocked on the door. On the other side, her voice said, "Who's there?" Was she expecting someone else?

"Your coffee delivery man, Carson."

The door opened, and she offered a slight smile as she let him in. He glanced at the balcony, expecting to see out, but the curtains were drawn over it.

He nodded toward the balcony. "Don't want to see the sunset tonight?"

She followed his gaze and looked back at him with something akin to fear in her eyes. "I, uh, I didn't want people looking in."

What a strange comment. She'd had them open the last time he was there. He raised an eyebrow. "Do you have a voyeur?"

"No, well, maybe. I just want to be safe, not sorry."

She was acting strange, even a bit jumpy.

He grabbed her by the arm as she turned away from him. "Abby, what's the matter? What's going on?"

Her eyes darted around the room as she quickly closed the door. She looked as though she was going to answer him, but Emma came running into the room.

"Hi, Mr. Carson!" She spread her arms for a hug.

Carson bent down to give her a hug. "Hi, Emma. Did you have a good day today?"

The little girl nodded. "Yes, sir. I had fun."

"That's great! Maybe I should go to daycare, because it sounds like it's a lot of fun."

Emma's forehead creased. "You're too big!"

"I am? Well, that's not fair."

"You can go with me someday if you want to."

"Why, thank you, Emma. Maybe I'll do that someday."

"Emma, go wash up for supper, okay, honey?" Abby scooted her away.

When she was out of sight, Carson said, "Can you tell me what's going on?"

She lowered her voice. "I'm probably being silly, but a man came into the store yesterday and looked at me in a strange way. Then today, he went back to the shop and asked Robin about me."

"Do you have any idea who he is?"

"Yes, his name is K. E. Lawrence. He and his wife are tourists. They have a sailboat anchored in the harbor. He told Robin I reminded him of someone he knew, and he asked about my family."

"You don't think he's following you, do you? It could be just a coincidence that you look like someone he knows. Happens all the time."

"I suppose so, but doesn't it seem strange that he would go back to the store to ask about me when I'm not there?"

"Maybe he thought you'd be there, and he'd ask you himself. How would he know you weren't going to be there?"

Abby twiddled her hair, appearing to think about what he said. "Of course you're right. I guess I'm just a little paranoid."

Carson lifted an eyebrow. "Any reason you might be?" She glanced up at him with a look of fear in her eyes. "Never mind. You don't need to tell me."

Emma came back into the room, and Carson decided to change the subject.

"Well, I have an apartment now. Or I will have when I move out of the inn. Thanks for the help."

"So you met Mrs. Norton?"

"Sure did. We're best buds now." He chuckled. "Well, not quite. But she did allow me to sign a short-term lease, for which I am very thankful."

"That's good. Glad it worked out."

"Mommy, I'm hungry." Emma tugged Abby's shirt.

Carson remembered he'd promised not to stay long, even though he hated to leave. He really did have work to do. "Hey, I better let you two get on with supper." He turned to leave and glanced at a sketchpad lying on the breakfast bar. Curiosity propelled him to check it out, so he picked it up and studied it. The picture was a rendering of the keeper's house, with a view of the exterior and the interior. The interior rooms were labeled, and furniture was placed in them. He faced Abby. "What's this?"

Her eyes widened, and her face reddened as she hurried over and reached for the pad. "I was just playing around with ideas. Kind of in my blood."

"It looks good. Could I use your suggestions when it's time to decorate?"

She shrugged. "Sure, if you like what I came up with."

"Are you kidding? Decorating is not my thing. I'd *love* for you to decorate the house."

Abby smiled. "I'd love to do it."

"Wait a minute. What do you charge? I'm not sure interior decorating is in my budget."

She laughed in her priceless way. "It's negotiable. Maybe we can barter, and you can take us out to dinner."

"I might be able to afford that. So, about tomorrow. Can you go to the island with me, or do you need to stay here with your mother?"

"I think I can, but I'll have to check on her first thing in the morning and let you know."

Noise from the kitchen diverted their attention. Emma was dragging a stool to the counter.

"Emma! What are you doing?" Abby rushed over to her.

"I'm making supper."

"I'll let myself out. Good night, girls." Carson unlocked the deadbolt, opened the door, and turned to wave. "Don't forget to lock up after me."

***

Abby reheated the coffee in the microwave after she put Emma to bed. She sat down on the sofa with the sketchpad and studied it. She'd forgotten she'd even made the drawing because she'd been focused on other things at the time. She picked up a pencil and made a couple of changes to the design. Carson really wanted her to decorate the keeper's house. Her heart sped up at the idea.

She'd have so much fun doing that. Her mind began to source products, furniture, fabric, and accessories. She couldn't wait to get started. But reality struck her as she considered the cost involved. She couldn't buy everything herself. She'd have to ask Carson for more than a dinner out. She shook her head. Why did she even make that suggestion? Was she flirting? Her face heated just remembering what she'd said.

He was a nice guy and comfortable to be with, but only as a friend. He hadn't teased her about being afraid of being watched, but he did give her reason to doubt her fear, herself. No, she wasn't going through that again. On the other hand, if she were being followed, it'd be nice to have Carson around. She'd certainly feel safer. But that would be using him, and she didn't want to do that. And he was probably right about her worry anyway. Abby blew out a deep breath. She could handle this. Couldn't she?

What would Granny do? Abby picked up the journal and began where she'd left off.

April 30, 1945

Mr. Reynolds brought my groceries today plus a copy of the Portland newspaper. There was a sad story on the front page about one of our boats blowing up right here off our coast. Everyone on board was killed. What a tragedy. Mr. Reynolds says the boat was torpedoed, but the paper says nothing about that. It just said a fire on the boat resulted in an explosion. Why wouldn't they say it was a torpedo if it was? He thinks the government doesn't want us to know the Nazis are that close.

But Mr. Reynolds says we are winning the war in Europe. With the Russian Army coming from one direction and our forces from the other, the Germans are running scared. So when will their submarines leave our coast? I'll ask Michael when I see him again. But I wonder when that will be. It's been two weeks since he was here. And I'm afraid he's tied up with that boating tragedy that happened. I shouldn't think this, I suppose, but I've missed him. I never know when he'll show up, but it feels like it's been a terribly long time that he's been gone, even though it hasn't really been.

Many times I think of something I want to tell someone, but Charles is gone and Grace can't understand. I'm thankful for Mr. Reynolds's weekly visits, but there are some things I don't talk to him about. Knowing Mr. Reynolds, whatever I tell him might as well be on the front page of the paper since he shares gossip from town and would likely do the same with any information I gave him.

He brought me seeds, so I started working in the garden, trying to get the soil ready to plant them, but my goodness, there are so many rocks in this ground. Thank God, the weather was pleasant enough to be outside. I tethered Grace to the fence so she wouldn't wander off while I worked. True to his word, Michael had the Coast Guardsmen build my picket fence. It hasn't been painted yet, but I can do that myself if they don't get around to it. I can probably use the same paint we use on the lighthouse. The garden is just outside the fence, so Grace won't get into it, much as she'd love to play in the dirt. But I've got to get these seeds going without her "help."

I almost had a heart attack before I fashioned a leash from one of Charles' belts with some rope to tie her to the fence. She had followed me out because my hands were full, and I couldn't close the gate behind me. I didn't realize it until I heard her giggle and looked up to see her going after a butterfly. I fear she would've climbed right over the edge if I hadn't grabbed her. She sure scared the living daylights out of me! The townsfolk would probably scoff at my tying up the child like a dog, but it's the only way I can watch her, and she has enough room to move around so she can play without me losing her.

Grace is growing so fast and learning so much. She's picked up a few more words, but what words she doesn't know, she makes up for in her own language. I usually know what she's saying though. Funny how that is even possible, but she makes it pretty clear what she wants. The little "smarty-pants" has even learned how to pull the footstool over to the counter in the kitchen if she wants to reach something. I worry that she'll do that when I'm not near and maybe fall. I don't want to scold her too much, because I let her stand on it while I am making cookies so she can watch or even roll out the dough—or try to. One of these days, she'll be big enough to make the cookies by herself.

Goodness, I hate to think of her growing so fast. But I do want her to grow normally, of course. I wonder if she'll be tall or not? Charles was tall and slender, and I'm fairly tall too. I've always been pretty slim, although now not as much as I used to be. Maybe if Grace is tall when she grows up, she'll favor us more. But right now, she's a little chunky. I don't think I'm overfeeding her. She gets fresh milk from the cow and she's got some teeth, so I'm feeding her adult food, mashed up. I tried a jar of baby food Mr. Reynolds brought, but she didn't care for it at all! Can't say I blame her. I tasted the stuff and it was awful!

Oh my goodness! The radio just announced that Hitler committed suicide! They interrupted the broadcast like they did for Pearl Harbor. What a terrible day that was. Thank God that awful man is gone. So I wonder if Germany will surrender now? Surely they will, without a leader. So is the war going to end soon? Will our boys come home now, or will they be sent to the Pacific instead? Will the Coast Guard leave our island? I've gotten used to their presence over the past year.

So much has changed since the war started. I went from having a husband and not having a child to having a child and not having a husband. It doesn't seem fair, but I know so much of life isn't fair. Shame on me to be so selfish when many in town have lost sons and fathers and brothers in the war. I've had a good life, and I have the opportunity to give this child a good life too. I hope I can. I hope her life can be happy even without a father. My mother used to tell me when I started bellyaching about something that I should count my blessings. I've tried to do that whenever I want to feel sorry for myself.

So let's see. I don't have perfect hair like a fashion model or movie star, but my hair doesn't look too bad, and I've learned how to do finger waves if I want it to look stylish. I don't have an hourglass figure, but my figure is good enough. I'm not fat and I'm healthy, which were two things Charles liked about me. I don't have the latest fashions, but I don't really need them here on the island. I don't have any women friends, but Mr. Reynolds and Michael have been good friends. I don't have the opportunity to go to picture shows, but my radio works (most of the time), and I can listen to radio shows. I don't have anyone to hold me and dance with me, but I can hold Grace and dance with her. I don't get to go to church often, but I can listen on the radio and read my Bible. I don't have a car, but I have a boat. Well, it's not mine. It's the station boat, but I can drive it. I don't get to go out to restaurants, but I have enough food here. I don't have one of those new dishwashers, but we don't have many dishes to wash, between Grace and me. We don't have a lot of anything, but we have enough.

I do believe what Mama said works. Thinking about my blessings has made me feel better. I hope I can teach Grace to do the same.

Chapter Twenty

Carson chuckled to himself. Abby had thought about decorating the keeper's house. How cool. And now she had agreed to do it. What a relief to know that was one thing he didn't have to worry about. He couldn't wait until they got to that part of renovating, because the house would be finished. But maybe he should consult with her about the kitchen backsplash and countertops before he ordered them.

His phone chirped.

"Carson? I can go. Want me to meet you at the dock, or do you want to swing by Mom's and pick me up?"

"You're at Grace's? I'll stop by there and tell her hello. See you in a few."

***

Carson was surprised to see Grace's lack of energy. Her normally vibrant eyes had lost some of their sheen, and even her skin color wasn't right. She definitely looked worse than she had before. He gave her a hug and a big smile, trying to cheer her up. He sure hoped it was okay to leave her alone.

"You won't get into any mischief while we're gone, will you?" Carson asked Grace.

Grace offered a weak smile. "Maybe I will, maybe I won't. But you'll never know."

"Mom, you're a mess," Abby said and gave her mother a shoulder squeeze.

Grace waved them off. "You kids go to work and leave me alone."

"We better leave. Her boyfriend's probably waiting for us to leave so he can come over," Carson said, winking at Grace.

Grace just shook her head as they went out the door.

In the truck, Carson thought it best not to comment on how bad Grace looked. No need to make Abby worry any more than she already did.

"I'll try to make sure we don't stay too late so you can get back to check on her."

"Thanks. It's hard to know what to do for her. But she doesn't want me to babysit her. That really irritates her."

In an effort to keep Abby from dwelling on her mother, Carson changed the subject.

"Well, now that you're my decorator, I need to get your opinion."

"Opinion? It's a little early, isn't it?"

"No, actually, it's not. I have to order the backsplash, countertops, and other things for the kitchen. The plumber is almost finished, and then we'll get the floors ready."

"Are you using the wood floors in there?"

"Yes. Once we got the old linoleum up, they looked pretty good, so we just have to sand and stain them. So, do you have any suggestions for the other things?"

They'd reached the dock, and Abby considered his question as they walked to the boat. "What do you think about white subway tile for the backsplash? That's rather classic."

"Yes, I agree. I was thinking along those lines too."

"Are you going with granite or quartz for the countertops?"

"I don't know. I thought about wood or concrete too."

"Let me take a look when we get there. You know, Maine is known for its fine slate. Homes back in the twenties used it for sinks. It comes in different colors too. And I would suggest bronze fixtures on the sink instead of stainless."

"Okay. That sounds good. I'll check into those options. Thanks."

They climbed in the boat, and Carson started the engine. On the way out the harbor, Abby glanced around nervously.

"Anything wrong?" Carson said, seeing Abby tense up.

"Oh, I'm just noticing that there are more boats than usual. Pleasure boats instead of lobster boats."

"I suppose the early tourists have arrived. Don't worry, I won't hit any of them." He gave her a goofy smile. "Wow, would you look at that one!"

The sleek yacht was dazzling white, at least fifty feet long, a sharp contrast to the other boats in the harbor. Abby turned to look just as a man came out on the back deck, stretching and gazing around. She sucked in her breath and gripped his arm.

"Abby? What's wrong?"

"It's that man, Mr. Lawrence."

"Who? Oh, the man that you thought was watching you."

She nodded, then ducked her head, pulled her cap lower over her face, and turtled into her hoodie. "Do you think he saw me?"

"I don't think so. He couldn't be watching you from his boat. He wasn't even looking this way."

"But what if he did?"

"What if? He's not going to follow you in that boat. That'd be pretty obvious." He patted her hand, which still clung to his arm. "Abby, really. You don't have to worry about him today. He isn't going to come to the island. He doesn't even know you'll be there. Relax, okay?"

After he'd put some distance between their boat and the other one, he said, "You can quit hiding now. We're well past them, and they're still anchored."

She slowly lifted her head and glanced around to make sure. Her shoulders relaxed as the harbor shrank behind them. "I guess you think I'm acting ridiculous."

"I haven't thought that at all. I can tell the guy freaks you out." He wouldn't go so far as to call her behavior ridiculous. Paranoid maybe, but who was he to judge?

"It's just so strange the way he keeps turning up."

"Well, Abby, Hope Harbor is a small town, and it's easy to notice people who aren't local. Heck, I've only lived here a couple of months, and I can already spot the tourists from the locals. Besides, there's not that many places for them to go in town. Right?"

Abby nodded. "You have a point."

"The guy's obviously got some money."

"I had some clients in California who were in that income bracket. But I don't remember him or his wife. But maybe he saw me out there, and I didn't see him."

"Sure. That's possible. And maybe he was just curious because now you're both on the other side of the country."

"Yeah, you're right."

Carson didn't ask, but he still wondered why she had such a fear of the guy. He didn't seem all that threatening to Carson. He studied her face a moment, then turned back to look ahead.

"Okay. You must want to know why I'm acting this way. Back in California, I volunteered in a soup kitchen. I tried to treat everyone with respect and kindness, be friendly, you know? Well, this one guy kind of fixated on me and started following me all over the place. He even found out where I lived and ended up trying to camp out in my yard. I tried to make him go back to the shelter, but he wouldn't leave. Kevin was deployed, so it was just me and Emma at home. I hated to call the police on him, so I called the shelter and they came and got him. After that, I looked over my shoulder constantly. When Kevin got home, he was really angry about it."

"I guess he would've gotten rid of the guy if he'd been home."

Abby looked away, then back. "He was more angry with me than the man. He said I led the guy on by being overly friendly."

Carson shook his head. "What? Like you meant to encourage a homeless person? That's not right. The guy obviously had some mental problems."

Abby shrugged. "I don't know. Maybe so, but maybe I encouraged him and didn't realize I was doing it."

Carson faced her. "Abby. I may not know you all that well, but I do know one thing about you. You're sincere, and you don't do anything that would mislead anyone. You were not to blame for that guy stalking you. You know, there are people in this world who have issues. I'd say that guy was one of them."

She looked at him with wonder in her eyes. "Thank you for saying that."

"Hey, I'm not just saying it. I mean it. And if nothing else, I'm honest."

His phone vibrated in his pocket. He pulled it out and pushed speaker. "Hey, Nick. I'm on my way. What's up?"

The contractor's next words hit him like a weight attached to the anchor, thrown overboard into the deep.

"We have a problem. The basement's flooded."

Carson digested the information, trying to stay calm. *Lord, what now?* "Should I turn around and go get something we need to fix it?"

"No, come on. You can see it for yourself, then we'll figure out what we need to do."

***

Carson looked like he was going to be sick. When he got off the phone call, his whole demeanor had changed, and a look of dread shrouded his face.

"What's wrong?" She was almost afraid to ask. She hadn't been able to hear the conversation over the noise or the boat engine, but knew the news wasn't good.

He forced a swallow. "The basement's flooded."

There was no point in asking any more questions because Carson wouldn't know the answers at this time. Poor guy. Another problem? What would he do? What could she do to help?

Her heart went out to him. He was such a nice guy and almost always upbeat. Just a few minutes ago, he'd been telling her she shouldn't worry and actually sympathizing with her about the stalker incident. Unlike Kevin, Carson hadn't made fun of her or called her stupid for being upset, much less acted surprised about what had happened to her. He'd made it clear he was her ally. So now, the tables were turned, and she wanted to help him however she could.

When they reached the dock, Nick was waiting for them. They hurried to secure the boat and get up the hill, then rushed past the lighthouse to the other side of the keeper's house. A door in the lower part of the house stood open. Abby noted that not only had she never been to that side of the house, she didn't know there was a basement either.

"How bad is it?" Carson asked, planting his hands on his hips.

"Got about two feet of water in there. We're gonna need to get a pump quick and suck the water out before it can do more damage."

"Where did the water come from? We haven't had a downpour out here, have we?"

Nick shook his head. "Nope. Pipe's busted. We managed to get it closed up to stop the water, but we have to get a new fitting for it."

"How much damage is there?"

Nick rubbed his hand across his face. "Don't know yet. Depends on how high it got. The electrical's in there, the panels and breakers. It could be bad."

"Then we better hurry and get the pump. Have you tried finding one yet?"

The foreman nodded. "Closest one is about an hour away by water. I think it'll take longer to go back to Hope Harbor and drive. Maybe we can get them to meet us at the dock with it. Let's pray it doesn't rain in the next day or two."

"Then let's get right on it. Call and make arrangements to get the pump. Can I get the fitting in town?"

"Maybe. I can check on that too." Nick pulled out his phone.

"Excuse me, where can I find Carson Stevens?" A voice came from behind them.

They jerked around to find a man standing with a clipboard in his hand.

Nick's groan was low, but Abby heard it.

"I'm Carson Stevens." Carson stepped over with his hand extended. "Can I help you?"

"Yes, I'm Tom Wilson, the county inspector."

Carson blanched. "I didn't expect to see you today. I thought you'd schedule an appointment."

"So today is not a good time?" Mr. Wilson glanced over at the house and the open basement door. "Is there a problem?"

"Yes, sir. You might say so. We had a busted pipe in the basement. But we're on top of it."

"You know things of that nature can ruin your electrical outlets and receptacles. Plus, if it's wet down there very long, you'll get mold. Things like that can really delay getting your inspection passed."

"I understand that. We'll make sure everything is dry and in working order. I'll get my electrician back out here right away."

"You do that. Hope your situation doesn't run as long as some I've seen with similar problems. You could be looking at a two-month delay."

Carson swallowed hard. "Two ..."

"Yes, that's true. Flooding in the basement is no small problem."

Carson drew himself up. "We'll take care of whatever needs to be done. When will you be back out? Or should I call you for an appointment?"

"You can call me, and I'll see if I can work in another visit. I'm pretty busy this time of year with folks getting ready for the season."

"Yes, sir. Well, I appreciate your coming out today. Did you want to look at anything else while you're here?"

"No, that won't be necessary. I can't write up a complete inspection until you find out what your damages are and get them fixed." He lowered his clipboard to his side. "Well, I guess I'll be off now. Good luck getting ready for opening."

Mr. Wilson turned and walked away, while Carson and Abby stared after him. Once he was out of sight, Carson spun around. "Nick, did you know he was coming today?"

Nick shook his head. "Nope. Surprised me too. What bad timing though."

"No kidding."

A worker came out of the basement wearing rubber boots and eyed Nick. "Boss, can I speak to you a minute?"

Nick gave a quick nod and hurried over to the man. The two spoke in low tones while Carson and Abby waited.

When they finished talking, Nick's brows were knitted.

Carson stepped forward. "What is it?"

Nick glanced around, then lowered his voice. "Sir, that busted pipe was no accident. My man here said the pipe was cut. It didn't just break by itself."

Carson's face reddened. "Cut? Who would do such a thing? Do you think it was one of our men?"

"I really doubt it. I've known these men a long time, and I can't imagine any one of them doing such a thing. If I find out one of them did, he'll have to deal with me." Nick pounded his fist into his other hand.

"Go ahead and make the call for the pump. Will you go get it?"

Nick nodded as he punched in a number.

Carson focused on the man who spoke to Nick. "Would you please get me the measurements of the pipe and tell me what to buy?"

The man nodded and sloshed back inside.

Carson looked at Abby, a sheepish smile on his face. "Welcome to my world."

"I'm so sorry for all your problems, Carson."

"Yeah, me too. I never did like surprises. Especially bad ones."

"I wish I knew how to help you," she said.

"Since there's no point in doing any other work today, you can keep me company when I go back to town to pick up the part. I can leave you there, and you can go see about your mother. She'll be surprised to see you back so soon. No need for you to come out here again today."

The man returned with the measurements, and Carson jotted them down. Nick got off the phone and verified the size. "All right, I'm off to get the pump."

"Right behind you."

Carson and Abby headed back down to the boat. Nick left in his boat and turned east. The creases between Carson's eyebrows had deepened as he was lost in thought.

"Carson? Who do you think would have cut the pipe? And why?"

Carson shook his head. "Abby, I really don't know. I didn't think I had any enemies around here."

"Do you think it was a prank?"

"I almost wish it were. But I have other suspicions."

"Someone doesn't want you to finish?"

"Seems like it, with all that's been going on. Unless I'm just a real unlucky guy."

"But why would someone not want you to succeed?"

"Competition? Somebody doesn't want me, an outsider, to do something in their neck of the woods?"

"Or just plain meanness, like Granny used to say. I thought people around here were nicer than that."

"I suppose desperate people will do anything for money."

"So you think someone was paid to cut the pipe?"

"I don't know. I'm just trying to look at all the possibilities."

Their boat hit the huge wake of a larger boat, splashing them. With water dripping off their noses, they laughed, and Abby was thankful Carson let some tension go.

"What a coincidence for that inspector to show up today at the worst possible time," Abby said.

Carson's frown returned. "I don't think that was a coincidence either."

"You don't?"

"Nope. Most inspectors schedule their inspections with the builder or the owner. They don't usually just drop by. Especially on an island."

"So you think he could have been bribed by the same person who cut the pipe?"

"The same person who paid someone to cut the pipe."

"Whoever it is must have money to throw around."

"Uh-huh. Who do we know with lots of money?"

Abby's mind flashed back to the yacht they saw in the harbor. "Not that Lawrence guy!"

Carson glanced at her with a puzzled look on his face. "No, I wasn't thinking of him. I was thinking of someone local. Someone who doesn't want me to open a B&B."

"Mr. Harding? Surely not."

"Well, I don't know who else has that kind of power and money around here."

"But maybe there's someone you don't know."

He jerked his head to look at her. "Who else could be against me?"

"I don't know. Maybe they don't even live in Hope Harbor. What about some preservationist group that might be against your making changes to the property?"

"That's a thought, but I don't know of any, at least around here. Seems like they'd contact me if they had a problem with my plans."

"So somebody wants you to quit and abandon your plans. Would you, if the effort wasn't worth the hassle?"

Carson stared at her. "Abby, this has been a dream of mine my whole life. I've been saving for years and checking the government excess list for good deals on lighthouse property. There's no way I'll quit, as long as they only mess with material things and don't cause any harm to anyone. And I can't imagine anyone that ruthless to get their way."

Chapter Twenty-One

As they returned to the harbor, Abby searched for the Lawrence boat.

"I don't see the yacht."

"Me either. I guess they'd seen enough of our little town and left to find more exciting places."

"You're probably right. It doesn't take more than two days to see all of Hope Harbor. Once they've seen the lobster statue in the town square, there's not much else."

"So now you can relax. No more stalkers." Carson offered a sincere smile.

"Thank God."

"You know, there will be a lot more tourists pretty soon. I hope they don't bother you."

"I'm not afraid of people, Carson, just creepy ones."

"Well, I'm glad I'm not in that category." He made an ugly face, and she laughed.

They reached the dock, tied up, and climbed out.

"I'm sorry you wasted a trip to the island," Carson said.

"Don't be. I'm sorry you're having so many problems. I wish I could do something to help."

"Pray I get the house finished with no more problems and pray we can take care of the ones we have."

"I'll be happy to do that. And I might work a little on your decorating too."

"Thanks. I appreciate your optimism."

Carson drove Abby back to her mother's house but decided not to go in, in case she was resting.

"Call me if you need anything," Abby offered.

"Ditto," Carson said.

***

Grace's skin had a healthier color when Abby got home and found her clattering pans in the kitchen.

Abby sniffed and inhaled the aroma of cookies baking. Her mother must be feeling better.

"Mom, you're making cookies?"

Grace glanced up. "Abby! You snuck up on me. Don't give me a heart attack!"

"Sorry, Mom, I didn't want to disturb you if you were sleeping."

"I've slept enough today already. I need to do something besides lay around all day." Grace pulled a pan of cookies from the oven. "What are you doing back so early?"

"Problems at the keeper's house. Carson had to come back to town for a few supplies."

"Problems? What kind of problems?"

"The basement's flooded. It looked like someone cut the water pipe on purpose."

"My stars! Who would do such a thing?"

"Carson would like to know." Abby planted her hands on her hips. "Mom, do you think Mr. Harding would stoop so low?"

"You think Fred Harding went all the way out to the island and into the basement?"

"No, Mom. I don't. But he could've paid someone to do it."

"Hmm. I know he's pretty important around here, but I just can't see him being that underhanded."

"Who else could be causing the trouble?"

"Are you sure there's one person responsible for every problem Carson's had? Couldn't it just be a string of bad luck? You know, sometimes life is like that."

"I'd think that, too, except that the pipe was cut. It didn't just break."

Mom chuckled. "Could be a ghost."

"Oh, Mom. Seriously?"

"You haven't heard about the ghost at Hope Island?"

Abby checked her memory bank. "Oh, that. We used to talk about the ghost when we were in grade school. An Indian brave's love fell off the cliff and died, so he threw himself off too so he could join her."

"And their ghosts now roam the island together."

"You don't believe that stuff, do you, Mom?"

"No, I don't. But when I went to school, I'd make up stories about ghost sightings on the island that kept the other children enthralled." Mom's eyes twinkled with mischief.

"Did you really? Shame on you."

Mom chuckled again and coughed. "I sure did. It was fun. Then Mother found out what I was doing, and I got a scolding, and she made me quit. Said I was lying, and God hated lying, but to me it wasn't lying, just storytelling."

Abby shook her head. "I keep learning things about you." She snagged a cookie and reveled in the warm, gooey deliciousness.

"Save some of those for Emma."

Abby rolled her eyes. As if she'd eat them all. "Sit down and rest. I'll put the cookies on the cooling rack." Abby took the spatula and began removing the cookies from the pan to the rack. "You know, I never even knew there was a basement at the house until today. Carson hadn't shown it to me, and I'd never been to that side of the house before."

"Oh dear. I remember that basement. I was scared to death of it."

"Why?"

"I'm not sure, but Mother warned me not to go there, said it was dangerous. I used to have nightmares about it."

"Dangerous? Wonder why?"

A shudder shook her mother's shoulders. "I don't know. But I know it was dark and mysterious. I thought goblins lived in it."

"You didn't."

Mom nodded. "I really did. Whenever I heard noises coming from below, I thought it was the goblins, but Mother said it was rats or some other critters."

"So she didn't go there either?"

"She did. I think she put the canning in there. I don't know what else, but she said she was the only one who could go there."

"That's odd."

"Thinking about it now, it does seem strange. But for some reason, I didn't challenge her on it."

Abby couldn't imagine what the basement looked like, since she didn't go in it herself. "So a goblin cut the pipe. Wonder what the goblin's name is?"

Mom shrugged, lifting her hands.

"Oh, and right after we got to the island looking at the basement problem, an inspector showed up. Talk about bad timing!"

"My goodness. Poor Carson. He does have his hands full, doesn't he? Well, we'll just have to pray for him."

"Actually, he asked me to."

"Well, God bless him. We sure will, won't we?"

Abby nodded and smiled at Mom while scanning the small kitchen. The harvest-gold appliances had been there as long as Abby could remember. They matched the wallpaper that featured fruit baskets full of apples, oranges, and lemons. Mom had added straw baskets to the décor, lining them up along the top of the beige cabinets. Over the small center island was a metal pot rack where copper-bottomed pots were suspended.

"Carson asked me to help him decorate the house."

"Good. I'm sure you'll do a wonderful job."

"He asked me to help choose things for the kitchen today. You know, I should help you redecorate yours."

Mom glanced around. "Why? I like it just the way it is. It's what we picked out when we moved in forty years ago, and as long as everything works, I have no reason to change."

Always the practical one, Mom wouldn't believe the way Abby's former clients had discarded household items because the styles had changed. Of course, that was the kind of lifestyle that used to keep her in business.

"It's time to go get Emma. Shall I come back by?"

"No, I'm getting tired, so I'll turn in early. But get one of those containers and put some cookies in it for Emma. Take as much as you want. I made them for you two anyway."

Abby opened the cabinet where Mom kept an assortment of plastic bowls and mismatched lids. Mom wouldn't get rid of anything, even if she didn't need it, thinking someday the right lid would mysteriously appear. After finding two pieces that fit, Abby filled the container with cookies and snapped it shut.

She kissed her mother on the cheek. "Bye, Mom. Love you. Call me if you need me."

***

May 7, 1945

Well, it finally happened. I was outside pulling weeds in the garden when I heard the Coast Guard boys hooting and hollering from the gallery of the lighthouse. I walked around and looked up to see what the ruckus was about. They were waving their caps and jumping around like happy schoolboys on the last day of school.

I called up to them and asked what happened. They told me that Germany had surrendered, and the war was over. They'd heard it on their radio. Since I was outside, I missed hearing it on mine.

Thank God, it's over. Our boys will be coming home. I'm sure they'll be as happy to be there as their families will be to see them. When I went back around to the front of the house, I could hear church bells coming from the mainland. I'm sure there'll be parades and celebrations going on all over the country. Maybe I can go to town and get to see the festivities. Mr. Reynolds should know when there'll be a parade. They might wait until the Fourth of July and have a combined celebration. I'd thought of taking Grace to the mainland on the Fourth anyway. I wonder how she'll like her first parade.

I remember seeing the flags in windows of homes with blue stars declaring a family member in service. Some of those blue stars ended up covered by gold stars when the serviceman was killed in action. How sad those families must be that they won't be able to greet their returning soldier. Will they be consoled now knowing their fight was not in vain? I hope they find comfort in that, as I have, knowing Charles died in the line of duty, too, even though no one was shooting at him. Should I have a star in my window too?

I wonder how much longer our Coast Guard boys will be here. I haven't seen Michael for a few weeks. Maybe he isn't in this area anymore. Maybe he's already been transferred somewhere else. It grieves me that I have not had a chance to tell him goodbye, if that is the case. But he could just be too busy. After all, I'm sure he hasn't spent as much time visiting with other lighthouse keepers as he has with me. Of course, he may have spent more time with me because of Charles's death, and now he doesn't need to "hold my hand" anymore.

However, I'd knitted him a scarf for cold weather, and I wanted to give it to him before he left. I hoped he would be able to use it, especially when he was on the boat and it got so cold. I used navy-blue yarn that I'd used for one I made for Charles, so I thought it would go all right with his uniform. I suppose I can give it to Mr. Reynolds if Michael doesn't come back to the island. That poor mailman could use a new one anyway. The one I knitted him two years ago is practically worn out. Charles used to tease me about knitting for everyone within fifty miles, but I enjoy it, especially when the recipient appreciates it. I don't do much knitting in the summer though because there's so much else to do outside.

Perhaps I should do something special for these Coast Guard boys to help them celebrate. I think I'll bake them a cake. I have enough flour and eggs to do that, and they always show such appreciation when I bake anything for them. I figure it's the least I can do to give them a little "home away from home."

Oh, dear, I just realized the entire war isn't over yet. There's still a war going on in the Pacific. I wonder if they'll surrender now that Germany has? I sure hope so. I need to keep praying for the war to end completely!

***

Nick stepped out of the basement. "We got her all pumped out. We'll have to leave the door open to let air in so it will dry."

"What about putting some fans in there? Can we do that?" Carson eyed his construction manager whose wet clothes were covered in mud.

Nick rubbed his face. "We need to check those receptacles. Don't know how much water damage there is. Is the electrician coming out tomorrow?"

"Yes, he said he was."

"Then pray the electrical's not ruined, or you're looking at replacing a lot more. You don't want that breaker panel to short out."

"Nick, I've been praying nonstop." Carson looked around. "Was this door locked last night?"

"Don't know. I didn't check before I left."

"Well, we'll lock it tonight. I made sure the house and the lighthouse were locked, so maybe whoever did this looked for another way to get in and do some damage."

"So you think someone was here before we were this morning?"

"Or after, unless it's one of our workers."

"No, I'd bet my next dollar it wasn't one of ours."

"We need to pay close attention to see if anyone has been here whenever we show up. Wish I could hire a guard."

"I hear you. Maybe you should camp out here."

Carson pursed his lips. "I've thought about it. I could just sleep in the house, even without all the necessities hooked up. I'll get a sleeping bag and bring it next time. Know where I can get one?"

"Yeah, outside of town there's an outfitting store that sells all kinds of camping gear. I'd loan you one of mine, but my kids have pretty much ruined them."

"Thanks. I'll get one and maybe some other supplies when I get back."

"You got a gun?"

Carson drew back. "A pellet gun, just for target practice. Do you really think I need to protect myself? Whoever is messing with this place is just creating property damage. I can't believe they would actually harm anyone."

"But nobody has been around when the culprit has been here. What if you got in their way or they didn't want you to know who they were? I'd say that could be dangerous."

"I'll think about it. I don't intend to have a gunfight." Carson couldn't believe the situation had gotten this out of hand. All he wanted to do was make a nice, peaceful place for guests to enjoy. But where was the peace now?

Chapter Twenty-Two

"Hello, Abby? This is Carson."

Abby knew his voice without even seeing the caller ID. She turned down the volume of the music, then sat down on the sofa. Carson sounded tired. "Hi, Carson. Did you get the problem taken care of?"

"Sort of. We got the water pumped out, but I won't know until tomorrow when the electrician comes how big the problem is."

"I hope the water didn't hurt your electrical."

"Me too. I was worried about running out of time, but if things keep going wrong, I might run out of money."

"Oh, dear, I hope not."

"Hey, it's not your problem, and I'm sorry you've gotten caught up in my mess."

"Carson, I want to see you succeed, so I care about these things you're facing. I just hope there are no more."

"Well, that's one of the reasons I called you. I'm planning on staying out there to keep an eye on things, so I might not see you for a few days. I'll try to make it to church Sunday, but we'll see. There's no shower hooked up yet, so I'll be kind of ripe."

"You're going to stay in the keeper's house?"

"Yep. Got a sleeping bag and some camping gear after work today, so I can camp out in the house."

"What will you do if someone comes around? Aren't you scared?"

"You know, I think I'm more angry than scared, but I'll be ready. And I pray God will protect me from the bad guys."

Abby smiled at his sense of humor despite all he was going through.

"I'll pray for your protection as well. Is there anything else I can do?"

"Bring me coffee from Mo's? No, seriously, I even bought a camp stove so I can make coffee the old-fashioned way. Should be interesting. Coffee and a can of Vienna sausages—what more can a man want?"

"Well, keep in touch and let me know how it goes."

"I will, as long as my phone battery holds out. That reminds me to get my charger."

"You really will be roughing it."

"Hey, I was a Boy Scout. We did this stuff for fun!"

Abby laughed. "Your idea of fun and mine are not the same. For me, camping out is a nice RV with all the amenities."

"I thought about that, but I couldn't figure out how to get one to the island. Anyway, I'll be fine. Hey, how's Grace?"

"She's doing okay. She made some more chocolate chip cookies today. Too bad you don't have any to take with you to the island."

"Yum. Coffee, Vienna sausages, and chocolate chip cookies. Sounds heavenly."

"When are you leaving? I've got some here you can have."

"Seriously? That'd be great. You have enough to share?"

"Sure. Can't let a man go hungry."

"Ha-ha. If you insist, I'll swing by in a few and pick them up. I want to hurry and get back before dark. I don't want to leave the place unwatched."

"I don't blame you."

"I'm taking my computer and hope to get a signal so I can do some work while I'm there."

"That's good. At least you can stay busy."

"Right. Well, I gotta get going. See you soon."

Abby shut off the phone, mulling over Carson's situation. Could he be in danger? It was one thing to cut a pipe, but would someone try to harm him if they saw him there by himself? *Lord, please keep him safe.*

She grabbed a small tote bag and threw the container with the cookies in, then searched her cabinet for more. Surely he needed more food. She added some granola bars and a couple of apples and filled a small ice chest with bottles of water and herbal tea. It was the least she could do. He must feel like he had no friends here besides her and Mom.

She just couldn't believe Mr. Harding was behind all this trouble, but maybe she trusted people too much, like Kevin had said. She winced at the memory. Would she always hear his criticism? Why couldn't she remember the nice things he said? Or was it normal for people to remember the bad things instead of the good? She tried to picture good memories with him, but every scene that flashed through her mind reminded her of something else he'd said that wounded. She had to keep those thoughts away.

A knock on the door drew Abby's attention. Carson couldn't have gotten there so quickly.

She opened the door. "Hi, Robin."

"Hi, Abby. I hate to bother you, but could you come back to the store Monday? I sure could use you."

"Yes, I'll be happy to."

"Oh, good. More tourists in town this week."

But at least two of them had already left town, thank goodness.

***

The setting sun was blending into the ocean, coloring the water with orange, gold, and red waves when Carson arrived back at the island. He secured the boat and hoped anyone coming to the island to do mischief wouldn't expect him to be there. He slung his backpack with Abby's snacks and his laptop over one shoulder and his sleeping bag over the other. Then he picked up the cooler and the carrier with the camp stove and, glancing around, clambered up the hill.

After storing his gear in the keeper's house, Carson went around to all the doors to make sure they were locked. He checked the padlock on the lighthouse, the lock on the basement door, and the lock on the foghorn building before returning to the keeper's house and locking the front door behind him. The gray of dusk had settled onto the island as he surveyed the interior. A strange quiet filled the air without the daily cacophony of hammers, drills, and nail guns. Carson walked from room to room, checking to make sure the windows, as well as the back door, were closed and locked.

As he climbed the stairs, they creaked beneath his steps, disturbing the silence of the house. He looked into each bedroom, closet, and bathroom, his ears and eyes on alert for anything unusual. If someone had spoken to him at the moment, he would've jumped out of his skin. How strange and unsettling to be completely alone in the house. He hadn't expected to be so uncomfortable. Surely, when the house was finished, the atmosphere would be much more welcoming. *Carson, get a grip. You act like a kid afraid a ghost will jump out at you.*

After surveying each room, he deemed them void of any other presence, both human and ghostly. As he went back downstairs, he noticed he was trying to walk silently, as if on tiptoes to keep from making noise. What he really wanted to do was play some music on his phone or computer to dispel the quiet and release his anxiety, but he couldn't. The noise would alert any would-be vandals to his presence.

He sat on his sleeping bag and settled into a corner of the living room away from the windows with his back against the wall. Pulling his laptop from his backpack, he positioned it so its light wouldn't show from the outside and began to work on his paying job. Using his phone as a hotspot, he was able to connect to the internet, but he knew he was risking using up more of his phone's power to do so, so he switched to working on some documents instead. As time passed, his stomach rumbled, distracting him from the work.

Carson looked up from the computer, shocked at how much time had passed. He checked his watch and noticed it was after ten o'clock, but it wasn't very dark outside. He moved his laptop aside, reached inside the backpack for something to eat, and grabbed a granola bar. Why wasn't it darker outside? He went to the window and looked out, amazed to see how light it was. Moving from window to window, he found the source of the light. A brilliant full moon shone like a beacon as it created shadows on the ground.

There was some comfort in knowing he could see outside, but

would the moonlight keep intruders out or invite them in? At least he wouldn't need a flashlight. From one of the windows, he could glimpse the water, the moon reflecting its sheen. What a beautiful sight, one he'd love to enjoy with someone else. No not someone—Abby. He could imagine her reaction to the scene. She'd love it just as he did, he was certain. Wouldn't it be nice if there was a real possibility this would happen?

He stared outside for some time as he relived the last few weeks in Hope Harbor and how different his life had been than the way it used to be in corporate America. Fighting traffic and crowds, sitting in a cubicle in a sterile office building, rushing from one meeting to another—all that was behind him now. He'd stopped trying to climb the ladder to the next level and stepped away from a lucrative job. The shock on his employer's face when he turned in his resignation made him chuckle. No one understood, especially Jennifer, who loved the excitement and busyness of the city. And his father said he was crazy to "throw away" his career.

But he hadn't been happy. And he hadn't been healthy either. The stress had taken its toll on his blood pressure and his nerves. He couldn't sleep and had no appetite. The only time he felt good was when he went out of town on the weekends and found a trail to hike in the woods. The fresh air and sounds of nature called to him, invited him to join them. Then there were the pictures of lighthouses he pinned on his corkboard at his desk, some he had visited, that further intensified his dream to own one. Someday, he would live away from everyone else in his own lighthouse on his own island.

And that day was almost here. Almost reached. He'd put away as much money as he could and still pay his bills until he had enough to bid on one of the government's excess lighthouse properties. He didn't know where his lighthouse would be but was thrilled when Hope Island became available. When he'd visited Maine on vacation, he'd fallen in love with all the islands and lighthouses he'd seen there. And now he owned one of them. The spark of joy that came with that realization always made him smile. So close to seeing his dream come true.

But he hadn't anticipated the problems he'd encountered. Closing his eyes, he prayed silently. *Lord, you've fulfilled my desires. You've led me to this place and time. Please help me overcome these obstacles and find out who is trying to stop me and why.*

A noise outside distracted him. Someone was walking around the house. Carson ducked behind the wall away from the window and tried to see from that vantage point. The crunch of grass was nearby, and Carson had the impression someone was looking inside, moving from window to window. He pressed flat against the wall and sucked in his breath. Across the room from him lay his backpack, the gun tucked away inside. How could he get to it without alerting the intruder?

Carson's heart raced as he tried to decide what to do. A dark form passed the window, heading in the direction of the front of the house. Carson took the opportunity to dash across the room to his backpack. He grabbed the gun and waited. The front door rattled as the intruder tried to open it. When he was unsuccessful, he continued on around the house. Carson leaned against the opposite wall away from the windows on that side while the person passed by. At least he didn't break the windows.

Carson heard the back door of the kitchen being jostled. Obviously, the guy wanted to get in. But why? What damage would he do if he could get inside and no one was there? The noise stopped. Had he given up? Then Carson heard another sound. It was coming from the basement door. Thank God they'd bolted that shut. He had no intention of dealing with another busted pipe. Now was the time to confront the man before he got away. Carson grabbed the gun and quickly went out the front door, quietly moving around to the rear of the house toward the basement.

When he rounded the corner, he saw a figure at the door.

"Looking for something?" Carson said as he drew his gun.

The man spun around and, in a split second, raced away.

"Stop or I'll shoot!" That's what police said, wasn't it? Of course, they meant it. Carson just wanted to scare the guy and find out why he was messing around the place.

But his words had no effect on the intruder as he dashed into the woods. Where did he go? Carson wanted to follow him, but he had no idea what he'd get into, not being able to see once the forest snuffed out the moonlight. Carson didn't shoot as he threatened. What was the point? From the way the man acted, he was running scared. Carson listened for the sound of an engine starting down at the dock, but nothing. No sound other than nature's nighttime noises. So how did he get off the island? Could he possibly have landed somewhere else? From what Carson knew of the island, there wasn't another good place to land with the island's border of boulders.

He shook his head. Had he accomplished anything? Possibly. Maybe he'd prevented more vandalism. But he still had questions, and he'd have to wait until morning to investigate the woods and see if there was a trail that led to an answer.

One thing he knew—the guy wasn't armed. Or if he was, he didn't want a fight. Thank God for that. Carson didn't want one either.

Chapter Twenty-Three

Abby stared into her coffee as if she could conjure up a vision. What was happening to Carson? Had he seen anyone? Run into trouble? What if he were hurt? She shuddered at the thought and picked up her phone for the umpteenth time to look at it. No calls from him and no messages. Had his batteries died or something worse?

At church that morning, she'd lifted her hand when the minister asked if anyone had any silent prayer requests, needing the support of other prayers in case he was in danger. She couldn't believe she'd been so worried about him, but he was a friend, and she didn't want anything bad to happen to him. Mom hadn't felt like going to church, so she and Emma had gone alone. Abby couldn't help but look around to see if Carson had miraculously made it to the service, even though he'd said he probably wouldn't.

She was dying to go for a run afterwards, but wasn't comfortable leaving Emma with Mom when she wasn't feeling well.

"Come on, Emma. Let's have a picnic at the park." Abby set down her cup.

"Yippee!" Emma danced around while Abby grabbed a backpack and threw in some cheese and crackers, fruit and water. They headed to the city park where Abby spread out a blanket. She and Emma shared their refreshments before Emma asked to go play on the playground and Abby nodded, smiling at the child's joy.

Every time Abby looked at the water, she wished she had some kind of super-vision to see all the way to the island and check on Carson. If she had a boat, she might even go there herself. But it was probably best she didn't. Was she too worried? The sermon that morning had been about that very thing. What was the quote the minister said? "Don't be anxious about anything." There was more, but she couldn't remember it. She'd gotten stuck on those words and wondered how on earth she could live up to them.

Emma ran around with other children while Abby stayed on their blanket with Wonder Woman bear. She watched as tourists took selfies in front of the lobster statue before turning her gaze out to sea. More boats floated in the harbor now, and she scanned the floating vessels, hoping she wouldn't see the Lawrence yacht again. That was one more thing she shouldn't be worried about. Those people had left, and there was no reason they'd come back to little Hope Harbor. It wasn't like it was Bar Harbor or anything.

Abby glanced back over at the playground but didn't see Emma. She stood up and walked toward the equipment. Emma must be on the other side. But she was nowhere in sight. Abby's heart pounded as she called Emma's name.

"Emma! Emma! Where are you?"

Abby circled the playground again, looking under the bridge, into the tunnel, and on top where the little fort was. No Emma. Abby fought back tears. She should never have taken her eyes off her daughter. With strangers in town, you never knew what kind of people were there.

Oh, Lord, please help me find my baby.

A couple of other mothers stood nearby, chatting with each other. Abby approached and asked if they'd seen Emma, describing her. They shook their heads, then looked around for her too. Panic squeezed Abby's heart as all kinds of scenarios flashed through her mind, none of them good. What kind of mother lost her child so easily? She could just imagine what Kevin would say if he'd been around.

"Mommy!"

Abby spun around and saw Emma trotting over, a leash in her hand connected to a Newfoundland, a black dog twice her size on the other end. "See Posey, my new friend?"

"Emma!" Abby ran to embrace her daughter, glancing up to see a man and woman approaching with big smiles on their faces. "Where have you been?"

The man spoke up. "We were walking Poseidon, and Emma asked if she could walk him. We asked her where her mother was, and she pointed to you. We waved, but I guess you didn't see us. We just strolled around the park. Sorry to upset you."

Abby wrestled with emotions of anger and relief. "That's all right. Emma should've come to me and asked first." She faced her daughter. "Isn't that correct, Emma?"

Emma nodded. "Yes, ma'am."

"Okay. Emma, please give the leash back to these people."

Emma did as she was told, and the couple introduced themselves as tourists who had just arrived in town. Thank God, they were nice people. But what if they were not? Abby wouldn't let Emma out of her sight again.

Frazzled from the experience, Abby packed up the picnic supplies and they went home. She had spent too much time worrying lately. After swinging by Mom's house to check on her, Abby went home and made a cup of herbal tea, hoping to calm her nerves. Taking her drink out to the balcony, she sank into one of her patio chairs and propped her legs on the railing while Emma watched an old rerun of Barney, the purple dinosaur.

Her phone tune played, and she grabbed it as soon as she saw Carson's name on the ID.

She exhaled a sigh of relief. "Hello?"

"Hi, Abby. It's Carson. I just wanted to let you know I'm back, at least for a couple of hours. I'm pretty gross and need to shower and charge my phone and computer."

Abby pictured Carson and couldn't imagine him ever looking gross. "I've been worried about you. Did you see anybody?"

"Yes and no. Someone was there, but I didn't see them clearly."

"What happened? Did he see you?"

"Yes, but nothing happened. He disappeared."

"Disappeared?" Abby stiffened, tightening her grip on the phone.

"Ran into the woods. Strange thing is, I don't know how he got on the island. I never heard a boat, and I looked around the dock in the daytime and didn't see a sign of anyone there."

"That's odd. But I'm glad to hear you didn't run into any trouble."

"You and me both. Some of the men came out to work yesterday, so I walked around the island while they were there. I thought I might see another place someone had moored a boat, but I couldn't find any clues. Those woods are dense and filled with mosquitoes. They had quite a feast on me. That reminds me—bring bug spray."

"Well, I'm glad to hear you're all right. Thanks for calling me." Abby relaxed back against the sofa. "Are you going to stay there again tonight?"

"Yes, I think it's best for now. Are you going back to work at The Brass Lobster tomorrow?"

"I am. The tourists are multiplying."

"I noticed when I came through the harbor. Oh, I forgot to ask, how's Grace?"

"She's still not feeling well, but thanks for asking. She didn't make it to church today."

"I'm sorry to hear that. Please give her a hug for me."

"I will." Silence followed, and Abby considered telling him about the Emma incident that day but decided against it. He'd probably think she was a negligent mother.

"Well, I guess I better get ready to go back to the island. Just wanted to check in with you."

"Thanks. Glad you did. Bye."

Abby put down the phone, comforted by the call and the knowledge that Carson was not in any danger. But who was the person Carson saw? And how did he disappear? An alarming thought triggered a new wave of concern. What if the strange man was still there and he was waiting to catch Carson off guard? *Abby, stop!*

It was like the minister had said, "Most of the things we worry about never happen."

***

Monday morning, Abby stepped into The Brass Lobster, surprised to see gaps on the shelves where merchandise was supposed to be.

"You've been busy," she said to Robin.

"This weekend was crazy busy. I sure wish you had Saturdays free."

"I would have if I had someone to keep my daughter. Sometimes I can leave her with Mom, but her health has been rather poor lately, so I can't expect her to watch Emma for a whole day."

"I'm sorry to hear your mother's still not feeling well."

"Yeah, me too." Abby scanned the store. "Would you like me to start restocking shelves?"

"That would be great. Thanks. Mondays are usually pretty slow, but you never know what to expect from tourists."

At lunchtime, Robin went into her office in the back of the store to eat while Abby watched the store. Robin had shown her how to ring up merchandise so she could wait on customers. A man wearing a button-down shirt with the sleeves rolled up and khaki slacks walked in and glanced around.

"Can I help you?" Abby asked.

The man wore a golf visor low on his face with sunglasses perched on top his head. He studied her a moment before answering. "No, thank you. I'll just look around."

"Go ahead. Help yourself. Let me know if there's anything in particular you'd like."

He nodded, then slowly walked from one display to the next, picking up items, checking prices, then putting them back down. Abby watched but tried not to stare. There was something odd about him. Abby proceeded to restock, glancing up at the man every so often to see if he was still there. Plus, Robin had told her to look out for shoplifters. Every time she looked over at him, she found him staring at her. Not this again.

He was still in the store when Robin came back.

"You can take your break now," she said.

Abby nodded toward the man, then made a quick exit to the office to eat her lunch. It occurred to her that the man was not really interested in the merchandise at all. He didn't seem to be really shopping, just pretending to be. But why would he do that? Was he a shoplifter who was watching her to see if she'd notice if he took something? Had he taken anything? Oh dear, she sure hoped not.

When she went back into the store, the man was gone.

"Did that man buy anything?"

Robin shook her head. "No, not a thing."

"I hope he didn't steal anything. He acted suspicious to me."

"I'll check around and see if anything is missing." Robin pointed. "You look over there."

After a thorough investigation, they decided nothing had been stolen.

"Maybe I'm just too suspicious."

"That's quite all right. You need to be, or people will steal you blind," Robin said as she rearranged a display.

"I don't think he was really interested in buying, anyway. I wonder why he even came in."

Robin shrugged. "Who knows? A lot of people do that. They just want to see what kind of items we carry. Maybe his wife was busy elsewhere, and he was just killing time."

"Did you notice a wedding ring?"

"No, come to think of it, I didn't. But then again, he might still be in town with a friend. There aren't many male tourists who travel here alone."

"True. After all, not everyone that comes in buys something." Abby forced her fear aside.

"No kidding. I sure wish they did." Robin walked to the display in the store window and rearranged the merchandise. "Maybe I need to put something more attractive in the window that will entice them to buy. Got any ideas?"

"How about that book by the author who stayed on one of the islands? A lot of people want to know about the area."

"Good idea." Robin picked up one of the books and thumbed through it. "I thought this was pretty interesting. I met the author when he lived in the area, and we had a book signing here when it came out. I wouldn't want to live like he did—without any modern conveniences and comforts. Roughing it on an island is not my cup of tea."

Abby pictured Carson out on Hope Island, doing without such things as well. A romantic image of being out there with him flashed through her mind, and she felt her face flush. What was she thinking? Carson was just a friend. And why had it suddenly gotten so warm in here? She picked up a postcard from the nearby rack and started fanning herself.

Robin noticed and said, "Do you think it's too hot in here? I believe I'll open the front door and let some of that ocean breeze come in."

Abby busied herself the rest of the day putting out stock and helping Robin wait on customers. The strange man never came back, so she chalked him up as another tourist. He wasn't the only strange person who came in. Some of the other tourists were questionable, not in a frightening way though. Tourist behavior was almost laughable as they chose their souvenirs, oohing and aahing over what she would consider minor items. But Robin apparently knew what would sell, so she carried a vast assortment in the store.

A well-dressed gentleman came in and had a private conversation with Robin. He looked familiar to Abby, but she didn't know his name. When their talk was over, Robin glanced over at Abby and beckoned. "Abby, I'd like you to meet Mr. Harding."

So this was the person who had harassed Carson? He didn't look as formidable as she had pictured. She walked over and extended her hand. "Hello, I'm Abby Baker."

His eyebrows lifted. "Oh, you must be Grace's daughter. How is she?"

"She's doing all right. Thanks for asking."

"I've heard she was in poor health. Glad to hear she's okay. Tell her Fred said hello."

"I will." He seemed to be a pretty nice person, not the type who would intentionally cause trouble for anyone. Carson must have misjudged the man.

When Mr. Harding left, she turned to Robin. "I've heard of him before. He owns several of the bed-and-breakfasts here, doesn't he?"

Robin laughed. "Fred Harding practically owns the whole town. In fact, he owns this building. I just lease this space from him."

"So he's pretty powerful, I guess."

"For sure. He carries a lot of clout."

"He didn't act like a person with so much control, in my opinion. In fact, he seemed rather pleasant."

"Oh, he can be quite the gentleman. Just don't cross him."

"Cross him? What do you mean?"

Robin cut her eyes around the room as if the merchandise were listening and lowered her voice. "I mean, you need to stay on his good side. I've known of people who complained about various things he did or didn't do, and before you knew it, they'd lost their leases. And there's not many places around here they could relocate to."

So he could be a threat, like Carson suggested. But surely the man wasn't roaming around the island at night.

***

When Abby got off work, she picked up Emma from daycare, then bought a couple of meals from the deli at the grocery store. She was certain Mom hadn't cooked, since she had no energy.

Abby was right, finding Mom dozing in her recliner when she let herself in. Abby touched her finger to her lips so Emma would be quiet and took the food into the kitchen. Emma came running in and grabbed her hand.

"Mommy, come quick. Grandma is having a bad dream!"

Sure enough, her mother was writhing and moaning but still asleep.

"Mom?" She tapped her lightly on the shoulder and kissed her on the cheek. "I brought you some dinner."

Grace fought to open her eyes. As they came into focus on Abby, she sighed. "Hi, Abby."

"You must've been having a bad dream."

Mom nodded, a note of fear in her eyes. "I was."

"Do you know what it was about?"

"Yes, because I've had the dream before."

"You have? What is it about?"

"I'm a small child and I'm in a dark, wet place. I'm crying for my mother, but she doesn't come, and the water is rising up to my neck."

"Do you know where you were in the dream?"

Another nod. "Yes, it was in the basement at the keeper's house."

Abby glanced at the photo of Granny and her grandfather. Much as she liked the picture, there was still something not quite right about it. But Abby couldn't figure out what.

Mom took Abby's hand and looked up at her. "Where's Carson?"

"He's been staying at the island for the last few days to make sure nobody has another chance to vandalize it again."

"Has he seen anyone?"

Abby told her what Carson had said about seeing someone at night, someone who ran away from him.

"Carson said he had searched the island during the day but didn't find any sign of the man. Isn't that strange?"

"Sure is. Guess that rules out Fred Harding. Fred would never do something like that."

"I suppose you're right. But who else would? And why?"

Mom shrugged. "I can't imagine."

"I brought some dinner from the deli. Do you feel like coming to the kitchen and eating with me and Emma?"

"I'm not too hungry, but since you went to the trouble, I'll try to eat something."

Abby helped her out of the recliner and into the kitchen. Mom picked at her food but didn't eat much. Abby was worried that she wasn't eating enough, but Abby couldn't force-feed her.

"Granny, why did you have a bad dream? Were you scared?" Emma asked.

"I don't know why I keep having that dream. Do you ever have bad dreams?"

Emma nodded. "Last night, I dreamed somebody was chasing me

and trying to take my bear away from me."

"Oh, that's scary!" Mom said. "Good thing it was just a dream. And you know dreams aren't real, right? So we don't need to be afraid of them. Okay?"

"Yes, ma'am."

***

When they finished, Abby and Emma cleaned up the kitchen, then made sure Mom had all she needed before going back to their apartment.

As they parked the car, Abby noticed a black car she hadn't seen before. It was a BMW with Maine license plates, so it must've belonged to someone else in the complex. While climbing the steps to their apartment, Abby had a sense of being watched. She glanced around but didn't see anyone else. As she turned back toward her apartment, she saw movement in the black car. Someone was in it.

She hurried up the stairs and into the apartment, then deadbolted the lock behind them. *Calm down, Abby. No need to worry.* If only her fears were just bad dreams too.

Chapter Twenty-Four

May 15, 1945
I had the biggest scare of my life today.

The day started out like any normal day. It was clear and lovely, with the sky as blue as a bluebird and the sun reflecting like diamonds off the water. It was the kind of day that begs you to be outside breathing in the fresh air and celebrating life itself. A little bit windy, but not too cold, I decided it was the perfect day to do laundry, knowing it would dry well on the line. I hate to admit I've been a little downcast since I haven't seen Michael for several weeks and fear I may not ever see him again. But today was so pleasant it lifted my spirits.

So I washed our clothes and sheets, then I put Grace's little sweater over her blouse and coveralls so she could enjoy being outside with me. I tethered her to the fence while I hung laundry and she sat in the clover and grabbed handfuls of it, fascinated by the little flowers that grew among it. I had to scold her a couple of times about not putting it in her mouth, but she obeyed and quit tasting it, so I gave her a clothespin to play with. At least she can't open one yet.

I sang a song I'd heard on the radio that morning, "Accentuate the Positive," which boosted my mood even more. When all the sheets and clothes were flapping in the breeze, I went back around to get Grace. But when I returned to the spot where I'd left her, she was gone. The belt that was supposed to hold her was still there, but somehow, she had slipped out of it. I panicked. My heart surely stopped beating as I searched every inch of the yard. That's when I saw the open gate. I knew I'd closed it, but the wind must have blown it open.

I rushed outside the fence and ran around the house calling her. Where was that child? What had I done? I knew I wasn't fit to be a mother if I *couldn't keep track of one little girl. I ran all over the place, up and down the trail with tears streaming down my face. Horrible thoughts beset me as I imagined her falling down the hill into the water.*

I even called up to the Coast Guardsmen on the lighthouse gallery, and they came down to see what I wanted. Only two men are stationed here since the Germans surrendered, and four German submarines turned themselves in at our Portsmouth Naval Shipyard down east. The two young men immediately began scouring the woods looking for Grace. I was beside myself and prayed aloud to God to help me find her and that no harm had come to her.

I was in this distraught state when who should arrive but Michael! I must've looked a fright, but when I managed to tell him that Grace was lost, he put his arms around me and held me for a brief time. It was as if the arms of God Himself had surrounded me because I calmed down. Michael then walked back to the house with me and asked where she'd been, where I'd been, and so on, like a detective. I remember him standing there with his hands on his hips as he surveyed the area.

Then he asked me if I'd checked the basement. I had not because I thought Grace had gone out through the gate. Then I remembered the basement door had been left ajar when I went in there earlier that morning because my hands were too full to close it behind me. I followed Michael down five steps to the bottom where the door was now closed. The wind must've blown it shut. Michael pulled open the door. I heard her crying before I could see her in the dark corner where she had somehow gotten. I ran to her and scooped her up in my arms. I was so relieved to find her. The poor child must've been terrified in that dark, damp space, not knowing where she was or how to get out. But she was safe, thank God.

I don't know why I hadn't thought to look there before, but I think God sent Michael as his angel to help me find her today. I thought seeing him again would be the best thing to happen, but finding Grace was even more special.

Once both of us calmed down, we went inside and I cleaned Grace up, removing her muddy clothes and washing her hands. Michael even made a pot of coffee for us while I took care of Grace. He is so helpful. Imagine a man doing such a thing! But he told me he makes coffee at the station quite often. I gave Grace a bottle and put her down in her crib. She was so tired from her ordeal.

I was tired, too, worn out from the worry. Michael stayed and visited a long time. He seemed happy to be there, but probably not as happy as I was to have him there. He told me he had been down in Portsmouth when the German submarines surrendered and what that was like. He described the German sailors and how they were taken to the Portsmouth Naval Prison. Michael was quite excited as he explained all about the submarines and their advanced design, even though I admit I didn't understand much of what he told me.

What did interest me was all the things they found onboard, including a plane that was in sections. I wondered when and where they intended to put the plane together. Michael told me the German officers wore white gloves and polished boots with Iron Crosses hanging proudly around their necks. He said the whole event was quite the show, with newspaper reporters all over the place, vying for position to get the best photos of the event.

I was amazed to learn these subs had traveled in "packs," as he called them, with about four in a group as they moved up and down our coasts. Michael said more people had been killed by German submarines than died at Pearl Harbor. Just imagine! I shudder to think those things were so close to our country, especially to us here off the coast. I'm glad I didn't realize that before the war ended or I might not have stayed here.

I asked Michael if he knew how much longer he would be in the area, but he did not know. He said Japanese subs were still a threat on the West Coast, and he might be transferred there. I hate to think of him leaving, but these past few weeks without him have given me practice learning not to expect him. I also asked him to promise to tell me goodbye when he learned he was leaving, and he said he would.

Before he left today, I asked if he was named for Michael the Archangel, and he laughed and said no, he was not. He was named for his father who was a Michael too. But I told him I thought God sent him to be my angel, and he found that idea quite funny, saying he was far from being an angel. I hope what I told him wasn't an improper thing to say, since his purpose *here has been for military business, not to protect a widow and her child. But I can still believe God sent me my own angel Michael for as long as I need him. I am having a hard time accepting that I don't need him. Maybe I'm confusing my wants with my needs. Lord, forgive me for any wrong thoughts I've had about him.*

Abby put down the journal and wiped her eyes. Reading about Granny losing Grace was like reliving her own experience the day before. How well she knew the fear, the desperation, and the helplessness. She identified with the blame of being a failure to her child, of neglecting her duty as a mother. How frightening it must have been to think the child had fallen down the cliff. She could visualize Granny searching the area and crying in despair.

What a coincidence that Michael had arrived when he did. No, it was more than that. It was a blessing, or even a miracle. Maybe God did send him. He was such a special person, and Abby was thankful he had been Granny's friend. Something in Granny's words made Abby believe her grandmother wished he could have been more than a friend. But there was no doubt their relationship had been honorable.

As Abby replayed the story in her mind, she realized why her mother had the nightmares she had. They obviously had to do with being trapped in the basement, although there was no water involved. Bless her little heart, how frightened she must have been. Frightened enough for the fear to last her whole life. The next time Abby went to Mom's, she'd tell her what she read in the journal. Maybe it would help her mother deal with the fear and end the nightmares. She hoped it would. Mom needed peace from that fear so she could rest.

***

Carson stretched, sore from sleeping on the floor. He missed his bed. Since he hadn't seen any more strangers lurking around, he assumed the intruder had left after discovering someone was at the keeper's house. Carson sure would like to stay in town at least one night, but he couldn't risk any more vandalism. But he was definitely looking forward to going home for a shower and clean clothes. Home. He wasn't sure where that was now. He needed to get out of his current place and into the apartment soon, but the keeper's house is where he would stay when it was finished. Would he get tired of living out here?

One thing for sure, he didn't want to be alone forever. Even though he'd lived by himself since college, he still felt connected to the world. Out here, civilization hadn't caught up to the twenty-first century. He couldn't wait until the place was ready for guests. Hopefully, he'd have some. He missed seeing Abby. It was nice to hear her voice when he called, but it wasn't the same as being with her. Would she like camping out there with him or not? Carson shook his head. Abby had other responsibilities, and the possibility of just the two of them together was unrealistic. Unless … no, marriage wasn't even on the radar. His focus needed to stay on the situation at hand.

Carson was glad to see the crew show up Monday after taking Sunday off. Thank God, there had been no damage to the electrical from the water in the basement. While online, he'd ordered the kitchen flooring, backsplash, and tile. Hopefully, they'd arrive by the end of the week and could be installed. Meanwhile, they'd removed the cabinet doors, sanded, and repainted them.

The living room was shaping up too. They'd put new insulation in and were waiting for a plaster specialist to come replaster the walls. Once he was done, they'd be able to paint them. This week, he hoped they'd also get the bathrooms finished. At least he could take showers before the house was completely finished. As long as they had good weather and no more problems, they should be able to get back on schedule.

While the men worked on things he couldn't help with, Carson decided to hike the island again. There were probably still areas in the woods he hadn't explored yet. Stepping inside the woods, he pulled the hood up on his sweatshirt to keep the mosquitoes off his head. He'd used heavy-duty bug repellent on his face and hands and hoped the pests wouldn't bite through his clothes. The temperature inside the spruce woods was at least ten degrees less than it was out in the sun. Carson inhaled the rich fir scent of the forest, reminiscent of Christmas.

His boots sank into the pine-needle-covered ground, disguising the depth of the terrain. It was obvious that the island was just a big pile of rocks with trees and pine needles on top. Walking was slow going because there was no flat, dirt trail to follow.

It wasn't long before he lost his bearings. He'd entered behind the lighthouse and started walking uphill but finding his way through the maze of trees had him turning several times, so he wasn't sure what direction he was headed. He tried to keep going up, assuming he'd reach the top of the island eventually and maybe even glimpse the water if there was a break in the trees. In the darkness of the forest, it was difficult to tell what time of day it was. Fortunately, his watch still worked, and he'd walked an hour by the time he reached the highest point of the island. The trees thinned out at the summit, allowing him to see out and assess his position in relation to the lighthouse.

The land here was actually higher than the lighthouse, which had been built on the end of the island facing out to sea. Carson figured he was standing in the center of the island as he surveyed the area. A screech nearby announced the presence of a bald eagle. A higher-pitched screech answered, indicating the existence of an eaglet. Carson looked up. There must be an eagle's nest in the vicinity. He followed the sound, glancing upward occasionally as he tried to locate the nest. When he reached a tree trunk surrounded by an assortment of bones, the sound was loudest, and he stopped. At the top of the tree was the biggest nest he'd ever seen. The eaglet wasn't visible from that vantage point, but there was no doubt he was there. And there also wasn't a doubt that those birds ate well.

Carson continued walking until he got to a rocky ledge that jutted out toward the water. As he approached, he recognized the scent of burnt wood, like the smell of a doused campfire. He slowed his step and edged his way around the outcropping as the odor grew stronger. At the base of the ledge, he found an opening that looked like the mouth of a cave. Was someone in there? Carson's pulse raced, his heart thumping as he peered inside. It was too dark to see without a flashlight, and he didn't want to use up all his phone's power for a flashlight, so he held back, deciding not to go inside. A sense of dread hit him with the realization that he'd left the gun back at the house, making him vulnerable to attack. If someone was nearby, did they know he was too?

He quietly stepped away and tried to remember how he got there. He'd go back to the house and plan another trip to that spot, next time prepared for whatever or whomever he found. Maybe he could get Nick to go with him. Hopefully, he could find the cave again. As he hiked back to the house, he mulled over the possibilities. Had someone been camping out, someone totally unrelated to the progress on the lighthouse side of the island? Or was someone staying there especially because of the work that was going on? One thing for sure, it hadn't been long since there had been a fire because the remnants of smoke still lingered.

So who had been there? Was he gone now or still on the island?

Chapter Twenty-Five

Carson didn't call her yesterday, so Abby didn't know if he had come back or not. But when she checked her phone before she went to work, there was a text message from him saying he'd gotten back but was short on time. He'd returned to the island last night before dark and didn't have time to see her, much less talk. Abby was disappointed, but she had no control over what he did. At least he'd texted her.

She picked up a Big Mo on the way to Mom's even though she'd made herself a cup at home when she got up that morning and fully expected her mother's chastising for buying what she called expensive coffee. As she went through the drive-through, she looked inside and spotted the strange man who had come into the shop the day before. No one was with him, so perhaps he wasn't married, or his wife wasn't an early riser. He was sitting at a tall table when she pulled up to the window. He looked as if he were reading a newspaper, and Abby hoped he didn't see her. But just as she pulled away, he glanced up and made eye contact with her. Her heart raced, and she shoved her money into the cashier's hand, grabbing the coffee cup so fast, she almost dropped it before speeding away.

Mom was sitting in the kitchen, her Bible open in front of her, when Abby let herself in.

"Good morning, Mom. Feeling better?"

Emma bounded over to hug her grandmother.

Mom hugged her back, her eyes warm with love. She glanced up at Abby. "All right, I guess."

Abby sat down at the table with her. "Mom, I read something interesting in Granny's journal last night. Do you remember getting lost and ending up in the basement when you were little?"

Mom frowned as she tried to recall. "Not really, why?"

"Granny wrote about it in the journal. You were just over a year old, so you might not remember."

"Lord, no. That was a long time ago. But I know I was afraid of the basement."

"Well, I think that's the reason why. Granny said you had gotten in there while she was hanging out clothes, and it took a while before she found you. And you were understandably upset. I bet that's why you have those nightmares too."

"Maybe so. Did she say the basement was flooded?"

"No, but perhaps your imagination filled that in."

"Hmm. Could be, I guess. It certainly would explain why I was afraid of the place."

"Yes, I think so too." Abby stood. "Well, I better get to work. Do you need anything?"

Mom shook her head. "No, thank you. You go on. I'll call you if I do."

"All right. Love you!" Abby kissed her goodbye, took Emma's hand, and went out to her car. As she strapped Emma into her car seat, Abby sensed she was being watched. When she straightened and walked around to the driver's seat, she glanced up and down the street. Her heart froze when she spotted a black car parked alongside the road several houses away. She found it odd because most folks in town parked in their driveways, and the nearest ones were empty. Someone sat behind the steering wheel, but the visor was pulled down, and she couldn't see the person from that distance.

She backed out and drove to the daycare, keeping her eye on the rearview mirror. When the other car didn't move, she breathed a sigh of relief. Surely, it was just a coincidence. There was more than one black car in town, and it was entirely possible someone on Mom's street owned one, even though Abby hadn't noticed it before. She was being ridiculous, so she pushed her paranoia aside to do her job.

But when the kids went outside to play, she saw another black car parked near the school. When did the town get so many black cars?

Surely, they weren't all BMWs, even if the cars did look very similar. Abby strolled over to Kelly, a coworker.

"Do you recognize that black car parked over there?"

Kelly glanced around. "No, I don't."

"Have you ever seen it there before?"

"No, but I don't usually look at the parked cars." Kelly shrugged. "Why?"

"Oh, nothing. I have a friend who has a black BMW, so I thought it might be hers."

"Well, that's a BMW, all right. I can tell from here. The only person I know around here who drives one is Fred Harding. Looks like someone is in it, but I don't think it's a woman. It's probably his."

Abby nearly choked on the lump in her throat. Fred Harding? He couldn't be following her. Why on earth would he? But who else could it be? Maybe she'd been wrong about Mr. Lawrence, since he arrived on his yacht. But was it just a coincidence that she kept seeing a black BMW?

She wished Carson were in town so she could confide her fears in him. But hadn't he dismissed her worries about Mr. Lawrence? He'd probably do the same this time too. Did all men think she was a ninny? Totally irrational and hormone-driven? She had to quit imagining things.

Abby called her mother before she left work to see if she could bring her anything.

"No, I'm fine." Her mother coughed out the words and sounded anything but fine.

"If you're sure."

"Oh, a strange thing happened today," Mom squeaked out.

"What, Mom? Something about your cough?"

"No, no. A man came by asking if I knew anyone by the name of Lawrence. I told him no, but he looked behind me like I was hiding someone. "

Abby dreaded asking the next question.

"Mom, did you see what kind of car he was driving?"

"No, I just remember seeing him drive away in a black car."

She gulped. "Did you say Lawrence?"

"Yes, said he was looking for a relative."

Abby's hands were shaking when she ended the call. The only Lawrence she knew was the man who'd come into the store with his wife. The man with the yacht. Was someone looking for him? Was he wanted for a crime? Maybe he was, and he had been traced to Hope Harbor. But why would they go to her mother's house?

When she and Emma got home, Abby walked out onto the balcony of her apartment and looked around the courtyard. She didn't like being so paranoid and suspicious. But she also didn't like the worry and anxiety caused by strangers getting into her business.

"Mommy, can I go play outside with Samantha?"

Abby glanced down at her side at Emma, who was watching another child who lived in the apartments, on the swing set. Abby started to say no, her gut response based on the fear of strangers lurking around. But it wasn't fair to deny her child the opportunity to play.

She drew in a breath. "Okay, let's go."

Abby joined Samantha's mother on the bench to watch the girls play, but her eyes continued to scan the area.

She was laughing at something the girls did when Samantha spoke up.

"Abby, there's a man over there by the bushes who's taking pictures."

Abby's head spun toward the man standing between the wall and a shrub with his camera poised.

"What on earth?" Abby started to grab Emma and run back to their apartment, but a different emotion took over. Anger. She'd had enough of this game or whatever it was.

"Samantha, please keep your eye on Emma. I'm going to find out who this guy is and what he's doing."

Abby's inner mother bear stood and headed toward the man. When he saw her, he turned around and began walking quickly away. Abby sprinted after him. Just as he reached for his car door handle, she lunged and grabbed hold of his shirt, jerking him around.

"Who are you?" she yelled in his face.

The man glanced to either side, his face reddened, the camera dangling from his hand.

"Who *are* you? Why are you following me?" She stood inches from him, daring him to move. Fortunately, she was tall, and he wasn't.

"Lady, I'm just doing my job. I'm a private investigator." He squeezed his hand into his shirt pocket, pulled out a business card, and held it in front of her eyes.

"Private investigator? Then who are you working for?"

"I ... I'm not at liberty to say."

"Really? Well, what if I charge you with harassment and trespassing?"

"Um, look. I work for a very wealthy man. He can fix this problem."

"*Fix* this problem? Seems like he created the problem."

"Here." He took out his cell phone. "I'll call him right now."

Abby stepped back to give him space to move and planted her hands on her hips. She fumed and couldn't remember ever being so angry. But someone had messed with her family, and the mama bear had emerged.

"Hello? Yes, it's me, Jack. I have a situation here and need your advice. Mrs. Baker is standing right in front of me and wants to know why I've been following her."

The private investigator held the phone away from his ear at the other man's loud response.

"Yes, sir. She wants to know who hired me." There was a pause as he listened to the person on the other end. "Yes, sir."

The call ended, and the man focused directly on Abby. "He said he'll be in town in a few days and will explain everything."

"And who is *he*?"

"Kenneth Lawrence."

Abby's mouth fell open. "Kenneth Lawrence? What does he want with me?"

"He said he'd tell you all about it when he gets here."

"Well, he better, or I'll have him charged with harassment. I'm sure that wouldn't do much for his reputation."

The investigator held his hands up. "Please. Just wait a little longer. He's a man of his word."

"Hmmph! We'll see. In the meantime, I don't want to see you around town anymore or I *will* notify authorities and tell them not only did you harass me, but you harassed my dear, elderly mother too!"

"Yes, ma'am. You won't see me again, I promise."

Abby crossed her arms and watched him get in the car and drive away. At least she knew who was behind all this stalking. And she had been right about Lawrence when he was in town. He really *had* been staring at her. There was some relief in knowing she was right, that she hadn't imagined things. But she still didn't know why. Did it have anything to do with Kevin? A new wave of anxiety traveled down her spine. Was Kevin hiding something from her before he died?

When she returned to the courtyard, Samantha was standing, her brow creased.

"What just happened?"

"That man has been following me, and I wanted to know why."

"Did you find out?"

"Not quite, but I will. And he won't be bothering me anymore."

"Wow. Anybody ever tell you you're really fast? You took off after him like a rocket, like one of those superheroes."

Abby smiled. "Like Wonder Woman?"

***

May 22, 1945

Grace and I went to town today. I had planned to take the boat myself, but Michael came by and volunteered to take us. I honestly felt more comfortable with him driving the boat so I could hold Grace.

I hadn't been to town since Charles died, but now that our waters are safer here, I had the urge to get away from the island. When I've been away from town so long, I feel a little uncivilized and disconnected from the world. Not only that, but today is my birthday, and I wanted to treat myself to something special. I'm going to get my hair done, then Grace and I will go to the drugstore to celebrate with ice cream.

I hated for Michael to wait for us, but he said he had business to do in town, too, so it worked out fine. I didn't tell him it was my birthday because then I'd have to tell him how old I am. I'm forty-two today. Forty-two years old with a one-year-old baby. Does that seem odd to anyone? There aren't many women having children this late in life. In fact, some women are even grandmothers by this age, as I might have been if any of my other children had lived.

Everywhere we went, people made a fuss over Grace. I'd dressed her in her Sunday best. I guess I wanted to give a good impression to the townsfolk, maybe prove I could be a good mother. I still get questioning looks and raised eyebrows, and a young store clerk even asked me if Grace was my granddaughter! I wonder if anyone doubts that she is my daughter. Can they see the secret I've been hiding for the past year?

When I was finishing up at the beauty parlor, Michael came in looking for me. He complimented me on my new hairdo, and I know I blushed because my face got so hot. As we were leaving, the hairdresser called out, "Happy Birthday," letting Michael know it was my birthday. He fussed at me for not telling him, then said we needed to celebrate. I told him about our plans to get ice cream, and he was excited to join us. He even told everyone in the store it was my birthday, so the soda jerk put a candle on my ice cream sundae, and the whole store sang "Happy Birthday" to me! I was so embarrassed! But it was really nice of him to make a big deal out of my special day. And he never did ask how old I was.

Before we went back to the boat, we stopped to look in the store windows, and suddenly he pulled me inside and bought a lovely scarf for me to tie around my hair so it wouldn't blow on the way back. I told him he was spoiling me, but he said I deserved spoiling, especially today. While at the store, I wanted to get a few things for Grace, so Michael excused himself for a few minutes. I bought Grace some new socks and a plastic bowl and cup. She'll need to learn how to use a cup soon. When we were finished, we went outside to find Michael, and he was walking toward us with his hands behind his back and a sheepish grin that made me think he was up to no good. I asked him what he was up to, and he drew a bouquet of flowers from behind and handed them to me, saying, "Happy Birthday!"

I couldn't help the tears that welled up in my eyes and ran down my face. I was so happy, I thought my heart would burst. I can't think of many times in my life I've been so happy. Michael took his handkerchief out of his pocket and touched my cheek with it before handing it to me. I remembered the time I'd been in his arms crying over Grace and was tempted to fall back in them again. But that wouldn't have been appropriate. And what a heyday the town gossips would have had! Their tongues were probably already wagging, seeing us together, acting like a happy family.

But sadly, that's all it is. An act. I'm acting like a mother, and Michael is acting like a husband and father. Little innocent Grace is the only one not acting, or maybe she is but doesn't realize it. I'm so tempted to confide in Michael, to tell him the truth. Not that he needs to know, but I need to tell somebody. But I can't. I promised I'd keep the secret until I die, and I will keep that promise.

Abby stared at the journal trying to understand what Granny was talking about. What was her big secret that she couldn't tell Michael? What was the promise she'd made and to whom did she make the promise? Abby felt as if she were putting a puzzle together but missing some of the pieces. Would she ever find them?

Chapter Twenty-Six

"Nick, did you know there was a cave on the island?" Carson asked his contractor the next day.

Nick rubbed his chin. "You know, back when I was younger, I heard some kids say they'd found one over here. Never saw it myself though. Why?"

Carson told him about discovering what he thought was a cave. "There was the smell of old smoke coming from it, like someone had had a campfire."

"So did you go in?"

Carson shook his head. "Too dark. Plus, I thought it might be dangerous if someone was there. I was wondering if you might like to go with me and check it out."

"Yeah, sure, but I can't leave right now. But I agree that you shouldn't go alone."

"I'm thinking that somebody has been staying there until night, then coming over here to vandalize."

"Have you seen anyone lately?"

"No, not since that first night."

"Well, I think if someone has been waiting for us to leave then discovered you were still here, they're not coming back until you're gone."

"I've thought about that too."

"And your boat is down at the dock, a dead giveaway that somebody is here."

"You're right. Hey, I have an idea, but I need your help with it," Carson said.

"Sure. What do you have in mind?"

"Why don't you go back with me in my boat and let one of your crew take yours back? I'll go home and shower and get some things, then you can bring me back over here, say at dusk. After you drop me off, you take the boat back to the mainland. Then tomorrow, you can bring the boat back when you come to work. Can you do that?"

"Yeah, that'll work."

"Good. I'll need a little time to clean up and get some food, so let's leave a little early if you can."

"Okay. Things are moving along now, so we should be able to knock off around four."

***

When Carson got home, he took a quick shower and changed. Before he did anything else, he texted Abby.

HOME FOR A COUPLE OF HOURS. ARE YOU BUSY?

It seemed like a long time since he'd last seen her, and he really wanted to see her before Nick picked him up. He also needed to grab a few more things to take back over, one of them being food. He was starving, but figured he'd go by the diner and pick up a meal to go and give him more time to see Abby.

Her response came right back. JUST GOT HOME. CAN YOU COME BY?

Carson smiled at the phone. He'd hoped to go by her place, so he was glad she asked.

SURE. NOW?

THAT'S GOOD. HEATING LEFTOVERS. HUNGRY?

His stomach rumbled an answer. Frankly, he'd eat anything as long as he could see her. There was so much he wanted to tell her.

STARVING. CAN I PICK UP SOMETHING?

NO. THANK YOU.

SEE YOU SOON.

***

Abby's apartment smelled wonderful and made his mouth water, but the food wasn't as exciting as being there with her. She looked even better than she had before, if that was possible. Her silky, long brown hair cascaded down her back, and he fought the desire to touch it. Her eyes sparkled when she greeted him, making him believe she was as happy to see him as he was to see her.

He sniffed the air. "What's for dinner?"

She pointed to a casserole dish on the stove. "Vegetable lasagna. I hope you like it."

"I'm sure I will. Beats Vienna sausage."

She laughed. "I hope so. I made a salad too." She handed him a plate. "Go ahead and serve yourself. I know you don't have much time."

"You're joining me, I hope." He looked around. "Where's Emma?"

"In her room. She wanted to change her bear's clothes. I'll go get her."

Carson helped himself to the lasagna and salad, then put his plate on the table, waiting for the others to join him.

Emma came running in and reached for him. "Uncle Carson!"

Carson glanced at Abby whose face turned red. She shrugged. "I have no idea."

"Hi, Emma. Get your plate and come sit by me."

After they all sat down, and Emma said the blessing, Carson and Abby tried to catch up. But he had to speak in veiled language so Emma wouldn't understand. Abby, too, wanted to talk, but a glance at Emma then back at him suggested she also needed to speak without Emma.

"When are you going back?" Abby asked as she cleared the table.

Carson looked at his watch. "I can only stay about thirty more minutes."

"Oh, I'd hoped you could stay longer."

"Me too." He glanced outside. "Hey, why don't we go out to the courtyard and talk while Emma plays?"

Abby wiped her hands on the dishcloth. "Great idea."

Once Emma ran off to play, Carson and Abby sat down on a bench, and he told her about the strange man and finding the cave. "We thought maybe the guy hasn't come back because he knows I'm there. So Nick is going to drop me off later and bring the boat back here. We're hoping we can do that without being seen if someone is watching."

"Please be careful." Abby's eyes showed genuine concern, warming him inside.

"But what about you? What have you been up to? Anything exciting? How's Grace?"

Abby looked over at Emma. "Grace is okay, I guess. But something else happened."

He studied her face. "What? Did something happen to you?"

Abby shook her head. Then she told him about a strange man stalking her and how she confronted him to find out why.

"He said he was a private investigator working for Mr. Lawrence."

"The man with the yacht?"

She nodded. "The same."

Carson blew out a low whistle. "And why did Lawrence have you followed?"

She shrugged, lifting her hands. "He didn't say. But he called Mr. Lawrence in front of me who said he'll come back to Hope Harbor and give me an explanation."

"And you have no idea why?"

"No. I wonder if it has something to do with Kevin. But I can't imagine what."

"Do you know when he'll be here?"

"A couple of days. Mr. Lawrence was somewhere on the boat, so he has to get back here."

Carson placed his hand over hers and faced her. "I wish I could be here when he comes back. Give you moral support, you know."

"I wish you could be too."

For a moment, he almost promised to stay until Lawrence met with her, but he couldn't. He had to get back to the island. He glanced at his watch and saw that it was time to go.

"I'm sorry, but I have to leave." He stood and she did too.

"I understand." She looked away toward the playground.

"But soon, everything will be settled, and we'll have more time. I promise."

"Don't."

"Don't what?"

"Don't make promises about the future. You never know what the future holds."

Carson wanted to argue, but she was right. However, if he had anything to do with it, they definitely would get together again. He had the urge to kiss her goodbye, but he resisted and only squeezed her hand before letting go. She'd made it clear they were just friends, and he didn't want to jeopardize their friendship. But being away from her just a few days had been so difficult, and his feelings toward her had long passed the stage of friendship. But if that's all she wanted, he'd try to be content with that.

***

As Carson walked away, Abby studied him and realized she liked everything about him—the way he carried himself with excellent posture, the way his body moved in perfect cadence, his height, his square shoulders and muscular legs filling out his jeans just right. His thick, dark hair and chiseled face. But it wasn't just the outside she liked. He was kind and thoughtful, funny and intelligent, and comfortable to be with. He never criticized her and was always positive and encouraging. And the way he looked at her ... his eyes penetrating hers as if searching her soul. Yes, she really did like him, maybe too much.

She'd missed him while he was gone, missed him in fact as soon as he walked away. There was so much more she'd wanted to discuss with him—tell him what she'd read in the journal, talk about progress on the keeper's house, and help him make choices about its décor. She should be used to this scenario. Wasn't life like that when Kevin came home for a short time, only to be deployed again? She should be stronger now than she used to be, now that she'd learned to live on her own. But hadn't she done that when Kevin was gone? Why was it whenever he returned, she felt weaker? Was it because Kevin wanted her to be the weaker one? Abby shook her head to get rid of the negative thoughts.

She really wanted to quit comparing Carson to Kevin. They were totally different, and it wasn't fair to Carson. But she couldn't help it, mainly because of their differences. The question that lurked was one she didn't want to ask or answer, but it wouldn't go away. Which man did she like better? *Abby, stop. Just accept Carson for who he is, the same way you want him to accept you.*

He had expressed a desire to be with her when she met with Mr. Lawrence. She wished he could be, too, but had never expected him to be. Carson's presence would make her feel more protected, confident, and less afraid. But she couldn't rely on anyone else to face this situation with her, whatever it was. She had to do this alone. *Please, God, give me the strength.*

***

Nick slowed the engine as they approached the island, trying to minimize the noise. With waves splashing against the shore, Carson doubted anyone would hear the boat. As quietly as possible, they arrived at the dock, keeping their voices low as Carson hopped out with his backpack.

"Come back at daylight in case I need reinforcements," he told Nick before waving him off, and then he hurried over to the shore and up the hill to the keeper's house. Wearing his dark sweatshirt and jeans, Carson envisioned himself as an undercover character in an action movie. Hopefully, no one would jump out and attack him like they did in the movies.

He glanced toward the lighthouse and the woods as he approached the house, looking for any sign of movement. Wind blew off the water, stirring the trees. How would he know if a person moved them? He quickly unlocked the front door and slipped inside. Then he made a fast search of the house to make sure no unwanted guests had managed to get in. After eliminating that possibility, he settled back into the living room and unrolled the sleeping bag he'd left there. He took the gun out of his backpack and laid it down beside him.

Thanks to Abby, Carson wasn't hungry, so there was no need to make any noise getting something out to eat. He smiled at the thought of Abby's invitation. She was always thinking of others and, it seemed, always taking care of others—he, Emma, Grace, even the gift store manager, not to mention the kids at the daycare. She was obviously meant to be a caregiver and did so quite naturally and without expecting anything in return. People like that were rare—special. And Abby was certainly special, in more ways than one.

Carson inhaled the scents of freshly sawed wood and new paint. The smell of progress and the reassurance that he was reaching his goal. He ran his hand along the smooth surface of the wood floors that had been sanded and polished. Soon there would be furniture in this room and, hopefully, guests sitting on it.

Carson's ears tuned in to every sound. Tree frogs sang in unison with the occasional hoot of an owl joining the chorus. Beyond them, he could hear the waves of the sea as they lapped the shore down below. The hum of a mosquito made him reach for the bug repellent cream he lathered on his neck and face. Then he tried not to move so he could hear anything that didn't sync with the natural noises. The pounding in his ears reassured him that his heart still worked. How long he sat still, he didn't know, but he dozed off as the natural symphony lulled him to sleep.

Something cracked nearby and he jolted awake. He straightened, then glanced at his watch. It was almost one in the morning. He stilled and listened as the sound of steps through the grass alerted him. He had company.

Carson picked up the gun and slowly stood, keeping his back against the wall. This time he meant to see the man before he could get away. Carson had worked through several scenarios about how he could confront the guy. Most of them involved an unarmed intruder. What he'd do if the guy was armed wasn't too clear.

From his vantage point, Carson saw the man's form move past the windows. He walked hunched over, almost apelike, but seemed to be wearing a long, bulky coat and a cap on his head. Just then, the beam of the lighthouse flashed through the yard and Carson got a look at the man. He swallowed a gasp at the sight. What kind of person was this? Long hair and a scraggly beard covered the man's head so much that he could be mistaken for an animal—even a bear. For a second, Carson thought of the Bigfoot legend, but he'd never heard of Bigfoot wearing a cap. This was definitely a man, albeit a strange one.

As before, the man crept around the house testing the windows, then the back door. An idea sparked in Carson's mind. He snuck over to the front door, quietly unlocked it, then took his position behind it. Carson breathed a prayer. *Please Lord, let this work out so neither of us gets hurt.*

The doorknob turned, then the door slowly opened. Carson waited until the man came all the way inside. As soon as he did, Carson pushed the door closed and shone a flashlight in the man's face.

"You forgot to knock," Carson said.

The grizzly man held his hands in front of his face to shield it from the bright light.

"Who are you? Why are you in my house?" Carson kept one hand on the flashlight and the other on the gun in case he needed it.

The man shook his head and tried to look away, his eyes showing fear and confusion.

"Can you talk? Tell me who you are! Who are you working for?" Carson stood his ground, muscles tensed in case the guy made a move to escape.

"Get that light outta my eyes! Please!" the gruff voice pleaded.

Carson lowered the light so that it shone on the man's dirty shirt but still illuminated his face. The guy reeked of unwashed clothes and body odor, and Carson was tempted to back away.

"All right. I did. Now answer my questions."

"I didn't know it was your house. Nobody's lived here for a long time, so I claimed it."

"You … claimed it?"

The man nodded. "Yeah. Squatters rights, you know."

"This property belonged to the federal government before I bought it. So you had no right to claim it."

"Huh? I seen 'em go into the lighthouse but not in here."

"So you've been helping yourself to our tools? Did you think they didn't belong to anyone either?"

The man looked away and shrugged.

"So, tell me, who put you up to this?" This guy couldn't have acted alone.

"What do ya mean?"

"Did someone pay you to sabotage our work?"

The man looked confused and frowned. "I don't know what you're talking about."

"Hey, Mr. ... Do you have a name?"

"Leroy."

"Leroy, has anyone offered to pay you to mess up our work here?"

He shook his head with determination. "No. I haven't talked to anybody. In a long time."

Carson wanted to believe the man, but common sense told him not to. However, it was entirely believable that the man had limited social interaction. And he couldn't imagine someone as refined as Fred Harding having anything to do with such a person.

"How did you get here? Did someone drop you off here?"

"Wha—?" The man swung his head from side to side. "Nobody done nuthin' to me. I tole you, I don't talk to nobody. Unless I got to go to town for something, but I don't go but ev'ry 'tuther month or more. And I got my own boat, so nobody drops me anywhere."

"Are you saying you *live* here?"

Leroy nodded. "Been here a long time."

From the looks of him, Carson believed it. The man's graying hair hung in dreads and the beard hadn't been washed, much less combed, in quite some while. Carson shuddered to think what might live inside that mass.

"You lived in this house?"

"Only when it's too cold." He pointed a grimy finger out the window. "I got a place over yonder a piece."

"In a cave?"

The man's eyes flashed. "You seen it?"

It was Carson's turn to shrug. "Maybe. Where did you get your food?"

"Got traps. Fish. Whatever. Found some canned stuff down there in the basement."

Carson wondered if that "canned stuff" had been there since the '60s when Abigail Martin had left.

"So why did you cut through the pipe in the basement?"

Another shrug. "Figured you would go away and leave the place alone if it was too hard to fix."

"Well, Leroy, I hate to inform you, but I bought this place—this whole island—so you've been trespassing."

Fire flashed in Leroy's eyes. "You mean you're telling me I can't live here no more?"

"'Fraid not. I can't afford to have you coming around and creating problems." *And scaring off my guests.*

"So where am I supposed to go?"

Carson realized for the first time that Leroy was wearing an old camouflage shirt and pants. No wonder he was hard to find. But did that mean Leroy was a veteran?

"I don't know, Leroy, but if you keep messing with things around here, you could end up in jail. In fact, I can press charges right now."

"I been in worst places. Like Nam." Leroy sat down on the floor. "You'll have to carry me off if you want me to leave."

"That can be arranged."

Carson longed to open the windows and get fresh air to fumigate the room from Leroy's presence, but he didn't want to invite mosquitoes in. Carson grabbed a length of rope he'd brought and tied the old man's hands and feet together, pulling him over to the wall so he could lean against it.

"What you doing that for? I ain't going nowhere, I tole you."

"Sorry, but you haven't earned my trust. Tomorrow, we'll call the sheriff, who'll come take you away."

Carson moved back to his sleeping bag across the room where he could keep an eye on the man, as well as get away from the odor. But sleep was out of the question now. Good thing he'd had a little nap earlier. Leroy, on the other hand, fell fast asleep, snoring and snorting enough to wake the dead. Carson studied the old guy. So this was the man who'd been making Carson's life miserable. But he could only blame Leroy for what happened on the island. The man had no power to affect shipments or inspectors' visits. Maybe those things truly were coincidental.

How long had he been living on the island? He'd heard of homeless veterans living under bridges and in parks, but those guys at least had some shelters or soup kitchens where they could get food and rest. But out here on an island by himself? Carson couldn't fathom it. Still, he hated to be the one to put him out on the streets. But what else could he do? The man couldn't stay there. *Lord, please show me how to help Leroy.*

Chapter Twenty-Seven

Nita, the daycare director, called out to Abby who sat on the floor reading to a group of preschoolers. "Abby, you have a phone call."

"Who is it?" She hated to interrupt the story with the children sitting still and listening.

"A Mr. Lawrence."

Abby's pulse quickened as she rose and handed Nita the book as she went to the phone.

"Hello. This is Abby Baker."

"Abby, this is Kenneth Lawrence. I'd like to get together with you tomorrow. Is there a place we can meet?"

Abby racked her brain for a safe place. "What about Mo's Joe? It's the coffee place in town."

"Yes, I remember seeing it. Can you be there at ten o'clock in the morning?"

"Yes, I can."

"Then we'll see you there."

We? Was he using the royal "we" and talking about himself, or would someone else be present? The private investigator or his wife?

For the rest of the day, she tried to figure out, for the thousandth time, why the man was interested in her. She went by Mom's to check on her, discouraged with the lack of energy her mother had and frustrated by an inability to help her. She'd even bought some vitamins at the drugstore, hoping they would give Mom some vitality. But Mom argued that they were a waste of money and, besides, too hard to swallow. Much as Abby wanted to confide in her mother there was no need to add worry to the woman's life.

Carson texted her a message when she got home. MYSTERY SOLVED.

TIRED. GOING HOME TO SLEEP. YOU GOING TOMORROW?

She'd forgotten that tomorrow was the day she went to the island when she agreed to the appointment. She texted back. CAN'T. HAVE APPT WITH LAWRENCE.

YOU DO? NEED ME TO GO WITH YOU?

NO. I'LL BE FINE. MEETING AT MO'S.

OKAY. I'LL BE PRAYING FOR YOU.

Abby sighed. Thank God he was safe. She was dying to know more about what happened at the island. How was the mystery solved? But much as she'd like him to be with her when she faced Mr. Lawrence, she knew she had to do it by herself. She appreciated Carson's concern. And his prayers. Too bad she hadn't been able to talk to him. But his texts had somehow given her more strength to face tomorrow alone.

When she walked into Mo's the next day, she almost didn't see Mr. Lawrence seated in the back corner of the place with another, older man. He stood and waved her over. Abby willed her legs to join them, feeling as if she were walking into an interrogation. As she approached the table, the other gentleman stood.

"Abby, Mrs. Baker, this is my father, Kenneth Lawrence the Third." The older man forced a smile while scrutinizing her. She glanced between the two and the Mr. Lawrence she knew said, "I'm the fourth." He extended his hand toward a chair. "Please. Have a seat."

Abby complied. The two men reeked of money. Both were well-dressed with perfect hair and manicured nails. Gold watches and rings adorned their hands and wrists.

"Relax, Mrs. Baker. Can I get you a cup of coffee?"

Abby nodded. "A Big Mo skinny latte, please."

"Right away. Please excuse me." Abby thought he probably didn't often have to fetch his own coffee. He could just snap his fingers and his servants would bring it. An uncomfortable silence passed between her and the other Mr. Lawrence, who she guessed must be around her mother's age, until Lawrence the Fourth came back with her coffee.

She thanked him for the coffee, glad to get it because she needed something to do with her hands besides play with her hair. The older

Mr. Lawrence wouldn't take his eyes off her, and she squirmed in her seat.

"I know you're very curious. But we needed to be sure before we confronted you," Lawrence the Fourth said.

Confronted her? Had she committed a crime she wasn't aware of?

He turned to his grandfather. "I'll let you take it from here."

She gave her attention to the older man, who cleared his throat before speaking.

He clasped his hands on the table in front of him. "Mrs. Baker, I'm going to tell you a story. Many years ago, back in 1943, my father volunteered for service in the military when he was twenty-one years old. His parents didn't want him to go, but he was determined to be part of the war effort. You know, World War II."

His cleared his throat again, then continued. "So he left home for the army. His sister Beverly, who was only seventeen years old at the time, lived with their parents. But she fell in love with a guy named Paul Thomas, whom her parents didn't approve of because he didn't come from a family with the same standing as ours. My grandfather forbade her to see him, but she refused to quit seeing him. Paul was planning to join up as soon as he was old enough, but he wanted to marry Beverly first. But Grandfather would have nothing to do with it. And when Beverly told him she was expecting a baby, he threw her out of the house."

Abby listened to the interesting story, all the while asking herself what it had to do with her.

He sipped his coffee, then continued. "Apparently, they ran off and got married anyway. A year passed by with no word from them. Then in March of 1944, Grandfather received word that Beverly and Paul had drowned in a boating accident." He pointed a skinny finger toward the water. "It happened out there near Hope Island."

A tremor ran down Abby's back. "That's when my grandparents were lighthouse keepers there."

"That's right. It was your grandfather who tried to save them but couldn't. When the authorities contacted Grandfather, there was no word of a child being found, so it was assumed there wasn't one or it had drowned, too, and the body never recovered. My grandmother grieved for Beverly until she died and never forgave Grandfather for running off her only daughter. When my father came back from the war, he learned the whole story and also grieved the loss of his sister."

"So you wanted to tell me because my grandparents were the ones who found them?"

He looked to his son, who reached into his coat pocket and pulled out a photo, laying it on the table so Abby could see it.

"This was Beverly."

Abby's breath caught as she gazed at the photograph. She could have been looking in the mirror, except for the hairstyle. And she knew of another photo that was an even better match, the one in her mother's photo album that showed Grace as a teenager.

"You see the resemblance, of course. How could you not? When I saw you in the store, I was as shocked as you are. The coincidence was too uncanny."

Abby couldn't take it in. "But my mother is Grace. Grace Abigail Pearson, the daughter of Charles and Abigail Martin."

"Are you sure? We believe your mother was the baby of Beverly and Paul Thomas, and that the Martins found the baby and raised it as if it were their own."

Abby's heart sank as the words of Granny's journal came to her mind. Was this the secret Granny had been keeping? Abby didn't know what to say. She couldn't share her granny's private journal with these strangers.

"Your mother lives here in town, doesn't she?"

"Yes, but she's not in very good health. She has COPD."

"I'm sorry to hear that," the older Lawrence said. "You know, she could be my first cousin."

Abby stared. And that would make her…?

"And of course, you would be related to the Lawrences too," the younger Lawrence added.

Her world was shaking. If this were true, not only was Grace not who she thought she was, neither was Abby. And Granny wasn't really her granny.

"What do you expect me to do? Tell my mother she isn't the daughter of Charles and Abigail Martin? I'm afraid the shock could be too much for her."

"We understand," Lawrence the Third said. "Of course, I'd love to meet her, but I won't force myself into her life."

"Yes," the younger man said. "We'll leave that up to you. One thing you might not realize though is that your mother would be an heir to the Lawrence estate, as would you. Beverly's father never took her out of his will."

Abby gulped as she looked from one man to the other. "I need some time to process this."

"Of course you do. Take your time. We'll be in town until tomorrow. Here's my card. Please call me."

Abby left the coffee shop stunned. She rushed home and found the journal. Throughout, Granny seemed to indicate that she wasn't really Grace's mother. She never said it though, just commented about being "given" a child so late in life. She expressed insecurities about her mothering skills, but then so did Abby, and she knew Emma was her child. But other things about whether Grace looked like her or not were mentioned. Then the last entry she read about keeping a secret. She never came right out and said where Grace came from, but she did drop several clues that Grace might not be her natural child. Was this proof enough?

She needed a long run to clear her head. Changing into her running clothes, she checked her tracker and set it for five miles. She chugged a bottle of water, ran down Church Street, and then down every other street in town, past the bed-and-breakfasts and the shops and businesses. The burden began to lift from her chest as she ran, praying that she would make the right decision. Abby ran the bayside trail to the top, then sat a moment to reflect. If it were true that Grace was really a Lawrence, should Abby tell her mother? What should she do? How could she be sure?

An idea struck her, and she took off for Mom's. Her mother answered the door after several minutes. "Where's your key?"

"Sorry, Mom. I didn't bring it with me. I'm out for a run."

"Isn't this the day you usually go to the island?"

"Yes, but I had an appointment today."

"Are you okay?" Mom touched Abby's head.

"Yes, Mom. It was a financial appointment." Which in truth it was. "How are you feeling today?"

Mom shrugged. "Same old, same old."

Abby gazed around the modest home with its threadbare furniture. "Where's that old album of yours?"

"Over there under the coffee table. Why?"

"I just wanted to look at it."

Abby found the album and flipped through the pages until she found her mother's high school graduation photo. She stared in amazement at the similarity in the photo and the one Mr. Lawrence had shown her.

Abby then picked up the photo of Granny and Grandfather that was taken the month before her mother was born. It hit her what was bothering her about the photo. Granny didn't look pregnant. Sure, Granny was a thin woman, but even thin women looked pregnant that close to having a baby. Abby could vouch for that. So maybe Granny didn't really birth Mom. How was she going to tell her though?

Mom's coughing drew her attention. She turned as Mom dropped down in the chair. Her mother definitely needed help, more than her piddling monthly income or limited insurance would cover. What if she were a Lawrence? Would she be able to get what she needed?

Abby went to the kitchen and downed a glass of water before coming back to the living room. "Mom, I'll check back with you later. Can I get you anything for dinner?"

"I think I'll just open a can of soup."

"You need more than that. After I pick up Emma, we'll come back by." She kissed her mother then resumed her run.

As she ran in front of Eddie's barber shop, Carson stepped outside.

"Abby! Just the person I wanted to see."

She pulled up short. "Carson. I didn't expect to see you in town today." His fresh haircut and trimmed beard made him even more handsome than she remembered.

He rubbed his cheek. "I've been feeling pretty scraggly the last few days. Thought I'd clean out my room at the hotel and clean up myself too."

"But aren't you supposed to be at the island?"

"I needed to take care of some things in town, so I didn't go today."

"Oh, well then, I'm glad we ran into each other. I wanted to know about your text last night regarding the mystery being solved."

Carson beamed a smile that showed satisfaction and brought a sparkle to his eyes. She didn't realize how much she'd missed that smile the last few days.

"Have you had lunch? Why don't we get something to eat, and I'll fill you in."

"That sounds good." She looked down at her clothes. "Are you sure you want to be seen with me like this?"

"Abby, I'd like to be seen with you anytime."

Abby's face heated, but her heart warmed. She smiled at him. "All right. Where would you like to go?"

"Somewhere we can talk. How about the deli? I don't think it's as noisy as the diner, and it's nice enough to sit outside on their patio."

They walked over to the deli and ordered sandwiches to take outside. Abby got their drinks while Carson carried the food trays to an umbrella-covered table. As they ate, Carson told Abby about the vagrant who had been living on the island.

"I feel kind of sorry for him," Carson said, "but I can't have him staying there when I have guests. Abby, you should've seen him. He was pretty scary looking, not to mention the smell. Sorry, didn't mean to disturb your lunch."

"No harm done. So what will happen to him?"

"I don't know. But I found out he's been getting a military pension sent to a post office box. Apparently, he's friends with a couple of local lobstermen who helped him get things so he didn't have to go to town."

"Is he going to jail?"

"Well, that's where he is now. I'm not going to press charges because we found all our missing tools in the cave."

"It's too bad he had to go to jail." Abby tried to imagine what it was like for someone to lose their freedom after so many years.

"He won't be for long, but at least he's getting three meals a day and a bed to sleep on. The beds in jail aren't much, but they've got to beat sleeping in a cave."

"I suppose."

"I've called the veterans hospital, and they said they'd see him and check him out for any health concerns. I hope the sheriff's department can take him over there."

Abby toyed with her sandwich, removing the bread to eat the contents with a fork, deep in thought and wishing she could think of a way to help the man. But she couldn't even help her own mother.

"Abby? You're so quiet. I'm sorry, I've been doing all the talking. Did you ever find out why that Lawrence guy had you followed?"

Abby looked up and met his gaze. "Yes, I met with them today, and I *really* want to talk to you about it." She told Carson about the meeting with the Lawrences and what she'd discovered. "Carson, I'm not certain their claim is valid, but all the clues point to it."

"Wow. All these years, they thought she didn't exist, and Grace thought she was someone else. Have you told her yet?"

Abby shook her head. "No. I'm not sure I should. It might upset her too much. Just imagine. This kind of thing would rock her world. I just don't know what to do." Tears welled up in her eyes. "I just want to do the right thing. For everybody."

Carson put his thumb on her cheek and wiped away the tear that fell. He gazed at her with so much concern in his eyes. "Abby, you're such a thoughtful person. I love the way you always want to help others. You know, that's a gift from God, that caring nature."

She glanced up at him. "A gift?" Wasn't this the same thing Kevin had ridiculed her for?

"Yes, it is. Abby, most people are too concerned about themselves to care for others. Most people are selfish. I know I am."

Abby shook her head. "I don't see you that way."

"Well, I am. I'm so goal-focused, I don't see other people's needs. You're different. You look out for others first."

Abby offered a timid smile. "I'm glad you think so."

"Hey. I *know* so. So let's discuss this decision about Grace. If it were me, I'd want to know."

"But wouldn't that make her feel like Granny misled her?"

"Did your grandmother raise her? Did she take care of her and love her? Did she do the best she could for her?"

"Yes, of course she did. Mom and Granny were very close. They just had each other for many years."

"So she didn't suffer any neglect by being raised by her."

"No. Not at all. But I need to tell you something else. Something I've read in Granny's journals. She's alluded to keeping a secret and making a promise. I think she made a promise to someone to raise Mom as her own child and not tell anyone. Why, I don't know. Maybe Grandfather asked her to. But we can't ask them now. However, I do know that Granny had difficulty having a child of her own."

"Sounds rather incriminating. Maybe that's why she hid the journal."

"Yes, I think you're right."

"Have you finished reading it?"

"No. I've been reading about her life during the war and the Coast Guard men who were on the island, one in particular she really liked."

"Sounds interesting."

"Oh, and I read a story about Mom getting lost once when she was a toddler and being found in the basement. I'm sure that's why she's always been afraid of the basement."

"No wonder."

"Funny thing that her dreams about being in the basement also involved water. Do you think the basement ever flooded before?"

"It's possible."

"Carson! I just had an idea. If Mom's parents drowned in a boating accident, that means she was with them. Maybe the water has something to do with the accident. Maybe Mom's fears were lumped together so she thought the water was in the basement."

"Hmm. That makes sense, I guess. I don't quite understand dreams. But I'm sure they have to do with something in our heads."

"Carson, there's more to this situation. The Lawrences said that Mom and I would be heirs to the Lawrence fortune."

Carson blew out a whistle. "Wow."

"Yes, wow. I don't want to make a decision biased by that fact."

"Come on, Abby. That's just an added perk. I think I know you well enough that you wouldn't accept any money you didn't believe you had a right to. You're way too honest for that."

Abby put her elbows on the table and rubbed her temples. "I just don't know."

"It's your decision, but I think Grace could handle the news. She may be weak physically, but she's got a strong mind, from what I can tell. I bet she learned how to be pretty tough growing up on that island with just her mother. And I'm sure she did her share of the work too."

"Yes, she did. They used to talk about it."

"And another thing, Abby. If this is true and you don't tell her, won't you be denying her a family she's never known? Denying yourself?"

Abby's heart squeezed. He was right. She had to tell Mom. At least let Mom decide if she thought the Lawrences were right. And she'd take the journal with her.

Chapter Twenty-Eight

June 15, 1945

I haven't seen Michael in three weeks, since that day in town. That was such a special day. The very thought of it has warmed my heart ever since. I suppose if that's the last I'll see of him, it's a good memory to have.

The garden is coming along, and Grace has "helped" me pull weeds, as long as I watch, and she doesn't pull up everything. The flowers I planted last month are blooming now and attracting butterflies. Grace loves to try to catch them, and it's so much fun to watch her chase them. She hasn't wandered off from me again or tried to. I think that whole experience with the basement was enough to scare her and keep her by my side.

Every day, she's prettier and so much like her mother, that sweet young girl. I hope I did the right thing by making that promise to her to raise her baby like my own. I don't think Grace will ever know she was someone else's child. At least, not as long as I'm alive. Charles and I had mixed feelings about it, but he came to love her like she was his as well. I'm so sorry he didn't have a chance to see her grow.

I never knew what her given name was, so I named her Grace because I believe she was a gift from God, just like His grace is, something I didn't earn or deserve, yet now my life is filled with love I never had before. Charles always told me I'd be a good mother because I liked to care for things like animals and people when I had the opportunity. I'm so thankful I have Grace to care for now.

Mr. Mitchell brought me a letter just a few minutes ago, interrupting my writing. Now that he's gone, I'll finish. The letter was from Michael. He told me he had to leave because he was being transferred to the Pacific coast since that part of our country is still in danger from the Japanese. He apologized for not being able to tell me goodbye in person, but he told me he'd never forget me and that I'd been a true friend to him. He also said he'd miss us and wanted me to kiss Grace for him. I'm crying as I'm writing this because I hate knowing I'll never see him again. He signed the letter, "All my love, Michael." I'll treasure this letter and his special friendship forever.

But I'm thankful God gave me his company during my darkest time, after Charles' death. God knew I'd need someone to comfort me and encourage me, and Michael did. I remember how weak I felt after Charles died, how I didn't think I had strength to be alone, to take Charles' place at the lighthouse or to raise a child. Michael reassured me and made me believe I had strength I didn't realize I had.

I'm a stronger person now. Charles is gone and Michael is, too, but God is still with me, and His word says He will be my strength. And now I know that together—God, myself, and Grace—we will make it.

"And we did," Mom said, her eyes filled with tears as she looked up at Abby. "Mother and I did well. We were a team." Mom wiped her eyes, then patted Abby's hand. "Abby, it's okay. Abigail Martin will always be my mother. She fulfilled my birth mother's wishes. I am so blessed that someone as fine a woman as Abigail raised me. We weren't rich by worldly standards, but we were rich in every other way."

"Mom, what about the Lawrences?"

"The Lawrences? Well, it looks like I have some relatives to meet. And so do you. And so does Emma too."

Epilogue

"There! That's the last piece." Abby stepped back and admired the picture she'd placed on the wall of the keeper's house. "Now the place is ready for guests."

Carson smiled. "You've done a wonderful job making this place so nice and welcoming. Thank you." He squeezed her hand and kissed her forehead.

Abby surveyed the room, pleased with the way it had turned out. "And tomorrow you get to greet your first guests. Are you nervous?"

"Nah. I got this. Besides, you're going to be here with me, giving me strength and moral support, aren't you?"

Abby smiled. "I didn't realize I had enough strength to give."

"Oh, but you do. You're the strongest woman I know. You truly are a Wonder Woman, Abby."

Abby's face flushed. But the name didn't offend her anymore because Carson's comment was sincere. "So you won over Mr. Harding. That open house was a great idea, inviting the town's businesspeople over to see for themselves."

Carson gave her a wink. "Where's that Bible verse about feeding your enemies?"

"Somewhere in there with loving your enemies."

"I'm not sure I can go that far. I'd rather love my friends, my very special friends." He gazed at her before pulling her into a breathtaking kiss.

When he released her, she fluttered her eyelashes, teasing. "You're a special friend to me, too, Carson."

He lifted her hand and rubbed his finger over the diamond ring on it. "I certainly hope so, future-Mrs. Stevens."

"I'm still trying to get used to being related to the Lawrences."

"Grace seems to be enjoying her newfound family."

"They've been amazing and so welcoming to her. More than I ever imagined. In fact, they're paying for all her treatment. And with the money they put in her account, we're going to have her kitchen remodeled and get her some new furniture."

"And now that you're an heiress, I can marry you for your money."

"Is that so? What if I refuse the money? Would you still want to marry me?"

"Depends. Would you marry a lowly lighthouse keeper?"

Abby laughed. "Why would I argue with destiny? After all, my name is Abigail."

The End

WANT TO READ MORE?

I f you enjoyed reading this book, the best thing you can do to help Marilyn is very simple–tell others about it. Word-of-mouth is the most powerful marketing tool there is. Marilyn would greatly appreciate you rating her book and leaving a brief review at either amazon.com, goodreads.com, or bookbub.com. A review isn't a book summary—it's not that complicated. All you need to do is write a sentence or two telling what you liked about a book—was it interesting, suspenseful, romantic, funny, etc.? Did you like the characters, the story, the setting? Just look for the book on whichever site you choose, then click on "write a customer review," or "leave a review." It's that simple. Thank you so much for helping the author write more books!

If you'd like to subscribe to Marilyn's quarterly newsletter and find out when her next book is coming out, please go to https://pathwayheart.com/subscribe/, and leave your name and email. She promises she won't give your information away to anyone else or fill your inbox with too much stuff.

Discussion Questions for Abigail's Secret

1. Abby thought her grandmother possessed some special strength that enabled her to do what she did. In a survey I took of over one hundred women asking them who were the strongest women they knew, the majority said it was their mothers or grandmothers. Do you feel like your mother or grandmother was a stronger person than you are? Why or why not?

2. Carson has had a lifelong dream of owning a lighthouse, but his father and former fiancée thought he was foolish to pursue that dream. Do you have a dream? Has anyone made fun of you for having that dream? Where do you think dreams come from?

3. Abby's former husband ridiculed her for always helping other people, not seeing her behavior as a God-given gift of service. Do you have the gift of service? Do you know anyone who does?

4. From her past experience of being stalked, Abby is suspicious of strangers. Have you had any past experiences that made you more untrusting of other people?

5. Which characters did you like? Which ones did you dislike? Why?

6. Hope Harbor is a small town where the locals know each other and also know who's new in town. Have you ever lived in a town like that, where everyone knows everyone else's business? Did you like it or not?

7. Michael O'Brien was a good friend to Abigail at a time when she needed someone. Have you ever had someone like him show up in your life just when you needed them? Do you think God sent them for you?

8. Carson had never renovated an old building like the keeper's house before and didn't know what problems he might run into. Have you ever renovated an old place? Can you identify with what Carson went through?

9. What did you think about Leroy? Carson was able to help him, but unfortunately, many veterans are homeless. Have you ever worked to help the homeless?

10. Did you know German submarines were that close to the US mainland during World War II? If you'd like to find out more about what happened in the states during the war, read *The Gilded Curse* and *Shadowed by a Spy*.

11. Did you know that you can buy a lighthouse like Carson did? The US Coast Guard manages the lights in the lighthouses that are still active, but thanks to GPS on marine vessels, many lighthouses have been deactivated. These have been deemed "excess property" by the government and can be purchased by individuals or preservation groups. Would you like to buy a lighthouse too? If you could, what would you do with it? Live there? Convert it to a B & B?

12. Abby finally discovered the source of her grandmother's strength. What is the source of your strength? Do you have a favorite Bible verse that explains it?